Ex-National Hunt Champion Jockey John Francome is a broadcaster on racing for Channel 4 and is fast establishing himself as one of the front runners in the racing thriller stakes. He lives in Berkshire.

His previous bestsellers have all been highly praised:

'Francome provides a vivid panorama of the racing world . . . and handles the story's twist deftly'

The Times

'Francome can spin a darn good yarn' *Racing Post*

'Thrills, twists and turns on and off the racecourse. Convincing and beguiling' *Irish Independent*

'Move over Dick Francis, here's competition'

Me magazine

'A thoroughly convincing and entertaining tale'

Daily Mail

'The racing feel is authentic and it's a pacy, entertaining read' *Evening Standard*

'Irresistibly reminiscent of the master . . . a most readable yarn' *Mail on Sunday*

'Thrills to the final furlong . . . Francome knows how to write a good racing thriller' *Daily Express*

'Mr Francome adeptly teases to the very end and cleverly keeps a few twists up his sleeve until the closing chapters' *Country Life*

Tip Off

John Francome

HEADLINE

First published in 1999
by HEADLINE BOOK PUBLISHING

First published in paperback in 2000
by HEADLINE BOOK PUBLISHING

10

ISBN 0 7472 5927 5

Typeset by
Letterpart Limited, Reigate, Surrey

Printed and bound in Great Britain by
Clays Ltd, St Ives plc

HEADLINE BOOK PUBLISHING
A division of the Hodder Headline Group
338 Euston Road
London NW1 3BH
www.headline.co.uk
www.hodderheadline.com

Tip Off

Chapter One

I'd never much cared for Toby Brown. He'd always been too arrogant and pleased with himself for my liking. That's how he'd been when we'd first met as ten year olds at school. Twenty-five years on, not much had changed.

I was sitting on a battered wooden bench amid the sweaty air and nervous clamour of the changing room at Fontwell Park. Outside, the ground was heavy and the sky had the shade and texture of soggy porridge. There were ten minutes to kill before the amateur chase, and I wasn't looking forward to it.

I'd picked up a *Racing Post* from the seat beside me and one of Toby's quarter page advertisements had caught my eye.

'The Best Tipster in the Country' was how he modestly described himself. But then, he'd managed somehow to name seventeen winners in his last twenty selections and post a hefty profit. I didn't dispute the claim – a friend on the newspaper had told me all the tipping services were closely monitored. Besides, everyone in racing was talking about it.

Punters up and down the country were following him like kids after the Pied Piper, and for the first time in their corporate histories the big bookies were losing money like water down a drain. I guessed Toby was loving it.

He'd always been a clever dick – very quick with figures. At school he'd been best at everything from French to football, which may partly have accounted for the faint resentment I'd harboured towards him ever since.

I still saw him from time to time, when we would nod a greeting and talk a little about mutual friends. We got along all right because there was no point in falling out with him; besides, his mother, Jane, trained my horses.

But, like everyone else, I was still very curious to know how, in the past few weeks, he'd tipped a string of winners way beyond the scope of mere good luck.

The bell above my head jangled sharply through the steamy room to tell jockeys to get ready for the next race. As I pulled on my helmet, I felt the usual minor eruptions in my innards. It wasn't so much physical danger I feared as the possibility that I was going to go out and make a fool of myself publicly, yet again.

Nester, my mount, was frankly too good for me. He was a classy chaser and I was a less than moderate amateur. Under normal circumstances his trainer wouldn't have let me into his stable, let alone allowed me to ride him on a race-course. I was on him today only because I happened to own him. Officially the horse was called Better By Far; the nickname by which he was affectionately known came from his habit of shoving all the straw in his stable into one corner to make himself a comfortable bed.

If it hadn't been for me, Nester would have arrived at the knacker's a year ago and ended up as the contents of a greyhound's dinner bowl. For that alone, I reckoned I deserved at least one race on him.

The trouble with my riding was that I simply wasn't a natural. From the start, I'd found this lack of ability frustrating and acutely embarrassing, but I was determined to beat it.

I was competent at most of the sports I'd tried, but it seemed that none of the skills from these translated through to race-riding. Like a lot of late starters, I'd spent too much time worrying about the mechanics of the job, instead of just getting on with it, and no matter how much I tried to relax, I knew from the videos that I still rode as if I was in the advanced stages of rigor mortis.

There were always so many things to remember: grip with your knees; keep your head and shoulders low; don't pull the horse in the mouth; don't hold your reins too tight – except, of course, if your horse pecks after a fence, when you have to hold them as tight as you can.

I'd spent hours feeling like a fool on a simulator, trying to remember everything I'd been told. My friend and business partner, Matt James, came to watch a few times; he tried to encourage me with the opinion that I'd progressed from embarrassingly awful to just awful. My style may not have improved a lot since then, but I had grown a thicker hide and excused myself with the fact that I'd never even sat on a horse until I was eighteen, by which time the suppleness of youth was beginning to wear off.

When the starter let us go for the two-and-a-half mile handicap chase, Nester felt so good I found I could leave all these negative thoughts behind. If the old racing adage were true – that it's good horses that make good jockeys – then Nester should make me a champion.

Two years before, he'd been considered the outstanding novice of the season. He'd proved it by winning the Arkle Trophy at Cheltenham, when Lord Tintern still owned him.

The first time I'd schooled him myself, a few months ago, he'd taken my breath away – quite literally. Before that, I'd had no idea what a top-class horse felt like. I was used to plodders who tried to get as close to a fence as they could, to minimise the effort they'd need to get over it. Nester, by contrast, always wanted to take off at least a stride sooner than I expected.

But this was his first race over fences in nearly two years. Jane Brown had made her orders quite clear that morning. I was to sit three or four lengths off the pace, and get a lead for a mile or so to keep him well within himself.

But that wasn't at all how it happened.

After a huge jump at the first fence I found myself right at the front, and from the moment Nester's feet touched down I knew I would be no more than a passenger for the rest of the race.

I guessed that Jane was sitting at home cursing me, but the threat of her wrath was far outweighed by the thrill of riding a top-class steeplechaser. I'd never come across anything like Nester's massive strength. He was powering through the deep ground and leaping each fence as if he were jumping from a springboard. I was having the ride of my life.

It didn't last.

As the race progressed, my confidence grew. I was learning that a really good horse didn't need to be told precisely where to take off. Nester had such ability that he seemed able to reach the fence from just about anywhere.

As we galloped easily towards the first downhill fence, going away from the stables, I was more concerned with my style and how I looked to the people in the grandstand than I was about where Nester was going to take off. For a few brief, happy moments, I even convinced myself that I looked like a professional.

I pushed forward and committed myself to a magnificent leap for the benefit of the spectators. I wanted to give them dramatic proof that Mr S. Jeffries had become an amateur to be reckoned with.

Then, too late, I found there was a limit even to Nester's talents. With abrupt stubbornness, he put in a short one.

If my legs had been gripping properly I'd have had no problem, but I'd prepared myself for a huge leap. When finally Nester was airborne, I was already halfway up his neck; as he popped over the fence, I lost my irons and dropped neatly over his right shoulder.

I'd owned up to my mistake before I hit the deck. Blaming myself because it wasn't the first time. Cursing because Nester had been going so well, and I'd mucked it up.

All this went through my head in the fraction of a second it took for me to leave the saddle and thud into the mercifully soft Sussex turf.

As my hip dented the ground, I instinctively curled up into a ball while the rest of the field galloped past. When I could hear they'd all gone, I picked my whip out of the grass and walked dejectedly to the side of the track where the St John's Ambulance had just pulled up.

The driver leaped out. 'Are you okay?' he called breathlessly, running around the front of his vehicle towards me.

'Yes, yes. I'm fine, thanks. Soft landing.'

I declined a lift back to the changing room; it was only a short walk. But I had to put up with a ribbing from a spectator who'd been watching from the middle of the course. It wasn't meant maliciously, but it hurt just the same.

I'd been disappointed when Jane had said she'd be unable to make it for Nester's first outing in his new colours; I'd wanted the support.

Now I was deeply relieved she hadn't been there. I didn't doubt she'd seen my dismal performance on the Racing Channel, but at least I had time to prepare my excuses before I spoke to her again.

As the race finished, Nester pulled up with the other runners, looking none the worse for having galloped riderless for almost a circuit.

Sally, the girl who looked after him, caught hold of his reins and checked him for cuts. When I came up, she wouldn't even look me in the eye. I couldn't blame her. 'Sorry I buggered that up, Sal.'

'That's all right, Mr Jeffries.' She still didn't look at me but let half a smile flicker across her lips.

Feeling depressed, despite Nester's obviously complete return to fitness, I walked back to the weighing room to shower and change. After a quick cup of tea, I went out to my car and got in. I picked up the phone to check for messages. There was only one, from Matt.

'If you're still alive, can you come into the office about six?'

If my partner needed to see me that urgently, it would be something important and I needed a distraction from my fall. I dialled, got Matt's answerphone and told it I'd be there.

I drove towards Reading and tried to push the frustrations of the afternoon to the back of my mind. I knew for the rest of the season I'd have to be satisfied with using my meagre riding skills on Baltimore, my other horse.

He was a hunter chaser, also housed with Jane at a friendly discount. He was beginning to look quite businesslike under her regime, and she had agreed that he could run at Ludlow in a fortnight's time. She was, she said, far more worried about my fitness than the horse's. After my performance this afternoon, she'd have good reason to worry about my riding skills, too.

Angrily, I thumped the heels of my hands on the steering wheel. I would bloody well learn to ride properly, if it killed me!

Chapter Two

I walked into our company's new, hi-tech offices to be greeted with a dewy smile by Monica, our receptionist-cum-secretary. 'Bad luck, Simon.'

'I wish it was just bad luck – more a case of bad jockey, I'm afraid.'

Jason Williams, who was our office manager and did most of the work in the firm, saw me through the window of his own cubby-hole. He came out, grinning.

'The bad news is you fell off,' he said. 'The good news is I was too late to get a bet on – so I'm twenty quid up.'

It was this positive attitude of Jason's that had persuaded my partner and me to take him on soon after we had launched our technology protection service.

'Glad to hear it, but why are you two still here?'

'Just wrapping up a couple of new contracts,' Jason said happily, thinking of his bonus.

I nodded encouragingly and walked to the closed door on the far side of the reception area.

I found Matt James in his office, sitting at a functional grey steel desk.

At thirty-six, he was a year older than me, but

seemed to have ten years' more experience. Cool detachment and good judgement accumulated over fifteen years in the army showed in his ice-blue eyes. He was a private man, tricky to get close to. His ambitions were obscure, his priorities contradictory, and his relationships with women sporadic and secretive.

His antidote to sedentary work consisted of hard, relentless games of squash, in which I'd never beaten him, and long solo treks across the mountains of marginal Britain. Tough, supremely fit, quick-limbed and quick-witted, there was no one I'd rather have had on my side in a crisis.

Two years ago, he and I had set up as partners in a new security company, specialising in the protection of commercial information. We hadn't made our fortune yet, but from a shaky base we were beginning to build a reputation.

Although we'd been friends since our school days at Marlborough, we didn't have a lot in common. Matt had gone on to command tanks in a cavalry regiment and a squadron in the SAS, while I'd gained a 2:2 in history at Durham and spent the next ten years as an insurance broker at Lloyd's.

We also had very different tastes in recreation and women. That was just as well as neither of us was married and he was a good-looking man by any standards. But we had always shared a passionate interest in racing and a keen desire to beat the bookies.

On his face that evening was a grin as large as any I'd seen in the twenty years I'd known him.

'Either someone's just handed you a monster

cheque,' I said, 'or there's a girl under that desk.'

'I wish there were,' Matt laughed, and shook his mop of sandy hair, 'but you were right first time. Tomorrow morning Salmon Leisure Plc will be handing me a substantial cheque.'

'Toby hasn't done it again?' I asked, incredulous.

Matt nodded. 'Good old Toby, and not such a bad price today: nine to four. Mind you, it should have been double that but I suppose it came right in as soon as Toby napped it. I wonder how the hell he does it?' Matt shook his head.

'I should think every bookie in the country's tearing their hair out wondering that.'

Matt had been following Toby's tips for a few months, and over the recent spectacular run of winners had allowed himself to plough back a good proportion of his winnings into each subsequent bet.

His blue eyes gleamed at me across his desk. 'Anyway, I'm not complaining,' he said with a satisfied grin. 'But look, I'm sorry, Simon – in my excitement, I forgot to ring and tell you the appointment I made for you has been moved.'

'Oh,' I said, disappointed. 'Who's it with?'

'One of your contacts – Emma's father, in fact. He rang to ask if you could meet him this evening on Jockey Club business.' Matt glanced at me. 'Why are you looking so surprised?'

Emma Birt was a girl I wanted to see more of. Her father, Lord Tintern, was a senior steward at the Jockey Club. 'I've been trying to get a toe in that door ever since we started,' I said. 'The security guys in the

11

Jockey Club guard their territory very jealously. But I've been working on old Tintern for the last few months.' I nodded, pleased with myself. 'Maybe all my arse-licking has finally paid off. Mind you,' I winced guiltily, 'our relationship could go sour if Nester stays sound and finds his old form.'

'You mean, once he's got a decent jockey on board?' Matt's eyes flashed again, sharp to spot and point out a flaw. 'You know, Simon, on today's showing, I think you must be the worst jockey I've ever seen. It really is time you gave up.'

I was used to Matt's constant jibes. 'Don't rub it in! I recognise that my partnership with Nester is due for review, but I'm still going to race Baltimore.'

'God help him,' Matt smiled. 'Anyway, I suppose I can't expect you to give up the chance of Nester winning the Champion Chase just because it might upset Tintern, so there's not a lot we can do about that. Meanwhile, he rang half an hour ago and changed the appointment to tomorrow, at Portman Square. So you needn't have rushed back.'

'Too bad,' I said, on reflection glad not to have to see Lord Tintern this evening. 'Did he say what it was about?'

Matt shook his head. 'No, and I didn't ask.'

'I'll have to wait till tomorrow then,' I said philosophically. 'I was going to go over to Wetherdown, but I don't think I can face Jane yet. At least this'll give you a chance to buy me a drink to celebrate your win.'

'And the fact that you and Nester are still alive in spite of your pathetic performance!'

TIP OFF

'Toby Brown has always thought he was right,' Lord Tintern said with mild disparagement. He paused while he poured us both a hefty measure of ten-year-old Laphroaig.

The bottle and two heavy cut-crystal glasses stood on the polished mahogany surface of an elegant early-Georgian card table. The table stood alone in the middle of a small, panelled meeting room in the Jockey Club premises at Portman Square in the West End of London. 'He used to work for me, you know, years ago when he first left school. He's my godson, as a matter of fact. I took him on as a favour to his mother, as a sort of trainee racing manager.'

'Wasn't he any good, then?' I prompted.

Lord Tintern glanced at me down his long, slightly hooked nose. He reminded me of a golden eagle I'd once seen at a falconry centre, gazing disdainfully from high on its perch. I was interested to observe that only three generations away from the keeper of a tiny inn off the Great North Road, Tintern seemed to have acquired all the characteristics of a true aristocrat.

I had the impression that he was going to pounce on me for the audacity of my remark, but he restrained himself. 'As a matter of fact,' he said, 'he showed real flair for the job, but he was more interested in running the horses for his own gain than the good of their careers; we pretty soon fell out. I can't say I've given him much thought since then, but, as you know, he's the hottest property in the game now, tipping all these winners. And, I might say, causing a lot of worries.'

'Tell that to the millions of punters all over the country who are following him.'

'Quite frankly, Simon, I'm not particularly sorry to see the big bookmakers losing for once. But that's not the point – the fact of the matter is, Toby's up to something. Nobody in the history of horse racing has ever been so successful as a tipster. You and I both know that, no matter how clever you are or how hard you work, there's always an element of luck involved. Toby's found a way to dispense with that, and it means only one thing: he's cheating. The bookies are baying for his blood. They sent a delegation to us over the weekend, and I've been asked to look into it.'

'Why don't you use your own security people?'

'Because Toby knows them. We've been on his case for a while now and come up with nothing. I thought maybe a fresh approach would throw up something.'

'Okay,' I said. But I was still surprised that he'd turned to us. The Jockey Club employed at least two dozen full-time ex-CID men, as well as a handful of retrained old soldiers, to maintain the integrity of British racing. And if it was true that Toby knew them all, it was also true that he knew me, and that I was now in the security business myself.

I was glad this didn't seem to have put Tintern off. I'd been hustling for some Jockey Club business for months, but in the back of my mind I was concerned that my decision to run Nester against Tintern's horse in the Champion Chase hadn't struck home yet; I was sure that sooner or later it would get right up his nose and seriously affect our chances of working together.

So why was he giving me instructions now?

For the moment, I decided just to let things run. A job was a job. 'I'll let you have a preliminary report by the end of the week,' I said. 'But you must have considered the possibility that it's no more than just a lucky run?'

Tintern shook his head. 'Nobody stays lucky that long. He's on his own inside track, and we've got to know how he got there. But,' Tintern hesitated a second, 'take your time. You know – softly, softly catchee monkey.'

I nodded, thinking what a fatuous maxim that was. Besides, Toby was no monkey. 'Shall I report to you?'

'Yes, of course. Anything you need, just ask.'

Once the business end of the conversation was over, we spent a few minutes exchanging racing small talk. Lord Tintern was affable enough and I was careful to avoid anything that might lead to a reference to Nester. The entries for the Queen Mother Champion Chase had been published three weeks before and I couldn't believe he hadn't noticed Nester among them. I guessed he'd be more than a little irritated to see a horse that he had once owned and written off entered in any race, let alone a Championship. Especially as he knew that I'd bought Nester from his daughter for the same token payment she had made to him.

'By the way,' he was saying, 'Emma phoned from Florida last Friday. She said she was coming home tonight.'

'That's great news,' I said, trying to conceal my elation.

'I should warn you,' he said, looking directly at me, 'I don't think you'll get much encouragement from her. I imagine she has bigger fish to fry.'

I didn't speak for a second or two and decided, small fish that I was, not to rise to the bait. 'I'm sure she has,' I said mildly.

'You know, of course, that I wasn't too happy about her selling that horse to you,' he went on.

I shrugged my shoulders to hide my alarm that he'd decided to raise the subject now. 'I don't think anyone believed he would recover at the time.'

'That's not the point. The fact is, I'd virtually given the horse to her – I'd be very unhappy if he suddenly came back to form. However, we mustn't let a bit of sporting rivalry interfere with our professional relationship, must we?' he added, with a sudden gracious smile, holding out a hand to me. 'Don't take too long getting to the bottom of this business with Toby.'

When Toby Brown wasn't staying in his exotically decorated flat in Mayfair, he lived on his own in an exquisite Strawberry Hill Gothic cottage on the edge of his mother's estate at Wetherdown, near East Ilsley.

Besides his tipping service, Toby seemed to have fingers in every racing pie. He had a few horses in training – none, surprisingly, with his mother; he owned several brood mares and youngsters, and he regularly bought and sold foals and yearlings. He also had a newspaper column and regularly appeared on television to air his idiosyncratic views on racing.

Although there was rumoured to be a partner

involved in his telephone operation, everyone knew it was all Toby's making. His high profile had ensured that his success was well documented and the line had quickly taken off.

He claimed he'd devised an entirely new formula for picking winners. This took into account more factors influencing the outcome of a race than any rival tipster. He had measured every race-course in the country, made his own going assessments based on times, and even counted the number of strides taken by each horse to cover a furlong.

Business was booming for Toby. When I'd asked him two weeks earlier, he'd arrogantly told me that he netted an average thirty pence every time a punter called in for the day's selection and he was getting around five thousand calls a day, with up to twelve thousand on Saturdays. Not a bad income when you considered the overheads – all he needed was his formbook and a telephone; no office and no staff. I guessed, though, that since his recent run of winners, turnover must have trebled at least.

When Lord Tintern showed me out, I got into my Audi outside the Jockey Club and joined the traffic creeping round Portman Square, heading for the M4 to go back to the office.

My thoughts flitted between interest in the job I'd just been handed and excitement at seeing Emma again for the first time in over a year.

She'd gone off to the States soon after I'd bought Nester from her, saying she'd be back the following spring. But by autumn, she still hadn't reappeared; she'd gone to spend most of the winter ski-ing in Colorado. I guessed, reluctantly, that there were other, unstated attractions there for her. I couldn't blame her for that; I hadn't told her how much I'd wanted her to stay.

I had spent most of the two years before that with Laura Trevelyan, who had worked with my sister. Laura was neurotic, quick-witted, and one of the best-looking women on *Vogue*. But that relationship had ground to an inevitable and uncomfortable halt soon after Emma had left.

Emma had sent me a few postcards while she was away, asking after Nester and Baltimore and, as an afterthought, me. I'd kept her up to date, but the most recent communication had been at Christmas in which she'd asked only after the horses.

Now she was coming back.

Slowing for the perennial hold up on the M4 near Slough, I could summon up a vivid picture of how Emma had looked, fifteen months earlier at Jane's stables.

She'd been wearing a pair of cream-coloured, stretch jodhpurs, uninterrupted by any panty lines, and a thin denim shirt, open just far enough to show the top of her lively breasts.

Her light auburn hair, damp and dishevelled, fell in rat's tails around a peach-soft face and her large turquoise eyes gleamed with conspiratorial excitement. It would have taken a man of far steelier resolve than I not to fall under her spell. I remembered it as if it were yesterday . . .

★　★　★

It had been a darkening afternoon in November when I'd walked through the broad-arched gatehouse into Jane's handsome stable-yard.

'I'm very sorry, Gerald, but there's absolutely no point in shouting at me.' I could hear a rare tremor in Jane's voice. 'This horse will never race again and that's all there is to it.'

'Then you'll just have to shoot the bloody animal!' Gerald Tintern wasn't joking. That much was obvious from the pitch and vindictive edge in his normally mellow voice.

I'd caught the sharp exchange over the howl of a damp wind which blustered unchecked from Salisbury Plain. Not far short of a gale, it shrieked through the old brick archway.

I took in the tableau in front of me: a horse as fit and strong as any I'd seen – apart from a bulky dressing around its near forefoot – and three human figures, all apparently oblivious to the vortex of icy air whirling around the enclosed space.

Instinctively, I changed course, looking for cover from the weather and Lord Tintern's anger. I knew Jane had seen me, and that she might have valued some moral support, but I kept my eyes down and walked quickly across to the office in one of the near corners of the yard.

I let myself in. It was another world in here; warm and quiet except for the murmur of a television in the corner. Even the acrid smell of the head lad's cheap tobacco was welcoming. The sight of Lord Tintern's daughter with her long legs dangling over the side of an old desk was positively exhilarating.

'Hi, Si,' Emma said in her husky, lazy voice, and I grinned back at her, although up until now I'd always hated being called 'Si'.

'What's going on outside?' I asked. 'Your father doesn't sound too happy.'

Emma sighed. 'He can be very tough.'

Jane's head lad, Mick Mulcahy, was paging through the entry book. He looked up. 'He doesn't deserve a good horse.'

'What's happened?' I asked again.

'You know how much Dad paid for Nester?'

'Not exactly,' I said. 'Obviously a lot, I should imagine, but he'll get it all back on his insurance.'

'Dad never insures anything. He says he's rich enough to be his own underwriter.'

'The horse may not be a write-off in any case,' Mick Mulcahy muttered.

'The vet said he'd cracked his pedal bone, just below the coronet,' Emma said. 'He said it might mend if he pins it, but it won't ever be strong enough to race.'

Jane had told me that an injury so deep inside the foot was rare. If Nester could have been persuaded to lie down for six weeks, he'd probably have mended well enough, but that was way beyond the patience of any horse. As it was, with luck he'd recover enough to enjoy his retirement at least.

Emma was looking sharply at Mick. 'How long do *you* think it'll take for that foot to come right?'

'I don't know if it ever will – I've never seen an injury like it before.'

'Esmond Cobbold could cure him,' I said with quiet confidence.

'Who's he?' Emma pounced on the possibility.

I smiled, loving her enthusiasm. 'He's an old boy I know – a friend of my parents' and a kind of healer – brilliant at getting horses right.'

I picked up the phone on Mick's desk and dialled a number in Herefordshire. After a short conversation, I hung up and turned to Emma with a grin. 'He's on his way.'

'Who the hell is this fella?' Mick asked sceptically.

'Esmond Cobbold is the man who cured Harvey, my old hunter, when every vet who'd looked at him said he was unmendable.'

'He'll not cure Nester overnight, I can promise you that.' The Irishman didn't like to have his authority overruled.

'Maybe not,' I said, 'but he'll help more than anyone else I know.'

'What does he do exactly?'

'He can do anything to a horse, bar talk to it. I suppose you'd call him a faith healer, but he's not a crank.'

'Simon, are you sure you're not exaggerating when you say he really can do something?' Emma asked me, still sceptical despite herself.

I held up my hands. 'All I'm saying is that he's the nearest thing I've seen to a miracle worker.'

'Good!' Emma slid off the desk and walked to the

window. She looked through the wet glass at the group of figures, heading in different directions now. Jane trailed behind the owner through the arch. The bun on the back of her head had been demolished by the wind and turned into a mass of waving grey hair. She looked thoroughly deflated.

'Wait here. I'll be back in a moment.' On impulse, Emma reached up to the row of pegs beside the door and helped herself to the nearest Barbour which was five sizes too big for her. She heaved it on. A moment later, letting a quick gust of damp air into the stuffy room, she was outside and the door was banging shut behind her.

Five minutes later she came back, and after a modicum of persuasion I looked like being a thousand pounds poorer and the proud owner of a three-legged race-horse.

I could only hope my confidence in Esmond would be justified.

He was an octogenarian ex-cavalry officer and retired farmer. With his conservative background, regimental tie, drooping moustache and monocle, he was an unlikely character to find in the wild and woolly New Age world of personal auras and earth mysteries, but he seemed to accept his gift in a surprisingly prosaic manner.

How he had discovered his ability to heal people's injuries, he never told me, but he'd hinted that in order not to look foolish, he'd started with animals, successfully achieving a complete cure on his own labrador's failing hip. He'd done similar things with other people's dogs and then progressed to horses, which was how I'd first seen the results of his ministrations.

My continuing faith in Esmond's powers was rewarded. A week after he'd first arrived to see the horse at Wetherdown, I happily gave Emma the thousand pounds she'd promised her father, and wrote to advise Weatherbys that Better By Far had become the property of Simon Jeffries, Esquire.

Chapter Three

The morning after my visit to Portman Square, I woke early to ride first lot from Wetherdown on Baltimore.

As I splashed water on to my reluctantly opening eyes, I looked at my face in the mirror in front of me and observed that the fresh bloom of youth was no longer evident.

At thirty-five, I'd have been surprised if it were. But the strain of trying to keep my weight below twelve stone when I stood at just under six feet was starting to show, and my sybaritic tastes were beginning to cancel out the benefits of several squash games and four mornings' riding out each week.

I nodded philosophically, though, and grinned at my reflection. I was never going to win the Gold Cup, and I may not have been Leonardo DiCaprio, but I had a sneaky suspicion that the Honourable Emma Birt wasn't totally uninterested in me.

Pleased that I was soon going to see her again, I brushed my teeth, shaved and walked through to my bedroom to fling open the window and let in the first early calls of the hedgerow birds and the damp morning mist. I took a few deep breaths, glad that I'd restricted myself to one glass of wine with dinner and gone to bed before the midnight news.

I pulled on a pair of cavalry twill jodhpurs, a cotton shirt and a cable-knit sweater. I'd left my boots in the back of the car, so slipped on a pair of deck shoes to go downstairs.

I lived in what had once been the coach-house of a large Victorian mansion set a hundred feet above the small riverside town of Streatley. The view from the kitchen window was across the Thames and the flat meadows beyond. Ancient hedges and a few pollarded willows with ghostly spiked heads poked through the shroud of white mist which lay across the valley floor.

I made myself a pot of mega-strength Java Lava and hacked a few segments from a fleshy grapefruit. Whatever other disadvantages Baltimore may have been going to suffer, carrying overweight wasn't one of them.

A few minutes later I was in the car, driving with my headlights on. The day was still struggling to emerge through the moist blanket that lay in scattered patches over the folds of the downs, but by the time I drove between the high stone gate-posts at Wetherdown twenty minutes later, the sun had just appeared as a faint silvery ball above the long horizon behind me.

I by-passed the house, set in a circle of giant specimen pines, and parked close to the broad arch of the brick gatehouse to Jane's handsome Edwardian stables.

I climbed out and stretched while I filled my lungs with crisp dawn air. A thrush anticipated trouble and with a noisy 'chip-chip', fled to an ancient yew that guarded the entrance, scattering the dew that sparkled on the tree's dark green needles.

From within the yard, I heard the clop of hooves on cobbles, the snorting of the horses, the bustle of lads rushing to be ready to pull out their rides on the dot of seven-thirty. Baltimore would be tacked up and waiting for me.

I walked in through the arch. I didn't look for Jane immediately. I hadn't seen her since my fall at Fontwell, but I'd spoken to her at length on the phone the night before. First, I went to Nester's box and let myself in. He turned to look at me with what I was sure was a friendly nod. I glanced around with my eyes smarting from the sharp tang of a peeled onion dangling from a rafter. This was Jane's way of warding off the bugs and viruses that liked to plague a horse's stable.

I noticed with a smile that the straw bedding was neatly rucked up into what looked like a vast bird's nest on the clean side of his box – he was the nearest I'd seen to a house-trained horse.

In a separate corner, his empty manger was on the floor, since he'd shown long ago that he would only eat up if his food was offered at ground level.

I dropped to one knee and slid my hand down his tendon to feel for heat. There was none there and none in his feet either. There hadn't been since Esmond Cobbold had declared his task finished. I nodded with relief. You could never tell for certain how well injuries had healed until they'd stood the test on a race-course.

Nester had galloped a good two and a half miles over the sticky ground at Fontwell, and he was fine.

I also had to give Jane a lot of the credit for his remarkable recovery. She had started his exercise regime with great restraint. For weeks on end he'd barely walked a stride, but he'd swum miles, toning his muscles with no strain on his foot. Then he'd walked slowly and, eventually, begun to trot, but only on the grass or the softness of the all-weather gallop.

Then Jane had cantered and schooled him gently over her least demanding chase fences for another two months, while he rebuilt his formidable driving muscles. The only hitch in the programme so far had been my falling off.

It had been Jane's suggestion to enter Nester for Cheltenham. I was more than happy just to see the horse back on a race-course again, but she was convinced he was as good as ever. After my dismal effort at Fontwell, we still didn't know for sure.

I left Nester's box thinking of the Senior Steward's views on his return to the track, which led my thoughts inevitably back to Toby Brown.

So far I had no firm plan on how I was going to get an angle on his success. Matt's less than subtle suggestion had been to break into his cottage and his flat in London, bug his phones and conduct a thorough search. I had talked him out of this for the time being, on the grounds that Toby was too intelligent not to be alert to the possibility that this might happen.

Abruptly, though, all thoughts of him fled my mind. Walking under the arch into Jane's yard was Emma. It was the first time I'd set eyes on her in over a year.

She was dressed in Levi's and well-worn chaps, and shivering under a thickly lined Drizabone.

'Hi, Si,' she said, as if she'd seen me the day before.

'Emma! It's great to see you.' I grinned my welcome. 'You look wonderful!' I walked over to kiss her on both soft, tanned cheeks. 'What are you doing here? I thought you only arrived back late last night?'

'I did, and rang Jane as soon as I got home. She said you were riding out so I asked if there was something I could take as well.' She nodded at a small hurdler being led up from a box as we spoke.

'Great. I'll see you on the way up.'

I found Baltimore and joined Emma as the string drew out of the yard to clatter up the flinty track towards the deep green sweep of Jane's private gallops.

'So, what did you get up to in Florida?'

She glanced up from adjusting her leathers. 'I met a few gorgeous horses and a lot of hideous men.'

I laughed, looking at her and waiting for more, but it was clear that she didn't want to expand.

'How's Nester?' she asked.

'He's in great shape. I rode him on Monday.'

'I heard.' She made a face. 'Jane told me.'

'Don't you start,' I warned. 'I've taken more than enough flak already. Has your father mentioned it?'

'Not really. Mind you, I've hardly seen him. But it's fantastic that Nester's recovered so well.'

'One hundred percent.' I smiled. 'He hasn't had a lame day since Esmond came to look at him.'

'Dad'll go ape when he realises Nester's sound again.'

She winced at the thought. 'Are you still going to run him in the Queen Mother Chase?' she added quickly.

'He's entered. That's why I thought your father might have said something.'

'He wouldn't confide in me. Anyway, Nester's yours now. Will you run him before Cheltenham?'

'We might run him in another two-and-a-half mile chase. It would be too far, of course, but the ground's good at the moment and the conditions of the race mean he won't be giving away too much weight.'

We had reached the end of the lane and the gate that gave on to the southern slope of the down. Jane was already waiting in her Land Rover to shout instructions to each of the riders as they went by. Emma had to go on; Baltimore and I were going last so that I could keep him settled. For a slow horse, he could pull like a train; the problem was that, when you let him have his head, he would never go any faster.

I pulled up at the end of the gallop, looping round as I slowed to a trot then a long lazy walk. Jane stood and studied every horse as we walked back past where she'd been standing.

'What do you think?' I asked hopefully.

'Fine, absolutely fine. Which is more than I can say for you.'

'I didn't ask about me,' I laughed, as if she wasn't being serious.

'Just as well. I'll see you back at the yard – I'd like a word.'

As I hacked back, I wondered about Jane. Although I'd known her for years, I still couldn't quite tell what she was thinking. I had the impression she liked me, though nothing she'd said ever confirmed it; and I thought she trusted me, but that wasn't obvious either.

I was putting Baltimore away when she came into his stable. 'He's looking well,' she congratulated herself.

'So he should, with all that money I give you to feed him,' I retorted, rubbing the sweat off the horse with a fistful of straw.

Jane ignored that. 'By the way, Gerald Tintern's on his way over.'

I felt suddenly uncomfortable and wondered if he knew he'd find me here. He might already be expecting results from my enquiries, which I hadn't even started yet.

'What for?' I asked apprehensively.

'He's just bought another horse to run in the Champion Chase.'

That was news to me. 'Is it coming here?'

'It arrived yesterday. Would you like to see it?'

'I'd love to. What is it?'

'Purple Silk.'

'Bloody hell! He must have paid the earth to get Jimmy Doyle to part with it.'

Jane laughed. 'He didn't take any notice of what I said, or anyone else for that matter. I told him to try and buy Nester back from you but he wouldn't hear of it. Pride wouldn't let him.'

'Tell me,' I asked as she lifted the latch and drew back the bolt on Purple Silk's stable, 'why's Gerald so keen to win the Queen Mother Chase?'

'He wants to have his photo taken, shaking hands with Her Majesty.'

It had never occurred to me that this might seriously be a motive for winning, but maybe Jane was right.

Purple Silk was a beautifully built animal with all the characteristics of a classic two-miler.

I'd seen him race on television and my own impression of him was that he had an abundance of talent but had never been asked a serious question. I wondered, though, if push ever came to shove at the finish of a race, just how big his heart would be. Nester, I knew, would battle until he dropped.

We were leaving the box when Jane turned to me. 'Simon, I don't quite know how to say this,' there was a rare note of embarrassment in her voice, 'but Gerald has put me in rather an awkward position. As you know, he's got six horses here, including Purple Silk, and he's suggested that he might have to take them all elsewhere if I carry on training Better By Far. He was perfectly nice about it, but said he thinks no matter how good a trainer I am, I'll never be able to train two horses for a race as well as I will one. And he's right, of course.'

As Jane pulled the bolt across the stable door, my mind raced, weighing up the options and wondering what I should do. I couldn't ask her to forfeit six good horses and all the training fees, but I couldn't think who else would train Nester as well. She knew him inside out and he was thoroughly settled at Wetherdown.

'It's up to you, Simon,' she was saying. 'I'm not

going to be browbeaten by Gerald, and I'd almost rather he did take his bloody animals away.'

'But it's not that simple, is it?' I said with a smile. 'I can leave you with Baltimore, though, can't I?'

'Of course you can,' she said, without trying to disguise her relief. 'Are you sure you don't mind about Nester? Believe me, Simon, I wouldn't put up with this kind of behaviour if it wasn't for the fact that our families go back a long way. You know that Toby is Gerald's godson? I'm Emma's godmother, and my brother Frank was a founding shareholder in Gerald's King George Hotel Group. My brother still owns thirty-five percent of it. *And* my godfather, David Green, is Gerald's lawyer.'

'It all sounds very incestuous, but I do understand,' I said. 'It's not the end of the world. If you don't mind, though, I'll send Nester to a yard where you can still keep an eye on him for me?'

'Of course I don't mind.'

'I'll let you know where he's to go as soon as I can.' I dismissed the topic. 'Now, do you happen to know if Toby's around?'

'Yes, he is. He's going to Newbury this afternoon, but I'm sure you'll find him at the cottage now.'

Before I left the yard, I hunted for Emma to tell her the news I'd just heard.

I found her still rubbing down the horse she had exercised, with her helmet off and her hair, longer than before, falling in pale copper-tinted waves to her shoulders.

'Hi!' She looked up with a smile that stopped me in my tracks. 'That was great! How was it for you?' She opened big, innocent turquoise eyes.

'Please don't say things like that so early in the morning,' I begged.

'Down, boy.' She grinned. 'Now, are you going to take me to lunch and tell me what's been going on since I've been away?'

I knew I hadn't time to have lunch with her. With her father's brief and another new one that had just come in, Matt and I were at full stretch.

'Of course,' I said. 'We'll go to the Greyhound. Nothing's changed there.'

'It never does. I'd like that.' She stood back to inspect the horse. 'What did Jane want?' she asked casually.

I explained that her father wanted me to take Nester from the yard.

Her jaw stiffened with anger. 'God, I'm sorry. I don't know how he gets away with it.'

'Ask Jane.' I looked at my watch. 'I've got to go. I'll see you at one.' I gave her a quick kiss and left her in the stable.

I climbed into my car, guilty and delighted at the thought of seeing Emma later, but with an effort I refocused my thoughts and drove the half-mile to Toby's cottage.

To reach the cottage, I didn't need to leave Jane's land. When Gervaise Brown had died, he had left her the Wetherdown Estate and enough money to keep it going comfortably without ever having to earn a penny.

The main house had been built and the grounds re-landscaped for a London banker in the 1880s; Gervaise had bought it from the official receiver in bankruptcy in the early-sixties.

Toby had been just five and Jane less than thirty when her husband died. She'd been desolate at first to be left such a young widow, but she made up her mind not to be beaten by it, calling up reserves of energy which friends hadn't realised she possessed. With a little knowledge and a lot of enthusiasm, she'd set about turning the domestic stables into a supremely well-equipped racing yard, and one of the prettiest in the country. She never kept more than sixty horses, and I thought she'd probably lived on her earnings ever since.

Her greatest personal challenge had been not to over-indulge her only child. She had already told Toby that unless he produced an heir, Wetherdown would be left to an equine charity.

But Toby, proud and resourceful, had proved he was quite capable of looking after himself without any need to compromise the comfortable bachelor existence he'd chosen.

His mother had compensated for her firm stand by offering him the use of Yew Tree Lodge, a small exquisite Neo-Gothic dower house that pre-dated the main house by a hundred years, but he'd accepted only on the condition that he paid rent for it.

In the five years he'd occupied the house, a constant stream of interior decorators, special effect painters, curtain makers, antique dealers and creative gardeners had turned the eccentric but charming house into the celebrated centrefold of half a dozen glossy style magazines.

It was too over the top for my functional tastes, but I could appreciate the flair that had gone into achieving it. I hadn't been there for several years, and I was intrigued to see what recent improvements he'd made.

Driving through the wrought-iron gates, I was relieved to see his car parked on the neat gravel circle to one side of the house. It was a pristine DB5 in an implausible shade of metallic elderberry.

I parked my more pedestrian Audi beside it and walked beneath a long, vine-bearing pergola, in the same wrought-iron as the gates, to the Gothic-panelled front door. I tugged a small brass handle that prompted a chain reaction through a series of wires and levers inside the house and culminated in the tinkle of a distant bell.

A few moments later, Toby opened the door to me, tall and slender in a paisley silk dressing-gown. His straight, dark chocolate hair was, as always, perfectly groomed. When he saw me, his smoothly tanned face creased into an enigmatic smile. 'Simon, how lovely to see you. Come in.' He wrinkled his nostrils fastidiously as I passed through the front door. 'I sense you've been near a horse recently.'

I laughed, acknowledging the strong smell of horse sweat still on my hands. 'You can sprinkle me with rosewater, if you like.'

'There's some Roger et Gallet in the cloakroom.' He waved at a door halfway along his elegant hall.

I took the cue. 'Thanks.'

'Coffee in the conservatory when you're ready,' he called.

I made my way through to a lushly planted, almost tropical hall of glass, in the middle of which stood a well-aged iron table and some chairs, where Toby was ready to dispense dense black coffee from a small cafetière.

He waved me to a seat and poured. 'What brings you here, then?' he asked in a markedly more no-nonsense way.

'This place, as a matter of fact.' I gestured around the conservatory. 'I saw that piece in *Interiors*, and I'm thinking of putting something similar on to my own house.'

Toby's eyes lit up. 'You need a lot of time or a housekeeper with very green fingers to keep a room like this going.'

'I wasn't thinking of quite so much vegetation.'

'Here, let me show you the plans and drawings – they might help.'

I let him spend ten minutes on an illustrated lecture on how I could recreate what he'd done before the conversation moved on inevitably to horses.

'I've been meaning to speak to you,' he said. 'Mother tells me you're serious about running Better By Far in the Champion Chase?'

'That's right.'

'But I thought he was a total write-off?'

'That's what it looked like, but fortunately for me he's come right. He was going really nicely at Fontwell, would probably have won . . .'

'If you hadn't stepped off,' Toby interrupted disparagingly.

'Thanks,' I said with a dry laugh. 'But at least the horse was going well, which is all I cared about.'

'Perhaps I ought to nap him for the QM – unless you're thinking of riding him yourself again?'

'No, I'm not. But I presume you know there's another form horse just come in from the cold?'

'Purple Silk? Yes, of course I know; I persuaded Doyle to part with it. Mind you, if your horse is back to his best, he could give Purple Silk a run for his money.'

'Well, the way you're going,' I grinned, 'whichever horse you nap will win.'

Toby gave a quick, almost embarrassed grin, and shrugged. 'Maybe.'

'Oh, come on. You've hardly got it wrong for about three weeks,' I pressed, taking my opportunity.

'There have been one or two hiccups.'

'Even you couldn't predict horses being carried out or brought down. Your strike rate's still miles over the odds. How do you do it?'

'Pure luck,' he ventured, unconvincingly.

'Oh, come on. Luck doesn't last that long.'

'Well, I'm putting a lot of effort into it, too. The harder I work, the luckier I get.'

'Toby, just tell me what your secret is. What are you doing that you weren't doing before?'

He sighed and looked at me silently for a moment. 'Now, that would be telling.'

'Unless I've missed something, I can't see what your system is. All different courses, different jockeys and trainers, jumping and flat, anything from six furlongs to three and a half miles.'

'Goodness,' Toby said with more of his normal acerbity, 'you have been following me closely.'

'My friend Matt James has. He's won a small fortune following your tips – almost fifteen hundred quid on Monday.'

'Monday was exceptional. I knew that horse had been saved for a gamble.' Toby grinned. 'A few million punters must have got on to it, as far as I can tell. I've got twenty lines coming into my service now, busy the whole time. Of course, the big bookies all closed my accounts when I started backing some of my own naps, but the tipping lines are bringing great money, so who cares? And this Saturday, things will really take off. Just make sure you're watching television on Friday night.'

'I will,' I said, intrigued. 'Maybe we could meet up for a drink on Saturday evening, after racing.'

'Sorry.' Toby became suddenly awkward. 'No can do. I've organised a small party later.'

Chapter Four

I left Toby taking declarations for the next day's meeting
and half an hour later I was sitting with Matt in our
office. We were having what he called a debriefing.

'Okay,' Matt said, 'I accept that there's no pattern to
these winning naps of Toby's – or at least, you and I
haven't found one yet – but it's still possible to stimulate a horse in order to enhance its performance
dramatically, isn't it? At least, enough to give it a
substantial edge over its rivals for as long as it takes to
run a race?'

'You mean, did Toby dope them?'

Matt nodded.

'Out of the question,' I said, more brusquely than I'd
meant to. 'Of course I'd thought of that, but to get at
all those horses – from different yards and different
parts of the country? It's not possible. And even if he
had, something would have shown up in the dope test.
If they were consistently coming up positive for anything, Toby would have had his collar felt weeks ago.'

'Okay, okay.' Matt held up a pacifying hand. 'I was
just looking at all the possibilities. I'm sure he could

41

have had them doped if he was running a concerted campaign with a number of trainers, but I accept that the tests kick that option into touch.'

'Matt, it just wouldn't be possible to get deals together with dozens of different trainers anyway. For a start, not many of them are that bent, and several who have had winners napped by Toby, I'd stake my mother's life wouldn't dope a horse.'

'Your mother's dead,' Matt observed drily. 'So what's your explanation?'

I sighed. 'Frankly, I haven't a clue yet.'

'In which case we'd better send in an interim report to the Jockey Club, telling them that investigations are progressing and we'll keep them posted.'

'Sure.' I nodded. 'And I'll ask them to let us have the results of the dope tests carried out on all Toby's winners, just to eliminate that option.'

'But we're going to have to look harder and see if we can find anything at all to link them.'

I shrugged a shoulder. 'We can try, but I don't think that's the way. I have one other faint lead to follow up.' I glanced at my watch. 'In about twenty minutes.'

'What's that?' Matt asked.

'I'll let you know if it gets anywhere.'

'Okay, but be back here by six. I've arranged for us to go and interview a man for Wessex Biotech tonight. And I think, as it's the first contact, we should both be there.'

Regretfully, I abandoned any ideas of a candle-lit dinner with Emma, and tried to calm the apprehension that always ran through me before a night of information gathering with Matt. It wasn't what the other party might do under questioning that worried me; it was just how insistent my partner's questioning might become.

With a sharp twinge of guilt, I left the office and raced west down the motorway to meet Emma for lunch at the pub near Lambourn. I had managed to kid myself that there was some justification for this lunch as research on the grounds that I needed to fill in the gaps in my knowledge of Toby Brown. He had worked for Lord Tintern once, and I'd just learned from Jane how close her family and his had been for many years.

But despite the guilt I was looking forward to spending a few hours with Emma, to make up for the months she'd been away.

As I drove into the pub car-park, Emma slipped out of a black convertible BMW and walked towards me. I tried to view her dispassionately, and failed. She was looking stunning.

'Great timing, us turning up together,' I said.

'No, it isn't,' she replied. 'You're late. I've been sitting in my car waiting for twenty minutes.'

'Why didn't you wait in the pub?'

'I haven't been in there for fifteen months – I didn't feel like walking in on my own.'

We managed to find a table that gave us some privacy among the eager gossip-merchants in the busy pub.

We ordered some wine and lunch.

'Now,' I said, 'you must tell me everything you've been up to.'

'Everything?'

I nodded.

'That's greedy,' she said. 'I'll stick to censored high-lights.'

I wasn't surprised to hear that Emma had been widely entertained in Florida, New York and California, with a few spells in the snow at Aspen and a month on Mustique in the Grenadines.

I already knew some of this from the sporadic postcards she'd sent, and the half-knowledge had been tantalising. Now that she was here in front of me, confiding her impressions, it already felt as if she hadn't been away at all.

'Okay,' I said after a while. 'You were right. If you tell me everything now I'll get information overload. Save a few of the more sensational details until next time.'

'Fine,' she laughed. 'Tell me what you've been up to. How's Laura, for instance?'

I tried a blank, puzzled look.

Emma raised both eyebrows. 'Your sister's friend, Laura Trevelyan,' she said. 'The girl you were going out with before I went away.'

'Oh, that Laura,' I said. 'She's fine; she took over Catherine's job on the magazine. They say she's doing very well.'

'When did you last see her?'

'I've hardly seen her at all since you went to the States. It fizzled out just after you left.'

'That's a shame.'

I shrugged my shoulders. 'I'll live.'

Emma appeared to think about that for a moment, then, with a change of tone, she went on, 'Where did you disappear to this morning in such a hurry?'

'I went over to Toby's house. I wanted to catch him before he'd gone for the day.'

'Don't tell me – you were looking for a sure thing to back?'

'You've heard, then?'

'About Toby's winning run? Of course. My father was ranting on about it last night. I gather the bookies are furious. Though why that should worry him, God knows; he's always moaning that the bookies are taking all their profits out of racing.'

'Yes, it's a popular theme among the upper echelons of racing.'

'And I know he's not particularly fond of bookies generally. My grandfather lost the family business betting on horses.'

'Did he? I thought your father inherited the business from him.'

'So do most people, but he didn't. My great-grandfather, Arthur Birt, made the original family fortune. He started with a small pub near Stevenage and built up a chain of hotels – he was almost on a par with the Astors. He gave Lloyd George fifty thousand quid to be made first Baron Tintern. As soon as his son, my grandfather, got the title and the money, he went on a thirty-year gambling spree and lost the lot.'

'But if the business was gone, why on earth did your father go into hotels?'

'To prove how useless his own father was, probably. I

45

think he despised Granddad – I can remember he was pretty rude to him. Anyway, he was determined to make the King George Hotel Group a success, and worked like a maniac to get there. I hardly saw him for the first ten years of my life.'

'He certainly seems to know how to get what he wants,' I agreed, 'even when it comes to someone as strong-minded as Jane.'

'Jane wouldn't have agreed to lose Nester just to protect her own interests. She has too much integrity for that,' Emma said. 'I should think she doesn't want to fall out with Dad for her brother Frank's sake.'

'She mentioned him this morning. I knew nothing about him before.'

'He's lived in Menton for years but they're very close. And he owns a chunk of my dad's company.'

'So I gathered. And presumably you've known Jane since you were in nappies?'

'She is my godmother. I've always been very fond of her, and of Frank – he's a lovely man. Apparently her husband Gervaise was the same.'

'How well do you know Toby?' I asked.

'Well enough, but we've never been that close; he was often around when I was a kid. I can remember going with my mother to take him out to tea from Eton. I was about seven, and he must have been in his last year. He was in Pop and thought he was very grand. And a few years after that, just before Mum died, she took me to the South of France to stay at Frank's villa. Toby was there too, full of himself, claiming he'd worked out a system for beating the casinos.'

'He's told me about that. I think they all barred him in the end.'

'Do you know what it is he's doing this time?'

'Nope,' I said, as if I had no particular interest. 'But Matt's been doing well out of it.'

'How is that steely-eyed partner of yours? Still aching for action in a black balaclava?'

'Yes, no change there, I'm afraid. Mind you, we get a little excitement now and again.' I couldn't suppress a quick stab of anxiety at the thought of this evening's undertaking.

'That's just what I need. Maybe I should help you out some time?'

'I'll let you know,' I said, laughing.

'I mean it,' Emma protested. 'I've got to do something.'

'What's wrong with shopping and lunch?' I asked.

She made a face and narrowed her eyes to glittering slits of turquoise; but she knew I was joking.

'Look,' I went on, 'getting back to Toby, what do *you* think he's up to?'

'Toby's a clever guy and he'd do anything for money, provided he wasn't going to get caught.'

'Like what?' I asked.

Emma flashed me a quizzical glance. 'Like helping the winner he's napped, stopping all the others, bribing all the jockeys . . . Who knows?'

'Matt and I have already been down that alley,' I said quickly, not admitting we hadn't thought of the stopping option. I considered for a moment whether it would be fair or rash to tell her that we'd been instructed by the Jockey Club to investigate Toby. I decided there wouldn't be any harm in it and began to tell her, but halfway through my explanation of what Matt and I had been doing, she interrupted me.

'What about the other option?'

'You mean, having all the other runners stopped?'

Emma nodded.

'What do you think?' I asked doubtfully.

She sighed. 'Yes, all right, it just wouldn't be possible – unless they were all very small fields.'

'No. We looked at that. Some of the fields had twenty plus runners.'

Emma nodded. 'I don't think Toby would have done that anyway. He's too clever. What do you think?'

I shrugged. 'I couldn't honestly say. He wasn't giving much away this morning.'

Emma didn't speak for a moment then asked, 'Did my father tell you why he'd chosen your firm to do this job?'

'Not specifically, but he suggested that Toby already knew most of the Jockey Club investigators too well for them to be effective.'

'What you'll soon discover about my father is that he doesn't do anything without a damn' good reason,' Emma told me in a voice that had suddenly grown unusually serious for her.

A few hours later, Matt and I left the car-park outside our office, heading for a small hamlet near Bath and a house which a client had asked us to 'attend'.

Matt was looking forward to the job. It was fairly

straight-forward and promised him the chance to use his well-practised techniques in field work.

On the journey down in his car, I told him about my lunch with Emma.

'For God's sake, Simon, are you telling me you spent all afternoon with her and it was purely research?'

'Not all of it,' I admitted.

'Well, while you've been sniffing around the Honourable Emma Birt, I've arranged for us to see one of the bookies tomorrow. That may give us a new perspective.'

'Who's that?' I asked, annoyed that he'd stolen a march.

'Salmon Leisure. We're seeing the chief executive, Harry Chapman.'

We were only twenty minutes from our destination by the time I got round to asking Matt for more details of the job we were on. He had fielded the enquiry when it came into the office and had handled all the briefings so far.

'Basically, the company's developed a piece of equipment that they call Powderjet; it's an alternative to the old-fashioned hypodermic syringe.'

'That sounds like a useful product. I loathe jabs.'

'You and most of the population,' Matt observed unsympathetically.

'I suppose you don't even notice them?'

'An injection is a classic case of a psychologically induced trauma. The degree of pain is very small. It's the anticipation that causes the grief, not the needle.'

'I know that, of course, but I still hate them. Anyway,

how does this new method work?'

'They place a small disc on the surface of the skin; the agent to be introduced is released through thousands of tiny holes under very high pressure so that it's propelled straight through the epidermis and into the patient's bloodstream.'

'And that doesn't hurt?'

'Not a bit.'

'Like those nicotine patches that people stick on themselves to stop smoking?'

'In that the drug is absorbed through the skin, yes.'

'Sounds a winner,' I said. 'What's the problem?'

'Wessex Biotech's main research lab is out in the sticks down here, and kept heavily secure given the money they'll earn from royalties on the product once it comes on stream.'

'What'll that be worth to them?' I asked to get an idea of the scale of the problem.

'If the system goes into use world-wide, it will run into hundreds of millions of dollars. Think of it – needles will become a thing of the past. But they can't get a cast-iron world patent on the thing until all the tests are complete. They're nearly there but if any competitors got their hands on the technology now, they could still be pipped.'

'So, what's happened?'

'Two complete prototype systems with specially adapted drugs have gone missing. This guy we're going to visit is one of their research scientists. David Dysart, who's his boss and the guy I've been dealing with, thinks our man may have helped himself to them to sell to the opposition.'

'And we're looking for these samples?'

'Possibly, but more likely anything that will show the subject's been in contact with rival companies or,' Matt paused significantly, 'been getting large amounts of cash from other sources.'

'Will he be on his own?'

'I hope so, or we'll be wasting our time.'

'Does he have a wife or family?'

'Not married.'

'You like all this, don't you?' I said, seeing that hard profile crease into a grin. 'But what you seem to forget is that when you were doing it in the army, you were usually dealing with other professionals.'

He laughed. 'You've led such a sheltered life!'

'Not any more,' I muttered. 'Anyway, how did we get this job?'

'As a matter of fact, you're responsible. Apparently you met Dysart somewhere, told him what you were doing and gave him a card. He's in his early forties, I'd say, very entrepreneurial and full of himself. Ring any bells?'

I shook my head. 'Not off-hand. I've given away hundreds of cards and I do the sales spiel wherever I go.' In the first few months of establishing the business, and ever since it had got off the ground, I'd networked conscientiously, though not always methodically, using all my old insurance contacts as well as any social ones that were offered. 'Did he say where we'd met?'

'No.'

'We must ask him,' I said. 'Now I suppose I'd better apply myself to the map and talk you to the target.'

The target was a chocolate-box cottage of thatch and stone, nestling in a deep cleft in the eastern slopes of the Mendip Hills.

'That's a very des. little res.,' I remarked. 'So our chum is already doing reasonably well for himself. How old is he?'

'It's all in the profile. He's twenty-nine, and on thirty grand a year.'

'What's he called?'

'Brian Griffiths.'

'Right,' I said, trying to sound positive, 'let's go and talk to him.'

We were in the cottage for an hour. Our instructions were to make exploratory investigations only, at this point, and in no way to antagonise a key member of Dysart's research team.

As I looked around the small sitting room of his house, I was struck by the quality of the furniture and the pictures on the walls. From my patchy knowledge of eighteenth-century equestrian paintings, I judged that one of them, at least, was worth twice its owner's annual salary.

During a lull in Matt's questioning, I remarked on it.

'Yes, it's nice, isn't it? It's a Herring, as a matter of fact.'

'Must be worth a lot?'

Griffiths looked at me a little primly, as if I'd just committed some social gaffe, which, I supposed, I had.

Matt wasn't put off. 'I see you've got one of the new Range Rovers outside, too?' The subtle approach wasn't his style.

Griffiths looked at him like an owl through his big tortoiseshell glasses. 'I do a lot of hill walking. It comes in handy for getting up to good start points.' He stood up. 'Now I think I've told you all I can about the missing systems and I've some work to catch up on. So, if you wouldn't mind . . .?'

'What a complete bloody waste of time!' Matt fumed as we drove back towards Berkshire.

'Well, we discovered something.'

'Like what?'

'Like he has a painting on his wall that's worth at least fifty or sixty grand.'

Matt turned his head to look at me. 'As much as that? Where would he get money like that to spend on a picture?'

'Maybe he didn't.' I shrugged. 'Maybe he was left it.'

'Maybe, but I didn't think much of him. Did you notice how he kept putting his finger inside his collar and lifting his chin – almost as if it was too tight? That's a sure sign of lying.'

'That doesn't prove anything, though.'

'At least it gives us something to report, and I suggest next time we go there when Griffiths is out.'

Chapter Five

The following morning, on the way to see Harry Chapman in London, Matt and I talked about Jane's family connections with Gerald Tintern, and how her brother, Frank Gurney, was a long-term shareholder in Tintern's King George Hotel Group.

'Salmon Leisure own a chain of hotels too, so I imagine Chapman must know Lord Tintern.'

'If he didn't before, he does now.'

'Was Chapman one of the bookies who complained to the Jockey Club?'

'Salmon Leisure are one of the four largest operators. They always show a united front whenever anything threatens their interests. The rest of the time they do everything they can to trample on each other.'

'A metaphor for the human race,' Matt said drily.

'If it's philosophy, it must be Thursday,' I laughed. 'But what still worries me is why Tintern decided to hire us to do the job, given that he doesn't think I'm good enough for his daughter?'

'I thought we'd established that he came to us because you know Toby well enough to get close to him without having any particular loyalty towards him.'

'How the hell would he know whether or not I felt any loyalty? I think he just wanted to protect Toby from any heavy-handed stuff from the in-house security people. He's his godfather after all. I expect he thought we'd be more gentle.'

'Not necessarily,' Matt said with a wolfish grin.

The head office of Salmon Leisure Plc was in a handsome old building in Hanover Square. Inside, it was decorated with low-key paintings and furniture of a quality that suggested it had been chosen to contrast deliberately with the vulgar way it had been gained.

A pretty dark girl sat behind the long sweep of polished elm that faced the main entrance. With East End chirpiness, she pointed us to the lift which went straight up to the chief executive's office on the fourth floor. There we were directed into an ante-room hung with large equestrian canvases, where another girl, even more striking than her colleague on the ground floor, looked up. After a momentary frown, she broke into a glowing smile that instantly encompassed both of us.

For once, I heard a faint stutter in Matt's voice as he introduced us. 'Matthew James and Simon Jeffries,' he murmured, 'on behalf of the Jockey Club, to see Mr Chapman.'

The girl's black hair was cut in a short bob, setting off high cheekbones and slightly angled, electrifying blue eyes which lingered on Matt for a moment before she glanced down at the desk diary in front of her. 'Yes,' she said. 'Mr Chapman's expecting you. He'll be free in a few minutes.' She stood up. She was wearing a short black skirt that rode up a little over the dark nylon of her tights and I saw a twitch of approval on Matt's face at the sight of her well-filled blouse. 'Coffee?' she asked.

'Er . . . yes, please,' Matt muttered and I nodded.

'Take a seat,' she said, waving towards a cluster of squashy sofas around a low table. She disappeared through a small door behind her desk. We sat down. I looked at Matt.

'Which do you fancy most, the pictures or the staff?' I asked, sensing that he was unusually uptight.

'No contest,' he answered curtly and tried to relax back on to the sofa. It gave more than he expected, until he found himself almost supine. He heaved himself back and sat on the front edge, making a face; he hated to look foolish.

The girl came back in carrying a cafetière and two cups on a tray. A pleasing aroma of strong fresh coffee wafted through the air as she bent over to place it on the table.

'Thanks,' Matt said. 'Where would you like to have dinner?' he added hurriedly.

I was astonished; I'd never seen him move so fast. The girl straightened her back and considered the question.

'Tonight?' she asked, swinging her bobbed hair to one side.

'Of course,' Matt said clearly, having evicted the frog from his throat.

'Harry's Bar.'

Before Matt could reply, a deep voice resounded from an intercom on the desk. 'Sara. I'm free now.'

'I'll bring your coffee through,' she said with a mischievous smile.

Harry Chapman's office was so big, it could have been a small ballroom. Perhaps once it had been.

The chief executive of Salmon Leisure stood up behind his desk, with his back to a tall window that overlooked the bustling, rain-drenched square below.

But no outside sounds penetrated the room, and the deep quiet matched the subdued grey-green and heather colours of the decor.

As Harry came round the desk, his features became clearer. He was a tall man, not dissimilar in build to Lord Tintern. Facially, he could scarcely have been more different. His rubbery flesh was the pale pink of a peeled prawn, his nose bulbous and cheeks chubby. Beneath a mop of fluffy grey hair and heavy lids, his eyes radiated a wily charm. He held out his hand and shook Matt's then mine with flamboyant gusto.

'Good morning.' There was a hint of South London in the gravelly voice. 'Let me guess which of you is which,' he cut in as I was about to tell him my name. 'I've had a look at your company profile, and I see that Mr James was one of those covert heroes who do so much to protect our liberty. That would be you,' he said, looking at me.

So forceful were his gaze and conviction that I almost quailed from contradicting him. 'Nearly right, Mr Chapman,' I muttered. 'In fact, I'm Simon Jeffries.'

The big man let go of my hand and roared with laughter. 'Nearly right,' he guffawed. 'Very good.' He turned to Matt. 'Sorry. Someone once told me you SAS chaps all look like university professors. Very wise, I should think. But you look more of the James Bond type. Anyway, have a seat.'

He sat down before us in a large easy chair, while we sat opposite on another over-filled sofa. Sara came in with our tray and poured coffee. I saw her glance at Matt with a quick smile.

'So, what have you boys come to see me about, exactly? I see you're a client, Mr James.'

'It's nothing to do with that,' I said hurriedly. 'I understand that you approached the Jockey Club on behalf of the Bookmakers' Association, to register your concerns over Toby Brown's tipping service?'

Chapman nodded. 'Yes, I did. And I'd have gone to them with or without the other members of my association. I don't know how he's doing it, but it's costing all of us millions. It can't go on.' He stopped and looked at us squarely, as if we were the culprits, to add more emphasis to his words. 'It's giving racing a terrible name, and those pompous old buggers in Portman Square weren't doing much about it when it's clearly their responsibility. As you know, anything to do with racing in this country comes under their jurisdiction. If Brown were being palpably fraudulent, we could bring the police in, but we have nothing to go on and, as far as I can see, the powers that be have done little to mobilise their internal security people.'

'We received instructions from Lord Tintern as

chairman of the disciplinary committee the day before yesterday,' I told him.

'So, what do *you* think?'

'It's too soon to say,' Matt put in before I could reply. 'Do you have any theories yourself, sir?'

'Forget the "sir". You're not in the army now, you know.'

Matt allowed himself a quick smile. I acknowledged to myself the subtlety of his technique in gaining control of meetings like this.

'Thank you, but what are your ideas?'

'It's obvious, isn't it?' The question wasn't entirely rhetorical.

'You tell us, sir,' Matt prompted.

Chapman ignored the 'sir' this time. 'Well, it's not sheer skill, is it?'

We shook our heads.

'Or luck,' Chapman growled. 'He's cheating.'

'The reason we've come to see you is to hear what you've discovered so far,' Matt pressed.

'Like what?'

'Have you identified who's been your biggest winner since this run started?'

Harry made a face. 'Of course we've tried. But there isn't any one big winner – it's all of them. One guy phones the line and tells ten friends. It's killing us.'

'But there's no one individual or consortium?'

Chapman shrugged. 'No, they're all at it.'

'Have you ever experienced such a successful run for a tipster before?' Matt asked.

'No,' Harry replied emphatically. 'Never. There are

people who know their job and have winning weeks, but not regularly; and if it does get too frequent, we close their accounts. Now, if we stopped everyone who was winning, we'd have no clients left.'

'How much have Salmon's lost so far from all this, then?' Matt pressed.

The question hit a nerve. Chapman's face lost some of its colour. 'Too much,' he grunted. 'It can't go on – and you can quote me on that.'

I had the impression that if we didn't find out soon what Toby was doing, Chapman would do something about it himself. He lifted his large frame from the chair. 'Now, if you'll excuse me?'

We were already rising from our seats in anticipation of the end of the interview. I looked at Matt, showing only a hint of my disappointment at this lack of any fresh information.

'Thank you for your time,' I said.

Chapman shrugged indifferently. 'If you start making any real progress, let me know. Give my regards to Lord Tintern. Tell him I'm delighted he's put two such sharp young men on the case. I expect his relationship with Toby makes the whole situation a bit ticklish for him.'

'I didn't detect any particular reticence when he was instructing us,' I said.

Chapman laughed. 'Yes,' he said, 'you're probably right. Well, good day to you.' He ushered us from his office with another hearty shake of his hand.

We walked through to the ante-room and Matt closed the door behind him. Sara was sitting at her desk. He lifted an eyebrow. 'What time do you finish work?' he asked quietly.

'About six,' she said, with an almost imperceptible glance at the door to her boss's office.

'I'll be here to pick you up then.'

We retrieved my Audi from its meter outside and headed for my sister's small house in Notting Hill which we used as a London base.

'Looks as though you might have scored,' I said.

'It's not a question of scoring,' Matt blustered. 'I just thought it might be useful to have a pair of ears inside that office. Those people have more reason than anyone to stop Toby.'

I restrained a smile. I'd always been rather curious about Matt's approach to women. I suspected that beneath the irrefutably tough and tightly controlled exterior there was an emotional vulnerability – perhaps the origin of the hardened outer shell. I had never encroached on this private area and thus our long friendship had survived.

'All right, but I bet you wouldn't have thought of it if she wasn't so attractive.'

Matt allowed this. 'Possibly not.' He picked up the phone. 'I'm going to call the office.'

When he was answered, he spoke for a few minutes to Jason who co-ordinated the half dozen men, ex-soldiers mostly, whom we employed on the bread-and-butter personal protection and surveillance work.

I gathered nothing new had come in on our present job, but David Dysart of Wessex Biotech had rung.

'At least we've got something to tell him,' Matt muttered.

'Come on,' I protested. 'We haven't much at all.'

'We agreed that Griffiths seemed to have more assets than his salary would account for.'

'That proves nothing, though.'

But Matt was already punching a number into the phone. When it was answered, he asked for Dysart and waited. After a few moments, he made a face. 'Right, I'll come down in person as soon as I can,' he grunted and put the phone down.

My sister Catherine had used all the money our father had left her to buy a pretty little house near Notting Hill Gate.

Fortunately for me, almost as soon as she'd bought it, she'd left her job at *Vogue* and gone to work on an American glossy in New York. She'd asked me to keep an eye on the house. In return, Matt and I used it as our London base. Catherine had installed her own dark room and we had converted the bottom floor into an office.

As soon as we arrived there, Matt left for Bristol to see Dysart and I dialled Toby's tipping line. I listened to a recording of his familiar voice offering his selections for the day, put the phone down, and went out.

I retrieved my car from where I'd left it, two streets away, and drove to Sandown Park. Toby's nap was a horse called Musicmusic in a two-mile handicap hurdle, and I wanted to see it run.

Wearing the winter racing uniform of velvet-collared

covert coat and brown trilby, I blended naturally into the crowd milling around by the stables. I watched Musicmusic being tacked up and led to the parade ring. I was looking for anything out of the ordinary. I watched his lad every step of the way. Studied the horse's distinguished trainer appraising him in the paddock with the famous rock musician who owned him, and kept an eye on the yard's travelling head lad.

I tried to detect any sign of interference with any of the other five runners.

I scoured the crowd around the ring, especially by the gate where the horses would leave for the course; I noticed nothing and no one that aroused my suspicions.

As the jockeys mounted, I walked round and placed myself near the exit so that I could follow Musicmusic as closely as possible while he was making his way down the laurel walk to the track.

He was a well-made horse who looked ready to run and was being ridden by Jimmy McBain, the season's leading pilot. He would probably have been offered by the bookies at around 3/1 favourite without Toby's recommendation; with it, he looked likely to start at even money.

He was a big, strong, imposing horse; if you'd never seen a horse before in your life, he'd have taken your eye. Maybe, I thought, Toby was just doing a thorough job after all, as he'd claimed. Having been so impressed by Musicmusic beforehand, I wasn't surprised by the ease with which he won.

He was two lengths clear at the last, and on the run in gained another two. What was more conspicuous was the cheer that greeted his win. I wondered how much Harry Chapman and his rivals had lost from people here on the course, and another few million punters in betting shops around the country.

Through my binoculars I studied the winner coming back. Jimmy McBain had wheeled him round and he was still jogging. I thought that if I owned him, I'd think about running him over longer distances.

I'd seen nothing that could be called suspicious in the way the horse had run. I wondered if the stewards would dope test him. They only selected a horse to test after a race was run. It wasn't always the winner. If they took a urine sample from Musicmusic I didn't expect the horse to show any symptoms of doping.

But neither could I see any of the other, losing horses coming back showing signs of undue distress.

I felt utterly frustrated by the lack of evidence of any irregular influence on the result of the race. Moodily I made my way back towards the stands. Near the doors, I heard a female voice call my name from somewhere above. I looked up and saw Emma.

'Come on up,' she called when I returned her wave.

I knew my way to the Tintern box, and a couple of minutes later, I was walking into it. To my relief, His Lordship wasn't there. Emma, though, was surrounded by three other men who appeared to be at least as interested in her as I was.

'Si!' she greeted me with apparent relief, offering a cheek to be kissed and leading me by the elbow out on to the empty balcony. 'God, I'm glad I saw you.' She pulled a face but didn't expand. She filled a glass for me from a bottle of wine she'd picked up on the way. 'Is there any way you could give me a lift back to London?'

'Where's your car?' I asked.

'I came with Jane, thinking I'd go back home afterwards, but there's a party this evening. I wasn't going to go, but if you can come, I think I'd enjoy it.'

I thought about the job Matt and I were on, and wondered what else I could have done that evening to further it. 'Where is it?'

'Some gallery near Bond Street – I've got the address. It's a preview party for an exhibition by a horse sculptor. He's rather good.'

I winced. 'I don't know if I can take another room full of leaping bronze nags.'

'We could have dinner afterwards?' Emma played her trump with a flourish.

Chapter Six

The party was pretty much what I'd expected – more appreciation of points of the horse than points of art. But at least there seemed to me to be genuine merit in some of the bronzes that went further than just figurative images of the thoroughbred.

The place was full to bursting with racing people who might have been expected to write cheques easily for at least a few thousand pounds if something took their eye. I'd already seen several of them at the races that afternoon.

While Emma had drifted off to talk to friends, I found myself standing beside an old acquaintance, Daniel Dunne, a racing mad estate agent I'd known since schooldays. We both found ourselves looking at Emma. Despite the sculpture on show, she was easily the most attractive object in the room.

'I'm just about to buy a property for her father,' Daniel said, in a way that implied he'd like to get his hands on Emma as part of the deal.

'Where's that?' I asked, not really interested.

Daniel touched the side of his nose. 'The deal's not

done yet, so I can't say, but if it goes through, I guarantee he'll be a very happy man.'

He drifted off, and I took the opportunity to duck out into Bond Street and find a quiet haven in a shop window recess where I could use my mobile in privacy. I punched Matt's number and was answered almost at once.

'How did it go?' I asked.

'Fine, I'll tell you later. Why don't you meet me at Harry's Bar at nine?'

'I thought you were with Sara?'

'I am.'

'But I'm with Emma.'

'That's okay.' Matt sounded relieved. When I didn't answer at once, he added, 'I'll pay.'

At a hundred quid a head, that made it a better proposition. 'Fine. Nine o'clock.'

When I'd finished the call I decided I'd had enough of the preview party and went back inside, hoping that I might persuade Emma to leave.

To my relief, she was looking for me, already impatient. 'God, what a load of stiffs,' she said, not quietly enough. 'No wonder I decided to go to the States. The Yanks may be naïve, but at least they're not all full of crap.'

'I gather you've been talking to someone who doesn't agree with you?'

'Don't start,' she said, then laughed. 'Let's go somewhere else.'

As we walked out, I told her we were meeting Matt later. She looked surprised.

'It's okay, he's having dinner with a girl.' I laughed. 'You won't believe it but he just asked her out when we met her in Harry Chapman's office this morning.'

'How amazing. I was beginning to wonder if he was gay.'

'I think I'd have known before now if he were,' I said. 'Let's go in here.' I nodded at a small quiet pub that seemed to have got lost in the elegant canyons of Mayfair.

Once I'd got us both drinks, we sat on a comfortable sofa by a fake log fire.

'This is cosee,' Emma said in a Sybil Fawlty voice. 'At least,' she said, resuming her own, 'it's better than being pushed around by a lot of pompous, braying oafs.'

'You aren't in a very charitable mood, are you?' I said. 'What's the problem?'

'Seeing my father always winds me up.'

'He's not that bad, is he?'

Emma looked at me a moment. 'The awful thing is that I've started to think maybe he isn't my father at all.'

I put down the glass in my hand and stared at her. 'That's a bit radical.'

She shrugged. 'It's just that he and I are so different, it's hard to imagine we have a single gene in common.'

'I thought you were being serious for a moment.'

'I am.'

She took a sip of her vodka. 'Do you remember I told you the other day how my mother and I stayed with Frank Gurney in Menton – when Toby was doing his system at the casinos?'

'Jane's brother?' I asked.

'Yes.'

'You think he and your mother were lovers?'

'Well, whenever I was with them, I couldn't help thinking it was much more like being with my mother and father than it was when we were with Daddy.'

'That might just have been because they got on better.'

'Yes, I realise that, but I don't think that was all of it.' She picked up a beer mat advertising Irish stout and flicked it into the fire, where it blazed fiercely for a few seconds. 'Even at that age, I could sense something between them. If Mum hadn't died soon after that, I'd have asked her.'

'But if they got on so well, why didn't your mother leave your . . . Lord T?'

'I think she might have done if she'd lived but I don't think she and Frank were lovers any more, and I suppose it might all have been too disruptive.'

'How were your mother and Lord T getting on then?'

'Not well. He can be a real brute when he wants to be.'

'You mean, physically?' I was quite shocked by the idea of the outwardly distinguished bastion of the Jockey Club beating up his wife in the privacy of their own mansion.

'No.' She shook her head. 'He's not quite that bad.'

By the time we joined Matt and Sara at Harry's Bar, they had already been there a while.

'Well?' I asked Matt after he'd done the introductions.

He shrugged. 'Dysart wasn't very impressed.' This was a lot for him to concede. 'Brian Griffiths complained about our questioning.'

I was surprised; even by my standards, we'd been restrained. 'Do you think he exaggerated?'

'I don't know, but Dysart wasn't too happy,' Matt said dismissively.

If we lost the job, and nothing else came out of last night's trip, at least it might serve to cut Matt's overwhelming confidence down to size. 'Suits me,' I said lightly. 'Anyway, Emma's starving, so let's order.'

Emma and I left before Matt and Sara. How he was planning to spend the rest of the evening was none of my business, but I had decided to drive Emma home.

I was too preoccupied with the problems of both our current jobs to relax with her; besides, though she showed every sign of being pleased to see me again, I sensed she'd react better to a patient approach.

I drew up outside her flat in a Belgravia mews. She threw me a quizzical glance. 'Drink?'

'No, thanks. I've got to get back to check things at the office.'

'What, now?'

'We've got two big contracts on the go. We're spread a bit thin at the moment.'

I saw a momentary frown on her face; she didn't believe me, but she wasn't going to question it. I kissed her gently on the lips and waited until she was safely inside the house before driving off.

★ ★ ★

I spent the night alone in Notting Hill and drove to our offices near Reading first thing next morning. On the way, I tried to raise Matt on the phone, but there was no answer.

Monica greeted me with a smile, a cup of coffee and a string of messages, all of which I delegated to Jason. In my own small office, I made out a full report of the previous day's race won by Toby's napped horse.

It was the tipster's twenty-third consecutive winner, excluding three who had beaten themselves either by falling or suffering some other unpredictable mishap. None of the racing journalists had yet offered a plausible explanation for the record-breaking run – not surprisingly, I thought, unless they wanted to be sued for libel.

I spent the next hour carefully studying the digital shots of the race and people on the course and reviewing every other race won by Toby's nominations, but came no nearer a theory.

I was trying to decide what our next move should be when Matt finally came in. I knew better than to try and quiz him on his activities the night before and instead passed him my report. He read through it quickly, with his usual concentration.

'What were you looking for, exactly?' he asked.

'Anything that might give us a lead.'

'And?'

'Nothing. Frankly, it looked like a pretty straight run race to me, and the form horse won.' I shrugged my shoulders. 'Do you know, I sometimes think maybe

Toby is just very good at his job.'

'For God's sake, the chances are right off the board. Look, I know you won't like this but we're not getting anywhere otherwise. I think we should bug Toby's place.'

'Which one?'

'Both. At least if there's any discussion about his choices with anyone else, we should hear it.'

I was reluctant to go along with this. 'As far as I know, he just spends a few hours a day entering new data on that program of his. I doubt he consults anyone else.'

'Simon, if he's cheating – and logically he has to be – he's bound to talk to someone about it. Deception on that scale takes a lot of organising.'

'All right,' I said, resigned. 'We'll do it. I can probably do Wetherdown and you could do London, if you go when he's out and the cleaner's in. She doesn't know you, and it shouldn't be hard to think of an excuse.'

'Fine. We'll have to mike close to his phones, rather than in them. They're too easy to detect inside the mechanism.'

'But suppose he uses his mobile?'

'If he does, that's too bad. We could still get a print out of the calls he makes; that wouldn't be difficult. And if we do what I say, we might hear something useful. Besides, we'll be able to hear anything else that's said in the rooms where we place them.' Matt stood up decisively. 'I'll go and sort it out.'

Within the hour he was back with two DAT-recorders and six ultra-compact radio microphones which we could place in both Toby's residences. The mikes would be tuned to the sound-activated tape-recorders hidden nearby. That way we'd be able to pick up at least one side of all Toby's telephone conversations, and most of any that took place in his flat or in his country house.

Privately, I was doubtful about the efficiency and value of such an exercise, but we didn't have much else going for us and at this stage anything was worth a try.

Chapter Seven

'Simon, what are you doing here again so soon?' Toby asked as he opened the door to me; I wasn't sure if I'd heard a note of suspicion in his voice.

'I need to borrow a tie, as a matter of fact. I was on my way from your mother's to a meeting in Swindon when I realised I'd come out without one.'

He raised one eyebrow a fraction as he opened the door wider. 'Come in then. I was just going out, but I'll see what I can find.'

He showed me into his drawing room and disappeared upstairs. Once I could hear him moving about in his bedroom, I took out one of my magnetic bugs and attached it beneath the lip of an old carriage clock which stood beside the phone.

Toby still seemed to be busy upstairs, so I slipped into the kitchen and placed the second bug behind the phone there.

I needn't have hurried. In the time he took to fetch the tie, I felt I could have rewired the whole house; he'd obviously chosen it very carefully.

'Don't lose it,' he said when he came back down into

the drawing room and handed me a wide, garish-looking strip of silk. 'It's one of my favourites.'

I promised I wouldn't, and left, glad that I didn't actually have to wear the thing.

I drove a few miles to the side of the downs, from where I could still see Toby's house. I parked and waited until I saw him drive away. With no pretence at caution, as if I'd forgotten something, I went back to his house and hammered on the door to make certain there was no one else around. But no one came and I guessed it was safe to have a snoop around for a suitable spot to place the sophisticated compact DAT-recorder Matt had given me. It came with its own powerful battery pack and I found a place to tuck the whole apparatus under the eaves of an open-fronted barn, where I could easily recover the tapes.

To check that everything was working, I pulled out my mobile and punched in Toby's number. The hidden mike immediately picked up the ringing in the house and triggered the DAT-recorder, which dutifully registered Toby's message. It ran on for another ten seconds before it acknowledged that was all there was, and clicked itself off.

That evening, as Toby had insisted, I watched him being interviewed on TV by a witty but aggressive chat show host who all but accused him of cheating, though stopping just short of libel. To his credit, Toby didn't even begin to get ruffled. He revealed next to nothing about his methods of selection, which could only have added to the fascination of anyone interested. And I guessed that the millions of punters following him didn't give a damn how he was picking his winners, so long as he kept on doing it.

He looked handsome and likeable in the studio, and I wondered why producers hadn't made more of him. He came across well, apparently modest and as surprised by his success as anyone else. But the interview had highlighted his extraordinary lucky run. I didn't doubt that a vast horde of new punters would be trying to get through to his line next morning.

The following day, Toby's selection was running at Newbury, and I intended to have a close look at it. It was one of the big days of the season and I set off early to avoid the traffic.

As I was on my way, Matt phoned to say he was about to ring the bell to Toby's London flat in Hay's Mews, Mayfair. A few minutes later, I pulled into a lay-by on the A34, picked up my mobile and dialled Toby's London number.

When Mrs Hackney, his affable cockney housekeeper answered, I kept her talking for what I hoped was long enough for Matt to position two more midget microphones. He had arrived ostensibly to deliver a case of wine purportedly from a satisfied customer, confident that it was heavy enough to ensure he would have to carry it up to the flat.

I drove on to Newbury race-course, parked and went to look for Larry Johnson. Larry was one of our most resourceful employees. I'd got him a press badge and assigned him to photograph as many people as possible around Toby's nomination of the day, giving me a chance to focus on other aspects of the running. He was where we'd arranged to meet, near the lorry park. I checked he remembered all the details of the horse we were watching and left him to wait for it to arrive.

I didn't see Toby until much later. He was standing by the paddock for the second last race in which his nap was running.

'If I'd known you were coming racing, I'd have brought your tie,' I said, as I leaned on the rail beside him.

'Just bring it back when you're passing,' he said with unusual curtness. I sensed he was nervous about something.

'What's the matter?'

He shook his head. 'You've no idea how heavy the pressure is to keep coming up with winners. There's so much going on to our naps now that I'd probably be lynched if I hit a losing run.'

'*Our* naps?' I asked sharply.

'You know,' he back-tracked, 'my company's. It's got to stop soon, though,' he muttered.

But his horse won, to a mighty cheer from the stands.

'Well done,' I said. 'Twenty-four in a row.'

He nodded, but didn't answer. Restraining an urge to ask more, I left him in the stands and went to watch the horse come back.

I left the race-course before the last and on my way home called in to see how Nester was settling in at his new home. When Jane had asked me to move him, I'd arranged to have him trained at Derek de Morlay's yard, about half a mile from Wetherdown.

Apart from his stable and lad, nothing much had changed for Nester. He would be training on the same gallop, and Jane's feed merchant had agreed to carry on supplying his hay and hard feed.

The horse seemed almost happier in his new stable. Derek's yard was smaller than Wetherdown – more a converted farmyard, with a lot of dogs, chickens and goats roaming around. There was so much for Nester to look at, he hadn't even begun to dig his box up.

I left him with a pat and a Polo mint, though he hardly noticed; the head lad was just beginning to feed, and Nester could hear the buckets rattling.

I told Derek that I'd be coming to ride out in the morning, and left the yard to drive round to Jane's.

Jane had been disappointed to see Nester go. She had put a lot of work into him and taken a great deal of care and patience with his recovery. I was also sure she realised he was coming back to his best.

But she was glad to see me, and as we talked about her ideas for his continued training, she mixed us a couple of throat-chilling dry Martinis and we settled down in her office. Soon the conversation turned to Toby's latest winner.

'Do you know how he does it?' I asked.

She shook her head. 'He always had an eye, of

course. Even when he was fourteen or fifteen it wasn't unheard of for him to pick four winners in an afternoon from the paddock; but he could never have done that on the form alone. I haven't a clue how he's getting it right so consistently now.'

'Poor chap's in misery,' I said. 'If his nap loses, he's worried he'll be lynched; if it wins, he seems to feel guilty for having got it right again.'

Jane nodded. 'I know, I've seen the pressure on him. I told him to give it up if it's such a strain. He rather pointedly replied he had to make his own way in life, and there was no way he was going to walk away from the kind of money he was earning from it now. The only certainty is that it will all go pear-shaped sooner or later – there's no other way for it to go. Anyway,' she said, with a change of tone, 'how's Emma? I gather you're seeing a bit of her now she's back.'

I shrugged. 'She's fine. I've seen her a few times. I'm not certain her father thinks I'm good enough for her, but then he's probably right.'

'She's her own woman – that's what worries Gerald. When her mother died she left Emma the twelve percent of the King George Hotel Group she owned – I think deliberately. So Gerald only owns forty-seven percent himself and he's paranoid that if Frank doesn't agree with him on some major corporate decision, Emma might not go along with him either.'

'Then who owns the other six percent?' I asked, thinking it might be Jane herself.

'David Green, my godfather. He was responsible for setting up the legal structure of the deal with Frank and Gerald; and David would always side with Frank.'

I liked the idea of this potentially troublesome factor in Lord Tintern's business affairs. He was a man who always expected to get his own way; he must have loathed the thought that his own flesh and blood could stop him.

'But how did Emma manage to hang on to her shares? I should have thought her father would have done everything he could to get them from her when she was a kid.'

'David wouldn't let him. He was a great fan of Susan's.'

'I'm delighted to hear that Emma's so independent.'

'I bet you are,' Jane replied, taking it the wrong way.

'I only mean in the sense that she can tell her father to get lost without worrying too much.'

'I wouldn't want to tell Gerald Tintern to get lost, even if I was his daughter.'

I came back to my converted coach-house in Streatley to find that Emma had left a message on my answering machine, asking me to rescue her from a bad date later that evening. I decided I couldn't face driving to London and rang her back to tell her that if she'd known it was a bad date, she shouldn't have accepted in the first place.

I put the phone down feeling a little guilty, but glad of an early night.

I was just nodding off when the telephone trilled beside my bed. I grabbed it with my eyes still shut and croaked into it.

'Simon?' It was Emma. I opened my eyes and blinked at my alarm clock. It was twelve forty-five. 'Sorry, did I wake you?' The softness in her voice made me tingle.

'It doesn't matter. How was your dinner?'

'I've been bored rigid for four hours – *that's* how it was.'

'Sorry to hear it.' I tried not to sound too smug.

'Are you riding out tomorrow?'

'No, it's Sunday,' I growled.

'What do you usually do on a Sunday morning?'

'That depends.'

'On what?'

'On who's with me.'

'What if I was with you?'

I groaned. 'Don't tease, Emma.' As I was speaking there was a loud bang on my front door. 'Hang on,' I said, startled into waking completely. 'There's someone at my front door. Don't go away – I'll phone you right back.'

I dragged on a dressing-gown as I stumbled down the stairs. I couldn't think who might be knocking me up at this time of night; I lived in the middle of nowhere. Warily, I unlocked the door and pulled it open.

Standing on the doorstep, a mobile phone wedged between ear and shoulder, and a big grin on her face, was Emma.

Chapter Eight

When I woke, the sun was shining, the birds were making spring noises and, beside me, Emma was still asleep. Her hair was a mass of auburn-gold curls and there was a faint smile on her soft, supremely kissable lips.

I thought happily of the previous night's activities and was feeling the stirrings of a new erection when Matt phoned. It was nine o'clock and I had my first opportunity to discover that Emma was not naturally a morning person.

She wanted orange juice and coffee, which barely evoked a thank you. I hadn't yet told her that Matt had rung to say that her father wanted to see us in a couple of hours, and we'd been invited to join him for lunch.

When I did, she groaned. 'Why does he have to stick his nose into my life? Do you mind if we don't tell him I was here? I'd much rather he didn't know.'

'Why? Do I embarrass you?'

She put her hand on my arm. 'No, I didn't mean it like that. It's just that he always wants to know everything I do, and it really irritates me.'

★ ★ ★

Two hours later, Matt and I walked into the hall of Lord Tintern's house, Ivydene. Tintern shook hands with Matt. 'I gather you were in the Blues before you went off to play dangerous games in Hereford?'

'Yes, sir, I was.'

'There are a few ex-warrant officers of yours on the payroll of the Jockey Club,' Tintern said conversationally. It seemed to occur to him then that he wasn't being a good host. 'I'm so sorry,' he said, waving an arm towards one of the half dozen doors that gave off the big black and white tiled hall. 'Come into my study and I'll organise some coffee.'

We went into the room he'd indicated, while he went off through another door. I wondered who would bring us our refreshments. I supposed Lord Tintern must have staff of some sort; I couldn't imagine him ironing his own shirts, and Emma had told me he never kept his mistresses long enough to domesticate them.

Matt had other things on his mind. 'He doesn't seem that bad,' he said.

'He's got a tongue like a razor sometimes. He doesn't often use it, but you wait till you cross him.'

Lord Tintern came back into the room. 'Coffee'll be here soon,' he said. 'It was good of you both to come in at short notice, especially on a Sunday. But I wanted to hear directly from you how your investigations are going.'

I was thinking about the best way to answer his enquiry when Matt started. 'Frankly, sir,' he said, 'we've been on the job since Tuesday, and we're still in the process of gathering facts. Simon has interviewed Toby Brown, and we've both visited the offices of Salmon Leisure, but we haven't got anything fresh to go on yet.'

I saw a twitch of irritation in Tintern's cheek, quickly dispelled when a woman with dark eyes and Mediterranean colouring carried in a tray of coffee and placed it on a side table.

Tintern looked at her with something like affection. 'Thanks, Filumena.'

She smiled back and scuttled out.

'So far,' Matt went on, 'we haven't established any particular connection between Toby Brown and the trainers and jockeys involved. We've seen no clear evidence of tampering with any of the nominated horses or any of the other runners.'

He stopped. I looked at Tintern for his reaction.

'Frankly,' he said, 'I'm convinced the answer lies in arrangements with the various stables involved.'

I butted in, 'Gerald, I just don't think that's likely. There are too many people – it would be impossible for Toby to organise it every day.'

For a moment, Tintern abandoned his charm. 'Well, he's obviously up to something, and the sooner you find out the better.'

'Would you be agreeable to us employing listening devices in Brown's two residences?' Matt asked.

Tintern gave the question some thought. 'No. That would be illegal, and the Jockey Club couldn't condone it.'

'All right.' Matt nodded. 'Then we'll arrange full surveillance on Toby and report back to you on the people he makes contact with. We'll also visit the Equine Forensic Laboratory in Newmarket.'

'Good idea, though you'll find the security there like Fort Knox,' Tintern said, and nodded in a way that seemed to terminate the discussion.

At Tintern's bidding, we moved into the drawing room. As it filled with familiar racing faces, our coffee cups were replaced with chilled dry Martinis.

When Emma came in, she walked straight over to where I stood with Matt. I wondered if, like me, she was still tingling from our recent love-making. From the sparkle in her turquoise eyes, I guessed she was.

She greeted and kissed me as if she hadn't seen me for days, whispering in my ear, 'Thanks for having me.'

'It was a pleasure.' I grinned. 'Come again, whenever you feel like it.'

'Mmm, I will.'

Matt made a face and moved away.

'What's his problem?' Emma asked.

'I don't know. He's my business partner, not my psychiatric patient.'

When lunch was over, the guests were invited back into the handsome drawing room where our host was preparing to hold court for a few more hours yet.

I found Emma and told her I was leaving; she said she was going to London in the morning and decided to stay. As Matt and I left Ivydene, I was pleasantly appalled by an unfamiliar sense of deprivation that Emma wasn't with us.

I envied Derek de Morlay. He seemed, at the same age as myself, to have achieved so much more, I thought, as I drove through the gates of the small farm where he had set up his training establishment five years before. It was not grand or picturesque, like Jane Brown's. He'd had no money to start his enterprise; every penny had been borrowed from the bank. But although the house and stables were modern and simple, a mass of flower-filled pots and baskets made it a pleasure to arrive. At the same time, the tidy yard was always simmering with activity, enthusiasm and plans.

He had told me the previous year that he had already paid back all the money he'd borrowed, and I didn't doubt him. He was a man for whom there was always too much to do to waste time with bullshit.

One of Derek's many enviable assets was his wife, Julia. She had been a top event rider before their children began to arrive, and was a widely admired expert in cross-country riding. In the several years I'd known her, I'd never seen her bad-tempered nor heard her say anything unkind about anyone. This refreshing lack of cynicism always attracted me back to Derek's household where the three children he and Julia had produced were showing signs of possessing a similar charm, as well as marked talent on their ponies.

I had no doubt Nester would do well at Derek's.

He greeted me with his customary brisk charm, and

urged me to hurry up if I didn't want to be late pulling out.

On the gallops, astride my pride and joy, all other topics were forgotten. As we thundered across the rich lay that covered the tops of the chalk downs, and the sun shafted through a rippled band of cloud over the eastern horizon, I felt that riding Nester that morning was one of the most supreme pleasures I'd ever experienced.

It was only as we pulled up, and I found Julia de Morlay coming up from behind on one of the stable stars, that I was brought back down to earth.

'Nester's looking fantastic,' she said, 'but do you know, he'd go even better if you rode him properly.'

Her voice was so natural, the sentiment expressed so honestly, I couldn't be offended; I simply had to accept the truth of what she was saying. I grinned sheepishly at her. 'Do I really look that bad?'

She nodded with a rueful smile. ''Fraid so. And I saw your ride at Fontwell last week. There were a couple of times when you just about got it right . . .' She stopped. Evidently something in my face told her she'd said enough.

'It's okay,' I prompted her, 'I can take it. What were you going to say?'

'It's not important, but what I was going to suggest was that you had a few lessons. I'd be glad to school you myself.'

What Julia had said made me conscious of two things: that Nester deserved better; and, just possibly, if I really could improve, that I might be able to justify riding him myself in a race again.

I gave her a resigned nod as we wheeled our horses into a walking circle to wait for Derek. 'Okay, that's very kind of you. When do we start?'

'As soon as you like,' she smiled, relieved that she hadn't upset me too much.

I came back down from the gallop, exhilarated by my decision and happy about Nester's state of health and mind.

'He seems to have settled in well,' I said to Derek as we ate a swift breakfast of croissants and coffee.

'Yes,' the trainer agreed. 'He's a super animal to have in the yard. He's got a lovely nature and the most peculiar way of shoving all his bedding into a corner of his box to lie on.'

'I know,' I laughed. 'Why do you think he's called Nester?'

Derek slapped the palm of his hand on his forehead. 'God, am I thick or what?' he laughed. 'I must say, I can hardly believe it's less than two years since he broke down so badly.'

I nodded with a grin. 'Nor can Gerald Tintern,' I said, 'which is why Nester's here.'

At her suggestion, I had my first lesson with Julia after breakfast that morning.

For an hour she had me on a lunging rein, riding her hack bareback – walking, trotting, cantering and jumping. When I finally dismounted, my legs collapsed beneath me.

Julia grinned. 'You only *think* you've been gripping with your legs up till now, but after two weeks I'll let you have your saddle back – *then* you'll think you're glued on.'

For the rest of the day, my legs felt as if there were no bones in them. Every time I had the chance I squeezed a football between my knees, in the way Julia had shown me, to work the muscles on the inside of my legs.

But as I left the yard, hardly able to walk, satisfaction at what I'd already learned vied with guilt at the neglect of my other work.

I vowed to myself that I would spend the next two days, as I'd agreed with Matt, following Toby's naps. I had to put my foot down to get to Monday's race in time, the last on the card at Leicester.

Once more there was no surprise at Toby's winner. I had diligently photographed most of the people round the ring, and snapped the horses going down, but had spotted nothing to suggest any fixing. It occurred to me that on this occasion too the horse had won entirely on its own merits.

When I got back to my car, I made a phone call to the Equine Forensic Laboratory. I pulled out of the Midland course at four-twenty and headed south-east towards Newmarket. A little over an hour later, I was driving along a straight, tree-lined road towards the old red-brick town that had been the headquarters of British racing since the reign of Charles II.

Before I reached the High Street, I stopped to ask

how to get to the laboratory, and was directed to a short cul-de-sac beside the heath on the west side of town.

I identified the place from a pair of tall, iron gates with a rearing horse motif centred in each, behind which was a long, overblown cottage-style building, like a rural Tesco's. I parked and walked down a fine gravel path between beautifully kept lawns and juvenile silver birches.

The entrance was a user-friendly timber and glass porch which opened into an area floored with natural coir and liberally adorned with large potted plants.

A receptionist who looked as if she'd had the same smile pinned to her face since she'd got up that morning, greeted me and asked me how she could help.

'I wonder if I could have a word with Dr Poulton. I phoned earlier.'

'Yes, of course, sir. Your name?'

'Simon Jeffries.'

'Won't keep you a moment, Simon.' She grinned and fluttered her eye-lashes while she pushed buttons on her switch-board.

I speculated on whether I could have been interested in a girl like that – as good-looking as any cat-walk model, though with a healthier figure, long black hair gathered up behind her head, big brown eyes and obviously well-shaped breasts beneath a cream silk blouse. A few weeks ago, I could have overlooked the fixed grin she put on for work and might even have persuaded her to meet me for a drink later, but now, I realised with a jolt, I had no desire to do any such thing.

She interrupted my reverie with the announcement that she was going home now, and Dr Poulton was on his way out to see me.

I sat down to wait and started to flip through the literature about the place that was stacked on a table beside me.

The Equine Forensic Lab took samples from race meetings and a whole cross-section of horse events all around the world, from show-jumping to endurance riding. From English racing alone they received over seven and a half thousand samples a year, of which, on average, a tenth of one percent proved positive – about ten a year. More recently, the Jockey Club had ordered random tests of horses in training, to prevent the use of long-acting performance-enhancing drugs.

It was a sophisticated laboratory that cost over a million pounds a year to run. Dr Philip Poulton was operations manager.

He was a bespectacled, mousy man who shook my hand weakly but welcomed me warmly enough.

'I had a message from Portman Square that you might be coming.'

I was grudgingly impressed that Tintern had bothered to do that.

'We'll go somewhere where we can be a little more private,' Dr Poulton went on.

He showed me into a small, general purpose room, furnished only with an oak table, chairs, a telephone and a couple of eighteenth-century racing prints.

'I won't keep you long,' I said. 'I just wanted to check out your standard procedures when samples arrive here.'

'You mean, from British race-courses?'

'Yes.'

'It's very straightforward, really. We're sent the sample containers and run tests for every known drug that might have been administered. If a sample tests positive for anything, we inform the Jockey Club.'

'And how do you know which horse's sample you're dealing with?'

'We don't. Samples are taken from horses chosen arbitrarily after a race – not necessarily the winner. The bottles we get are only marked with a bar-code label; the Jockey Club issue these, and no one else knows which horse or race-course they refer to. We give them the test print-out with the bar-code; they identify the horse.'

'So you have no idea what's coming in here?'

'No. It's an obvious but very effective precaution against malpractice. Of course, it's absolutely essential that the system is incorruptible, and I'm glad to say that there's never been a failure.'

I nodded my head, and asked him, by way of small talk, what were the oddest drugs he'd detected in his time.

'Well, of course, these days, it's very seldom anyone bothers to use anything to stop or stimulate a horse because they know it will be routinely detected. From time to time they try masking with other substances, but I don't think anyone's got away with it for years.'

'What sort of stimulants did they use, when they still thought they could get away with it?'

Dr Poulton seemed to savour the question with a pursing of his thin lips. 'All sorts of things,' he said, 'most of which wouldn't have made a lot of difference anyway. Quite commonly they'd use cocaine, administered through the mouth or nostrils, or caffeine, which can be injected. But it's a long time since anyone used either.'

I left Newmarket and drove home, turning over what Poulton had told me. On the face of it, he was right; the system was fool-proof as we'd always been told and confirmed our conclusion that whatever Toby was doing, he wasn't doping the horses he'd napped. The best hope of discovering the secret of his success must lie on the race-course itself.

To my annoyance, when I phoned Toby's line for his nap the following morning, it was running at Haydock.

But as I'd decided to log all the attendances I could of other parties at the affected races, the more distant ones were almost more significant. The northern tracks had their own followers, and it took a lot to get a southerner up for a normal day's racing.

I had to use the digital camera myself, as discreetly as I could, especially when I was down near the start. The race-courses had stringent rules about who was and who wasn't allowed to take pictures on the course itself.

At the back of my mind was the thought that I could always claim the protection of Lord Tintern and the

Jockey Club if anyone remonstrated with me. At the same time, I didn't want to be conspicuous by photographing without an official badge.

Chapter Nine

I arrived back late and exhausted on Tuesday night but was in the office first thing next morning.

Just after nine, Matt arrived, looking annoyed and perplexed.

'What's happened?' I asked.

'I can't believe it, but Toby's jacked in his tipping line.'

'What? You must be joking!'

'I'm not. I just phoned the line and the message says that, as of today, there's no more service.'

With my mind racing between frustration at losing the Jockey Club job and speculation about Toby's reasons for suddenly abandoning a large, easy income, I picked up the phone and dialled his London number. A machine answered; I didn't leave a message. I tried the number at Yew Tree Lodge. Not even a machine answered.

I was still stunned by the news. 'I can't understand it – he was making an absolute fortune. I can't see Toby giving it all up for no reason. Somebody must have put him up to it.'

Matt nodded slowly. 'That's what I'd have said.'

'But who?'

Matt shrugged. 'And how?'

'I wonder if he's okay?' I said, surprised to find myself suddenly concerned for Toby's welfare.

'If he's gone out of business, the Jockey Club won't need us to carry on our investigation,' my partner said flatly.

'I should think they'll still want some kind of report to justify the money they'll have to pay us.'

'Maybe,' he said, unconvinced. 'We might as well get hold of the tapes from his cottage and the flat. I could do it,' he added unexpectedly. 'I'm meeting up with Sara from Chapman's office for a drink this evening.'

'No,' I said. 'I'll do it. I might catch Toby if he's in and find out what's happened.' I also had plans to be in London.

Matt didn't object and we arranged to meet at six that evening at my sister's place to update each other.

As I drove up the M4, I rang Jane.

'Any sign of Toby?' I asked when she came on the line.

'No, and you're not the first to ask.'

'I'm sure I'm not. I hope he's okay.'

'Why shouldn't he be?' Jane asked sharply.

'You know Toby. It seems very strange for him to close down a lucrative line without a bloody good reason.'

'I also know that he was getting worried about it. So do you. I think he's probably decided to call it a day and take a break, though he normally phones to let me know when he does. The blasted bookies must be happy, at least.'

I agreed with her, extracted a promise that if she heard from Toby she'd tell him to contact me, and rang off.

I found a place to park right outside the building where Toby's flat occupied the second floor. I phoned his number but there was still no reply. Two minutes later I was pressing the button marked 'Porter'.

When he arrived, I blagged my way into the building, retrieved the tape from the recorder hidden behind the fire-hose under the stairs, and left.

I arrived at my sister's house shortly before six. I hadn't expected Matt to bring Sara with him, but when they turned up together, he said they were having dinner later, and he wanted me to hear from her directly what she'd just been telling him.

I sensed that Sara was already regretting her indiscretion but had let herself get caught up in Matt's urgency to find out what had happened to Toby.

We sat around the table in the basement office, but Sara couldn't sit for long. She gratefully took the drink I offered her and started to walk up and down the room.

'I shouldn't be telling you this,' she started. 'But after what's happened . . .'

'Come on,' Matt said quietly. 'No one's ever going to know it came from you.'

'They'd better not,' she said, and took a deep breath. 'Yesterday, Toby Brown napped a horse that opened in the morning at ten to one. Of course, a pile of money went on it in the first few minutes, and every one pulled it in to fives then twos. The small firms were all phoning, desperate to unload some of it. It won, of course. Matt knows because he backed it.' She glanced at him with marked fondness. 'Right after that, Leslie, the finance director, came in to see Harry. He was white as a sheet. He told Harry they were going to have to do something, and spelt out what the firm had lost on Toby's naps over the last three weeks.'

'How much was that?' I asked.

'Over ten million.'

'Bloody hell!' I said, looking at Matt, who nodded.

'I know,' he said, 'it sounds incredible, but you can believe it. The punters are hardly bothering with the other races now.'

'That's right.' Sara nodded. 'I heard Harry shouting, "How much longer can we go on losing like this?" And Leslie said no more than a week, or they were going to have to realise some assets.' Sara shrugged. 'I don't know the state of their balance sheet from day to day, but I should think it very likely they've swallowed up all their cash reserves and cranked up their borrowings to near the limit.

'It's a very tricky situation. You see, the profit from the betting shops is what paid for the hotel chain. Historically, they've consistently made a lot of money – until now, that is. But if they decided to sell the shops, they'd have to sell them very cheap because of the losses they're making; and if they didn't sell, and Toby's run continued, they would go bust.

'They've had buyers knocking at their door for most of the individual hotels, and several for the group as a whole. I guess the UK hotel market is still undersubscribed.'

'That's why they can charge such ridiculous prices,' I said, nodding.

'But Harry wouldn't let that happen. Don't forget – he came with the hotels.'

'So what did he do?'

'He came out and asked me to arrange a meeting yesterday afternoon with the chief executives of the other three big bookmakers. I made damn' sure I was around when they got there. I didn't hear everything they said, but the gist of it was that they were going to deal with Toby. They reckoned they had no other choice.'

'How were they going to deal with him?' I urged.

'I'm afraid I don't know. I missed the details; they clammed up when I was in the room.'

I looked at Matt. 'What do you think it means?'

'Could be anything. Did you get the tape from his flat?'

'Yes, but I haven't listened to it yet.'

'Have you talked to Tintern?'

'No,' I admitted. I'd been trying to put it off until I had something constructive to report. I couldn't help thinking that we should find Toby before we spoke to Lord Tintern. 'Let's play the tape first,' I said, hoping that might reveal something.

I pulled the small cassette from my pocket and slotted it into a DAT-deck.

It looked from the amount of tape used as if about an hour of material had been recorded since Matt had placed the mikes there four days before.

On the Saturday evening there had been a short conversation in the flat – more of an argument – with another man whom Toby referred to as Link. I didn't recognise the nasal London voice but it was clear that whoever it was resented the fact that Toby had arranged to have dinner with other people that evening.

I remembered that he had said he was holding some kind of a party on the Saturday night and for a moment I thought we were going to hear the whole event on tape, but it soon became clear that there had been a change of plan and he was going to the other people's house for dinner.

The banging of a door marked the end of that conversation; we assumed this was 'Link' leaving. After that, there was a quick one-sided phone conversation in which Toby arranged to have dinner at Le Caprice, rather than at anyone's home. We got the impression he was talking to a woman, but no names were used.

At what the recorder logged as 8.15 on Monday morning, we heard Toby make a call, recording the day's message for his tipping line. From that, we realised he had been away all Sunday.

Then there was nothing until Tuesday evening, when the recorder was activated by Toby playing very loudly a recording of *Rigoletto*. This lasted a frustrating twenty minutes before the phone rang when the music was switched off. We heard him answering.

'Toby Brown here . . . Oh yes? How can I help

you? . . . What about it? . . . If we come to an arrangement, it'll cost you a lot of money . . . All right, as long
as you know. Where would you like to meet? . . . Let
me write that down . . . Fine, I'll see you then.'

The next sequence must have occurred just a few
minutes later, obviously to an answerphone. 'Hello,
Link? It's Toby. I'm sorry, we'll have to cancel our
meeting this afternoon. I've made an appointment I've
got to keep. I'll speak to you later.'

From what Sara had overheard in her boss's office,
she was fairly sure that Harry Chapman had made
contact with Toby; it sounded like the meeting which
we'd just heard him arranging.

There was nothing else on the tape.

Matt looked at me moodily. We'd learned frustratingly little. And we had no clue to where Toby had
gone, or where he was now.

I picked up a phone and dialled all his numbers
again. This time, his mobile number answered with a
message. I left my name and contact number, and
begged him to get in touch as soon as possible.

I was encouraged; last time I'd tried the mobile, it
had been switched off. That it was now in answering
mode suggested Toby was still in circulation.

Matt, dispelling his gloom, took Sara off to have
dinner. I agreed to keep myself on stand-by in case
Toby phoned.

I settled down in front of a convincingly real fake log
fire in my sister's comfortable, quaintly old-fashioned
drawing room on the first floor of the house and
watched the early news on television.

I was just thinking about phoning Emma when my mobile rang.

I grabbed it. The caller's number hadn't been displayed. I punched 'yes'.

A male voice I didn't recognise asked if he was speaking to Thames Valley Protection Services. I told him he was.

'It's David Dysart here, of Wessex Biotech. I've been dealing with Matt James.'

'You've come through to his partner, Simon Jeffries.'

'Simon, how are you?' The voice had the hearty confidence of a man who obviously thought he knew me.

'I'm fine, thanks. But, forgive me, Matt told me you and I had met . . . I'm sorry to say I couldn't remember where.'

Dysart laughed. 'At least you're honest. I'll tell you exactly where it was – a party given by Lord Tintern a year or so ago at the In and Out. I think you were a guest of that lovely daughter of his.'

I remembered the party well, and Dysart vaguely now. 'Yes, of course,' I said. 'How do you know Lord Tintern?'

'He's an old friend. His venture capital fund took a stake in our company last year – not a large one, about seven percent.'

'I didn't realise that, though I know quite a lot more about your company now.'

'And our personnel.'

'Yes,' I agreed guardedly.

'Brian Griffiths was rather upset by your visit. I think

possibly I made a mistake asking you to go to his home, but anyway he's accepted it now. The reason I'm phoning was to tell Matt to continue with his investigations. I'd put him on hold for a while, thinking I was making more trouble than was necessary.'

That was the first I'd heard of it; I was glad I'd fielded this call. I reassured Dysart that we would take great care not to antagonise any more of his staff unnecessarily and he rang off sounding as if he'd believed me.

I thought about Dysart for a while after that. I found I could recall his face quite clearly now: a youngish-looking forty, ungreyed dark blond hair, with the eager, unsophisticated manner of an entrepreneurial scientist. Clever, bold and imaginative, I wondered why he was a friend of Gerald Tintern's.

My phone rang again.

'Simon?'

I recognised Toby's voice at once and my pulse raced with relief.

'Toby! How are you? We've all been worried shitless.'

'Have you?' He sounded surprised but grateful. 'I'm sorry. I thought it would be best if I took off for a few days after the line closed.'

'I'm not surprised, but what happened?'

There were a few moments of silence before he answered, 'Simon, there was a lot of money at stake, you know.'

'That's obvious. So, are you going to tell me about it?'

'I'd rather not talk now.'

'I understand, of course,' I replied, trying to disguise my impatience. 'Where are you?'

'Mother says there are still reporters hanging around the cottage, so I'm staying with some friends – out of London. I just thought I'd let you know. My mother seemed to think you were keen to get hold of me.'

'Yes, thanks. And, listen, if you get any problems that Matt and I can help you with, just ask.' Again, he didn't answer at once. I guessed he was weighing up my motives. 'After all, you and I go back a long way,' I added, cringing at my own insincerity.

'Yes,' he said, accepting my offer at face value. 'Thanks, I will.'

Chapter Ten

The following afternoon, as the last light was fading, I parked outside the grand but graceful red-brick front of Ivydene House.

The front door was opened by Filumena, the dark woman who had brought us coffee the Sunday before. I was struck by how exceptionally good-looking she was and couldn't help thinking that her duties in the household must be broader than merely domestic.

She smiled warmly. 'Good afternoon, Mr Jeffries. I'm afraid Lord Tintern is at the keeper's cottage,' she said in fluent English with a hint of an Italian accent. 'But he knows you're coming so I take you to his study.'

She showed me across the chequer-board hall and ushered me into a small library. 'Coffee?' she asked.

'Yes, please.'

She left me in the handsome room, not quite closing the door. I walked round behind Tintern's large walnut desk to look at a vista which led the eye up a fine avenue of chestnuts to the sweep of the chalk downs beyond, glimmering pink in the dying light. I admired the scene for a moment then turned to face the desk which dated, like the house, from the time of Queen Anne. Two telephones and a pen rack stood on the far side of the polished surface.

Guiltily, I found my eyes swivelling down to the shallow stack of papers lying on a large leather-cornered blotter.

I glanced at the door and listened for a moment before turning over the first few pages. There were letters about Jockey Club business, House of Lords arrangements, confirmations of transactions from stock brokers. Nothing that seemed of major importance to such a busy man as Tintern.

I was just shuffling the papers back into place when I heard a car crunch across the gravel in front of the house.

I walked briskly from behind the desk and sat in an armchair with a copy of the *Field* in my quivering hands, in time for the housekeeper to come back to the study with the promised cup of coffee on a tray.

As she went out, I heard footsteps in the hall and Tintern came in. I stood up to hold out a hand, which he shook perfunctorily before going to sit behind his desk, in front of the pile of papers I'd just been inspecting.

He put both hands flat down on either side of the pile, gazing apparently at the top sheet, evidently suspicious that I'd been prying.

After what seemed like minutes but was probably only four or five seconds he looked up and his eyes bored straight into mine. I couldn't help quaking a little as I awaited a rebuke.

Abruptly, he smiled. 'It was good of you to come, Simon,' he said, turning on the charm.

'Not at all,' I muttered. 'We just thought it would be sensible to put this Toby affair to bed.'

'Quite right,' Tintern agreed. 'But are you sure he's closed down for good?'

'I got the impression it was a permanent arrangement,' I said truthfully.

'You've seen him, have you?'

'I've spoken to him.'

'Did he tell you why he's stopped his line?'

'No, but I imagine he's made enough money and is getting out before his luck runs out.'

'Well, let's just hope he's given up for good. It's been a blessed relief to be able to tell the bookies that the affair is over.'

'I'm sure it has been, sir,' I said earnestly.

'Of course, we still want to know what was actually going on. We don't want someone else suddenly popping up and doing the same again.'

'I don't think that's at all likely,' I said.

'Even so, I'd like you to continue your investigations.'

I nodded. 'We still don't have any leads on what he was doing out of the ordinary to score his winners. The more I've looked at it, the more I think it was just a lucky run.'

Tintern sighed philosophically. 'Maybe, I don't know. But give it a bit longer.'

I finished my coffee and put the cup down. 'I'm sure I've taken up enough of your time already. I'll be off. I'll keep you in touch with any further developments.'

'Before you go,' he said, 'there was something else I wanted to discuss with you.'

I had been about to stand up but sank back into my chair, hearing a new, more personal note in his voice.

'How's Better By Far?'

'He's fine, thanks. Derek de Morlay's training him now.'

'I know, but how is he?'

'He's sound at the moment.' I shrugged my shoulders. 'I'm just keeping my fingers crossed he stays that way.'

'If he wins at Cheltenham, I'll sue my vet.'

I couldn't tell if he was being serious or not. Knowing him as I did, I guessed he was.

'We'll see,' I said as lightly as I could, and not wanting to encourage this conversation further, I said goodbye and left.

Three hours later, I walked from one of the courts at the squash club in Goring, sweating like a glacier in a heat wave but very happy. I'd just given my partner the most serious trouncing he'd received in months. I guessed this might have been a side-effect of the lessons I'd been having with Julia and all the new leg exercises.

Despite his antipathy to losing, Matt took it fairly well. 'I suppose that means I have to buy you gallons of beer now,' he said disparagingly, to underline his own abstemious taste for Perrier water.

'A couple of pints will do.'

When we were sitting down in a quiet Thames-side

pub, he became more communicative. 'Frankly, I'm not surprised Tintern's asked us to carry on with the job. I'm sure he didn't expect serious results inside a fortnight – investigations like this take months, not days – and the fact that Toby's packed up anyway doesn't mean we've failed.'

I had to laugh. 'You should take up spin-doctoring! Anyway,' I went on, 'we've got to keep our eyes open, just in case Toby decides to get behind someone else.'

'Since he packed up, I've been monitoring all of them. The only tipster showing a profit now is Connor McDonagh.'

'Oh, no!' I groaned.

'You know him, don't you?'

'Yes,' I said, 'but not that well.'

'Well enough to slip him some subtle inside information about one of Jane's runners?'

I nodded slowly as I saw where he was going. 'Yes, as it happens, I do.'

'Excellent! So, if there was anything from Jane's yard due to run that on its form looks like winning but which you happen to know is off peak . . .?'

'That's asking a lot. For a start, Jane won't run a horse unless she thinks it's got more than just a good chance.'

'But there must be times when owners are pressing for a run?'

'Yes, I suppose there are. Or,' I'd had a sudden thought, 'I might be able to persuade Gerald Tintern to run one of his against Jane's better judgement. He's about the only person she'd do it for.'

'Work on it,' Matt said.

'Hang on a minute. Let's wait and see how long he carries on winning. He might stop tomorrow.'

'Okay, but you start getting it lined up.'

'Talking of working on it,' I said, just to remind him we were equal partners in our business, 'I haven't told you about my conversation with David Dysart last night.'

Matt looked uncomfortable. 'What did he say?'

'He said he'd told you to drop the case last weekend.'

'He didn't actually tell us to drop it,' Matt muttered, caught on a back foot for once.

'Okay,' I conceded, 'he said he wanted it put on hold . . .' I enjoyed watching Matt squirm for a moment '. . . but I persuaded him to let us carry on.'

'Oh, good,' Matt said, showing more relief than he'd intended. 'Well done.'

'He also reminded me where I'd originally met him. It was at one of Gerald Tintern's parties in London.'

'Really? Tintern knows Dysart?'

'Yes.' I nodded. 'And he owns seven percent of Wessex Biotech.'

Matt considered this news. 'That's fascinating, though I don't think it necessarily takes us anywhere, do you?'

'No, but it's good to know that one of them has obviously recommended us to the other.'

'Maybe you just did a good selling job on him then.'

'Frankly, I can't remember. But anyway, in the meantime I'll see what I can do about setting up a nap for Connor. I'll have to be fairly subtle about it, though. He's pretty sharp, and if he thought I was positively trying to push a tip on to him, he'd have to assume I was backing something else. At least – I would if I were him.'

Emma hadn't ridden out at Jane's for the last few days, and I hadn't made any arrangements to see her; I'd been hoping she might have got in touch with me herself. She hadn't, and I guessed I'd have to take the initiative.

When I left the office, I decided in the interests of time and motion to go back to Ivydene House. I took the precaution of phoning first to see if Emma was there.

She was, and sounded pleased that I was on my way over. Her father, she said, was not on good form, and she needed cheering up.

I hoped Lord Tintern would be in a better mood by the time I arrived to ask his help over the running of one of the horses Jane trained for him.

When I saw him, he unbent enough to offer me a drink and let me tell him my plan. After a moment's thought, he nodded his approval and it turned out that he had exactly the horse I was looking for.

Sox O'Dee, one of his promising young chasers, was running in poor company in two days' time at Towcester, despite his trainer's view that the gelding was still feeling sore from a cut received during his last outing.

'I felt the horse's leg myself,' Tintern said. 'There's a bit of a scab but he's sound as a bell once he's warmed up.'

'But will Jane let him run?' I asked.

'I respect Jane, of course, but she's a perfectionist, and besides she's very protective of her strike rate. But really racing's a sport – you can't only send out horses that you think will win.'

'On the form, Sox O'Dee should win,' I said.

'Yes,' Tintern agreed, 'but he's missed a lot of work, I'm afraid.'

Emma came back into the drawing room, changed and ready to go out. 'Okay, time's up. I'm hungry.'

'I don't know why both of you don't just stay and have dinner here,' her father said, almost plaintively.

'No, thanks,' Emma said with no pretence at deference.

'Why are you taking me to the pub?' she asked, once we were in the car and heading for the gates.

'Because there's a fifty-fifty chance Connor McDonagh will be there, and your father, God bless him, has just handed me a gift-wrapped, ready-made nap to pass on.'

'But Sox O'Dee won't win. I heard Jane telling Dad he was mad if he wanted to run him.'

'I want Connor to tip a horse that's unlikely to win, then if it does, we can be bloody sure somebody's gone out of their way to make certain of it and may even be able to find out how, if it comes from Jane's yard. But I've got to talk to her first. Can you get her on the phone?'

Emma dialled Jane's number, and when the trainer answered gossiped with her for a few minutes before handing her over to me.

'Jane, hi. I'm glad to hear Emma's riding out again tomorrow, but what I wanted to talk to you about was Sox O'Dee.'

'What about him?'

'Is he running on Saturday?'

There was a moment's silence before she answered. 'Simon, I can tell from the way you've asked that Gerald has already told you he is.'

'True,' I admitted. 'But you don't really want him to?'

'He's had a cut on the outside of his fetlock; been on road work for two weeks. I don't think he's ready for a race. Personally, I don't want to chance it.'

'But you don't like arguing with Lord T?'

'No, frankly, I don't. He does it in front of the lads, and it looks awful. I've told him – if the horse breaks down, it's entirely his responsibility.'

'So he runs?'

'Yes,' she said, through clenched teeth by the sound of it.

'And how do you rate his chances?'

'Slim. I weighed him this morning. He's put on fifteen kilos.'

I put the phone down, pleased that I'd found the tip I needed for Connor McDonagh.

No one had seen Connor in the Greyhound for several days.

'He's on a roll,' the barman said. 'Taken over where Toby left off.'

'He's only had six in a row,' I said. 'That's not unheard of.'

'Maybe, but everyone's looking for someone to fill Toby's shoes. Connor's just started advertising as the new Toby Brown.'

'There's no reason why they should expect the same again.'

'There's no reason why anyone should expect to win the lottery, but it doesn't stop them doing it.'

I accepted that I wasn't going to get my chance to see Connor that night so concentrated on Emma instead.

After we'd eaten at the pub, she came home with me. This time it was an altogether calmer, deeper experience, which was to linger in my mind even more vividly than the first time. In the morning, we found it very hard to get out of bed before we both went to ride out.

Emma went on to do a second lot while I went to see Julia for another hour of torture on her hack; she seemed to be getting more bossy with each visit.

When it was over, my next task was to contrive a way of bumping into Connor McDonagh.

I drove in to Lambourn and from my car phoned his office, which consisted of two rooms above a saddler's shop in the middle of the town.

I'd known Joan, his secretary, for a long time; her father had been head lad in one of the great old yards in the town. She answered the phone and told me I'd just missed Connor. 'He's popped out to the chemist's. He needs more insulin. His diabetes seems to have got worse since this blasted line went mad,' she told me confidentially. 'And since he stopped riding out, he's been putting on a lot more weight.'

I thanked her and parked in the middle of the village. I got out and walked quickly towards the chemist. I'd almost reached it when Connor came out.

He was about fifty and had floated around the Lambourn Valley as long as I'd known it. There was a rumour that on his first visit to the Cheltenham Festival, in 1982, he'd had five thousand on the Irish-trained For Auction to win a quarter of a million pounds on the Champion Hurdle.

He'd bought himself a small house in the village, ridden a few amateur races and established his reputation as a pundit to the point where he'd started writing regularly for the racing papers. He had consistently been one of the top tipsters in the country, and was presumed to follow his own most judicious selections since he'd recently bought himself a much larger establishment outside the village. Like Toby Brown, he had within the last year opened his own premium telephone tipping line.

He was a handsome man in the classic Irish mould: wavy black hair, square craggy features, strong colour and bright blue eyes. But, by contrast, he had a rather melancholy air due, I guessed, to the onset of his medical condition.

He was walking from the chemist's shop, taking a plastic pill bottle from a bag he was carrying. When he saw me, he quickly shoved it back.

'Hello, Si,' he said.

'Hello, Connor. Joan said I'd find you here. She said the diabetes is causing you more problems than normal.'

We discussed his health as we walked back towards the village square.

'What did you want me for?' he asked when he reached my car.

'I couldn't get through to your line and wanted to know what your tip was today. You seem to be on a bit of a run.'

'Yes,' he agreed. 'You could say that. I've tipped Ferguson's horse in the opener at Devon. They say it's taken to jumping like the proverbial duck.'

'Thanks, Con. I'll give you one for tomorrow.'

He glanced at me sharply. 'What's that?'

'Sox O'Dee at Towcester.'

'How do you know? Have you ridden him?'

'Jane wouldn't let me ride one of her good horses,' I laughed.

Connor, oblivious to my feelings, nodded his agreement. 'What does she say about him?'

'You know Jane – nothing, but I can tell she's bullish from the way she was grinning after he worked yesterday.'

A glad light in the Irishman's eye told me he was nibbling at the bait. 'Is that so?' he said. 'Will you have a quick bevvy?' He nodded towards a gloomy little pub across the road.

'No, I must be going. I've got too much to do.'

As Connor walked back to his office, it occurred to me with a jolt that if Toby were behind him, Connor wouldn't have any part in the selection of the naps. And even if he did publicly select Sox O'Dee, I wouldn't know that Toby might not have gone for the gelding anyway. After all, he was the form horse in the field. Then again, Toby might have spoken to his mother about it.

All I could hope was that Sox O'Dee was the day's nap, and it won. If it did, it would give a strong sign that somehow the race had been fixed. There was a lot of 'ifs' in the plan, but I drove back to the office feeling that I was doing something constructive at last.

I phoned Connor's line as soon as it opened next morning and heard a string of rambling prognostications on the 3.20 at Towcester before I reached the real purpose of the call which was the day's nap: Sox O'Dee. While I listened, it crossed my mind that there was one distinct similarity between Toby's tipping line and Connor's – both of them offered only one selection each day. Where most tipping services gave at least three to improve their chances of finding a winner, Toby and Connor had always relied on quality.

I put the phone down and drove straight to Wetherdown where I was told that Sox was already on his way to the races with two other runners. I called Matt from the car and arranged to pick him up from Henley.

'Well done,' he said mildly as he got into the car. 'I hope the bloody animal wins.'

'You haven't backed it, have you?'

'Just a little; for interest. I backed Connor's nap yesterday and it scrambled home at two to one, which was okay.'

'You know, if the race is run straight, Sox O'Dee simply cannot win,' I said. 'Jane says he's only three-quarters fit.'

Matt nodded. 'Of course I know that. I'm betting that Connor's into the same game as Toby. I thought three to one that he was pretty good odds.'

I laughed. 'You could be right!'

Lord Tintern was in the stand talking to some friends. He looked relaxed and confident. Blissful ignorance was often an asset where horses were concerned and he was a lucky owner, there was no doubt about that. Maybe Sox O'Dee had more talent than Jane thought. It would be typical of Gerald Tintern's good fortune if that turned out to be the case.

I ignored the earlier races and went to have a look at Sox O'Dee before he ran.

There was nothing very conspicuous about me hanging around the open boxes behind the main parade ring. There were always punters who liked to go there to see the trainers with their horses before a race, hoping they might be able to read something from the expressions on their faces or the horses' behaviour. Ten minutes there could be worth more than an hour with the form book.

Sox O'Dee was a big brown gelding whom Gerald had bought after he'd won a good point-to-point in Ireland. Sally, who had looked after him since he'd been at Jane's, was leading him around until her travelling head lad arrived with the saddle. Jane, I knew, had stayed behind to avoid a confrontation with the owner.

The gelding looked calm enough and, if I was honest, in fairly good shape, but even I detected a hint of stiffness as he was first led out and started to walk around the small tarmacked oval in front of the boxes.

I'd arranged for Larry Johnson, one of our ex-squaddies, to take the photographs that day, and my eyes didn't leave Sox O'Dee as I followed the horses filing into the main paddock ten minutes later. From the corner of my eye, I saw Lord Tintern stroll casually into the centre of the ring and exchange a few words with Jane's head lad and Mike Jackson, the jockey.

The horse itself was moving well enough now. The wound on the outside of its fetlock, which Jane had mentioned, was barely visible as Sally led him past me, just a few yards away.

Mike Jackson mounted up with the other eleven jockeys in the race and they filed through the crowd.

I had made up my mind to watch the race from the lawn in front of the members' stand. Everyone has their favourite place for watching races. Some prefer being in the middle of the course, where they can feel more part of the action. Others like to put themselves close to one of the more challenging fences in a chase, and others only believe they are getting their money's worth if they are on top of the most expensive stand.

I felt that my spot on the rails, ten yards short of the winning post, offered the best all-round view. I knew that I'd also be able to watch the whole race from several angles on videotape afterwards, courtesy of RTS.

With my binoculars glued to my face, I followed the runners down to the start. Sox O'Dee put in a sharp buck as he swung wide of the main circle towards the small group of onlookers who liked to be down at the start, where Larry Johnson was positioned.

I heard the commentator call out the starting prices as they set off. Sox O'Dee was favourite, not only because he was Connor McDonagh's nap – although that had undoubtedly shortened his price – but also because he was the highest rated horse in the race. Nevertheless, there were two other runners who could have been classified as dangers.

Once the horses had jumped off, Sox O'Dee went straight to the front as he always did. He jumped like an old hand, measuring his fences and keeping his front legs tucked tightly beneath him. Nothing else could match his stride, and as they began the long climb from the bottom of the hill, the other jockeys were scrubbing along to keep in touch. I knew, though, that it was only a matter of time before Sox O'Dee began to tire. I'd seen the hill at Towcester bring horses to a walk.

I took a deep breath and rammed my glasses closer to my eyes. I wondered for a moment what Lord Tintern was thinking as he focused on the horse from somewhere in the stands behind me. I don't remember breathing again until the horses swung into the home run for the last three furlongs, with two fences to jump. Sox O'Dee landed a full eight or nine lengths in front; all he had to do now was to keep standing.

But, suddenly, he was labouring, and two contenders were fast closing the gap behind him. Sox looked as if he were galloping in slow motion and began to wander off a straight line. Mike Jackson gave him a sharp crack with his whip, but the winning post seemed to be moving away from him.

It felt almost cruel to watch but somehow Sox O'Dee found the reserves to hold on, and reached the post with just half a length in hand.

Half a length, though, was more than enough. When you had a bet to win, you didn't have to give the distance as well.

A few strides past the post, he was walking like a dying dog and his jockey jumped off. In the stands behind me there was a huge cheer – more, I guessed, for the money won than Sox O'Dee's effort.

I spotted Lord Tintern going down to collect his prize, looking thoroughly pleased with himself. I pushed my way through the crowd so that I was near enough to speak to him before he reached the winners' enclosure.

'Well done, Gerald,' I said thoughtfully. 'What do you make of that?'

'I'm very glad I insisted that Jane should run him, although I'm not certain we're any the wiser about Toby. I think Sox is just a very brave horse.'

Disappointed as I was, I thought Tintern might be right, but stayed to watch the unsaddling. Sox O'Dee had obviously pushed himself to the limit and the flanks of his loin had become deep, heaving hollows. His eyes were popping out of his head as he cast around anxiously and whinnied a couple of times for some company. His efforts had been beyond the call of duty, and I felt almost guilty to have been a part of it. I turned away and went to find Matt so that we could go home.

Chapter Eleven

The next day was Sunday. The phone next to my bed rang early. Emma groaned and put her head under the duvet.

'Morning, Mr Jeffries. I think we should meet.' It was Harry Chapman.

'Your place or mine?' I asked.

'We'll split the difference. Come and have lunch at Cliveden – on the river at Maidenhead.'

'I've arranged to have lunch with a friend.'

'Then bring her along.'

'Who's paying?' I asked, wondering how he knew my friend was a woman, and worrying at the inevitable cost of eating at one of the smartest hotels in the country.

He laughed. 'I am, of course. Though, God knows, I'm not feeling very rich this morning. But listen, I'll want a word in private first. Wait in the lobby and when you see a bronze Mercedes driving in, come out and we'll take a turn round the gardens. All right?'

It was surprisingly mild for a February day. The sun was shining through a thin layer of high cloud and flashed off the windscreen of Harry Chapman's Mercedes as it cruised down the drive between the towering Wellingtonias and parkland blue cedars, towards the ornate front of Cliveden.

I made sure Emma was comfortably installed near the bar with a glass of champagne before I strolled down the sweep of stone steps towards the formal Italian gardens in front of the house.

The Mercedes swished to a halt and Harry stepped out before his chauffeur had time to open the back door for him. He grinned at me with far more friendliness than he'd shown last time we'd met.

'Hello, Simon,' he called. 'Lovely morning, eh?'

'Super.' I nodded and fell in step beside him as we headed around the side of the building towards the privacy of the wide open lawns at the back.

'I take it you're still on the case for the Jockey Club,' Harry glanced enquiringly at me, 'even though Toby Brown's packed it in?'

'Yes. Their view was that someone else might take over.'

He nodded. 'They could be right,' he growled. 'These tipping lines are making us feel very exposed. There isn't a betting firm in the country that isn't looking at the possibility of crashing. It's crazy – one single operator like Toby or this bloody McDonagh and our whole industry is in jeopardy. If it goes on much longer, the only big firms to hold out will be the ones with the highest liquidity – and that could mean selling other major assets too cheap, just to get a quick deal.'

'So, why don't you just stop taking bets on those races?'

'We have to take them; none of us is prepared to be the first to cave in. I suppose we all think that sooner or later the naps are going to start losing, and whoever's taken the money on that race will have recouped a sizeable chunk of their earlier losses. Prices have been so short that the amount of money the punters are staking keeps going up.'

'Would your firm consider selling off other assets to stay in the game, then?' I asked.

Harry stopped and looked at me.

'What do you mean exactly?'

'I don't know. Selling your hotels, maybe?' I suggested, remembering what Sara had said.

Harry gave a short laugh. 'Do you seriously think I'd answer a question like that?'

I shrugged. 'It's the question the media are going to start asking soon enough, and they'll be speculating about potential buyers.'

I left the thought hanging between us. I wanted to get an idea of just how desperate he was, but he didn't react. Instead he looked straight ahead and carried on walking. The subject was obviously closed. 'So,' he said, 'what do you know about Toby and Connor McDonagh?'

I looked at him. 'Are they connected?'

'It looks very much like it to me.'

'Why do you think that?'

'Come on,' Chapman said sharply. 'It's obvious they're working together and Connor's taken over from

Toby as the front man. We lost a fortune on that horse yesterday.'

'Connor's had five out of five naps right. That's pretty damn' good,' I said, 'but it's not unheard of.'

'The punters already think he's the new Messiah.'

'And punters, as you well know, are usually wrong.'

'Your partner had a grand on that horse.'

When Sara had told us that Harry watched every aspect of the business like a hawk, I hadn't realised how close to the truth she'd been. I was amazed that Chapman had bothered to look up an individual punter's account. I was also surprised that Matt had had as much as a thousand pounds on the animal.

'He told me he'd backed it – I guess he shares your view that Connor has somehow taken over from Toby,' I conceded. 'But I still don't think there's any connection between Toby and Connor.'

'Well think again, my friend. There has to be a connection. Toby has stopped what he was doing because his very impressive skill in picking winners has now been bought by private interests. There's nothing illegal in that – just good business practice.'

'When did that happen?'

'Last Tuesday; the four big firms sent representatives to a meeting with him at a pokey little place in Half Moon Street where he runs his lines. We had a pretty fair idea of what he was drawing from it, so we doubled the sum and added five grand a week for him to supply his naps to us on an exclusive basis.'

'Good Lord,' I said, genuinely astonished at the size of the payment, but beside the losses they were incurring it would be insignificant, I conceded. Toby, it seemed, had cleaned up.

'This agreement,' Chapman emphasised, 'was on the clear understanding that his tips weren't offered elsewhere.'

'So I should think. And Toby's quite a sensible chap.'

'I think he's quite a greedy chap,' Harry said with deceptive lightness, and glanced at his watch. 'Now, I think it's about time we went in and had a bit of lunch.'

We crossed the lawns and walked through a garden door into the great house. Inside, we made our way through to the front bar where we found Emma talking to a good-looking, expensively dressed girl of about the same age.

Harry Chapman looked at her fondly and turned to me. 'This is Ingrid, my daughter.'

I'd seen Ingrid's type a thousand times before – a rich man's spoiled daughter, with implausibly blonde hair and dressed in flawless, clearly recognisable designer clothes.

I realised she must still have been in his car while we were walking away from it, and that he'd left her to make her own way into the hotel. I sensed Chapman enjoyed springing little surprises.

Over lunch, it became apparent that Ingrid's only interest was herself. She loathed racing and knew nothing about her father's business, beyond its capacity to finance her wardrobe and provide her with free accommodation.

Harry and I had no chance to talk any further

about our mutual interests, and I couldn't wait for lunch to end.

'That's the last time I come on one of your business lunches,' Emma said as we drove away from the hotel.

I laughed and gave her a squeeze as we reached the pair of gates at the end of the long drive. 'I'm really sorry. Harry on his own would have been fine, but if I'd known he was bringing that hard-bitten, make-up-encrusted piece of St Tropez yacht fodder . . .'

'You're forgiven,' Emma said with a grin. 'But I still haven't gathered why he wanted to see you.'

'Ah-ha. Just a bit of business,' I said mysteriously. 'Now, do you want to come with me to Wetherdown?'

'What for?'

'I owe Jane some money for Baltimore's training fees. And I want to use her mechanical horse.'

'In other words, you want an excuse to practise your riding?'

'You're beginning to know me too well.' I grinned. I'd been working away at the exercises Julia had given me, and wanted to see how much fitter I'd become.

Emma sighed. 'All right, but I'll only stay half an hour and that's it.'

The tension at Wetherdown was palpable as we walked in under the arch. It was most obviously visible in the tears of Sox O'Dee's girl, Sally.

She was sitting on a chair in Mick Mulcahy's office in the corner of the yard, dabbing at her eyes with the sleeve of a soggy Puffa. I looked at Mick.

'Has the horse died or what?'

'No. He's not great, though,' Mick said. 'He had one hell of a race yesterday.'

I nodded. 'I've never seen a horse so exhausted.'

'He couldn't have gone a yard further.'

'Anyway, he won, so what are the tears about?'

'Ah, well,' Mick said, raising his eyes to the roof. 'He may have passed the post first but he's liable to have the race taken off him.'

'But why?' I said with an ominous sinking in my stomach. 'No one objected; there wasn't any enquiry or anything.'

'No, but he may not pass the dope test.'

This time my heart gave a few double-time beats. 'What! You think he was doped?'

'No, not deliberately, like. But little Miss Florence Nightingale here forgot herself. Instead of Dermosil ointment, she'd been rubbing Dermobian into his cut, and that contains prednisolone which is basically a steroid. Anyway, it's a banned substance as far as the rules of racing are concerned and, just our luck, they chose to test him.'

I didn't know whether to be relieved or disappointed. Professionally, I wanted to know that the horse had somehow been got at with performance-enhancing drugs, though I couldn't see how or where that could have happened.

On the other hand, in these circumstances we could be fairly sure that the horse must test positive; certainly it was more than likely that if the girl had thoughtlessly plastered ointment on the horse's leg, it would show up. Jane would then be fined, and disallowed the race. And, presumably, if any other substance *had* been introduced, that would also show up, and then she'd be in real trouble.

In the meantime, I could understand why Sally was feeling sorry for herself. Mick must have made her feel two inches high.

'Where is the boss?' I asked.

'You'll find her back at the house, and not too happy.'

I looked at Emma. 'Maybe my cheque will cheer her up.'

'I doubt it,' she said.

Jane certainly didn't look happy. We'd let ourselves in through her kitchen door and found her, sitting in her own office, surrounded as always by stacks of newspapers, form books and sales catalogues, with a good measure of undiluted whisky in a glass at her side.

She looked up and tried to force her gloomy face into a smile.

'Hello, you two.'

'Hi, Jane. You don't have to put on a happy act for us, you know. Mick's just told us.'

'He's such a blabbermouth! You'd better not breathe a word of it to anyone, either of you. Your father will go potty when he finds out, Emma.'

'So you haven't told him yet?' I asked.

'No. He's on his way round, though. I think I'll have to tell him now; I can't just let him find out from the lab result. Perhaps you'd care to hang around for a while?'

I smiled. 'Sure, and Emma can calm him down.'

'Dream on! I'll keep out of his way, if you don't mind.'

'I can't think how often I've told them not to use that Dermobian. It's great stuff, but it takes about five days to clear the system.'

'I don't think Sally wanted him to run at all,' I said.

Jane looked down morosely at her glass. 'I wasn't that keen either. I'm ashamed of myself for letting Gerald badger me into it.'

'You won't convince him he's wrong, now the horse has won.'

'That horse may have won, but it took a hell of a lot out of him; it'll take him weeks to recover.'

We heard the front door bell ring.

Jane looked at Emma. 'Would you be a darling and let him in?'

'Sure,' she said, but Jane suddenly pulled herself to her feet.

'No, actually, I ought to do it myself. He'll only know I'm sheltering behind you. Come into the drawing room,' she said over her shoulder as she left the room.

We waited a few minutes before going to join her. I was already feeling for her as we walked into the big room at the front of the house. Through its tall, uncovered windows, the dying rays of the February sun could be seen over the tops of the downs.

Lord Tintern was silhouetted in front of one of the windows. I couldn't see his face until he moved back towards the centre of the room. From the way he looked at us then it was clear that Jane hadn't told him we were there. But whatever he felt about it, he wasn't letting on. He flourished the bottle of champagne he was holding. 'Come on, you must join me in drinking my horse's health.'

I shuddered. He obviously didn't know yet that the horse was probably going to lose the race on the dope test.

'I've just been telling Jane how proud I am of her – producing that horse so well. She didn't even want him to run, but I knew he was ready for it, eh, Jane?' He turned to her and almost winked.

She closed her eyes and tried to quell a shudder. 'Gerald, I don't know how he won; he wasn't fully fit, and he shouldn't have done. He just managed to hang on out of sheer will-power. And I don't think it will have done him any long-term good.'

Tintern laughed. 'Come on. We *won*, didn't we? Let's have a drink, for God's sake.' He put his bottle of champagne on a table. 'Jane, tell Emma where she can find some glasses and an ice sleeve to wrap around this.'

Emma was too relieved at the lack of confrontation to object. Jane told her where to find things, and Tintern carried on crowing about his decision to run Sox O'Dee. He seemed quite oblivious to the stilted- ness of our response as we drank his champagne. Then to Jane's obvious delight, after fifteen minutes, he announced that he had to be going.

Jane went to see him off. When she came back, the tail lights of his car were already disappearing down her drive. 'I don't know what he'll do when the results of the test come through,' she said sheepishly.

Emma nodded sympathetically. 'If he tries to make a scene, just tell him to take his horses somewhere else. At least you could have Nester back then.'

'Not necessarily,' I teased. 'He's doing rather well at Derek's.'

'I can't possibly tell him to move anyway,' Jane said morosely. 'He's got six of the best horses in my yard.'

Emma laid a hand on her arm. 'You're lucky, you don't live with him.'

Jane smiled and pulled a face at the prospect.

'In the meantime,' she nodded resignedly at her empty champagne glass, 'all that's happened is that the storm's been delayed.'

'Well, it's not just bad news,' I said, putting my cheque on the table in front of her. 'And all I want now is some time on your equiciser.'

'Help yourself.' She smiled.

I left Emma in the house with Jane and walked out to the hay barn where the equiciser was kept. This piece of equipment was basically a wooden horse, whose head and neck were hinged on a spring. It was designed to recreate the motion of a galloping animal. It didn't give much of an authentic feel, but it did entail the use of the correct riding muscles.

Used properly, a rider needed to be supremely fit to last more than five minutes on it.

I managed two, and was thrilled. I rested for a while and did another two-minute session, then a rest, until I'd done twenty minutes and called it a day, utterly exhausted.

★ ★ ★

The next day, I went out to investigate Sox O'Dee's win from another angle. I drove to Lambourn early and arrived at Connor McDonagh's office door without any warning. I knew that he tended to spend the first couple of hours ringing round gathering information for his next day's selections, and today was no exception.

Joan showed me straight into her boss's untidy lair. He stood up and came round his desk to greet me. 'Simon, good to see you! Thanks for the word last week about Sox O'Dee. I suppose I'd better buy you a pint next time I see you in the Greyhound.'

'Don't worry. I came to see you to let you know they may take the race away from him.'

Connor raised an eyebrow. 'Really?'

'Yes. I doubt he'll pass the dope test.' I looked at him hard as I spoke to detect any sign of culpability. 'But you wouldn't have had anything to do with that, would you?'

'Good God, no, man! I'm not a complete eejit.'

'His girl rubbed a whole lot of Dermobian on a scab, and that'll almost certainly show through.'

Connor looked excessively relieved. 'Then they'll not be pointing the finger at me?'

'I wouldn't count on it.'

He waved me to a chair and went back to sit down. 'I tell you, Simon, I don't know what the hell's going on. I mean, I shouldn't complain. I'm taking a frigging fortune on the line, but you and I know this is not down to me.'

'There are some people who think you're in partner-ship with Toby Brown.'

'But I barely know the man! I haven't a clue why he stopped, and I certainly haven't taken any advice from him. I haven't even seen him for weeks.'

'Well, there are people who were very keen for him to stop, and if they think you've somehow taken over, they'll want you to stop too.'

'The bookies, of course?'

'Yes.' I nodded.

'Jesus, Simon! I just pick a few horses. For sure I know what I'm doing, but I don't expect to get it right every day.'

'What's it been – five out of five so far?'

'Six out of six,' Connor corrected.

'Well, whatever, but I wanted to tell you that I have a professional interest in all this, and if you think you're in trouble, I can help.' I took out one of my business cards and scribbled an extra number on it. 'That's my mobile. You can get me on that any time. Just don't tell anyone, anyone at all, that I've told you this. Okay?'

'Sure.' He took the card gratefully. 'Thanks. Is there anything I can do for you?'

'You could save me a couple of quid and tell me your nap for today.'

He laughed, gave me a name and saw me out.

Back at the office, Matt was looking agitated.

'Tintern's been on, asking how much we know about Connor's activities.'

'About time too,' I said.

'I just wonder how he feels about his own horse being one of Connor's naps,' Matt murmured.

'When I saw him yesterday, he was happy as a sand boy – sloshing champagne around like a sailor on shore leave. Of course, Jane hadn't told him the mandatory dope test would show up positive.'

'What!' Matt exploded. 'Why didn't you tell me?'

'I haven't seen you.'

'But what happened?'

I told him about Sally and her over-enthusiastic ministering. 'But the results won't be released for a few days, so we'll just have to sit and wait.'

Matt sighed, hating to wait for anything.

I tried to deflect him. 'How are we getting on with Wessex Biotech?'

He perked up. 'I'm going down to see Brian Griffiths this evening. I want to run through various events over the last few weeks that I think may have some bearing on those missing prototypes.'

'Have you seen one of the instruments yet?'

'Not yet, but Dysart says he'll give us a demonstration when we meet him later this week.'

'Okay. In the meantime, I think I'll go and see Tintern up at the Jockey Club on Thursday when he's in. There are a couple of things I want to check out.'

'What are you planning to do for the next couple of days?'

I braced myself for a short skirmish. 'As a matter of fact, I'm going racing tomorrow.'

'To check Connor's nap?'

'Only if it happens to be running at Ludlow.'

'Why?'

'Because I'm riding Baltimore in the hunter chase there.'

Matt gave a disdainful shake of his head. 'I've told you, Simon, if you think we're ever going to make anything of our business, you've just got to get your priorities right.'

'As it happens,' I justified, 'we're involved in a racing investigation at the moment, so if it makes you feel happier, treat my day's racing as research.'

Any guilt that Matt might have wanted me to feel was utterly absent when I woke next morning, as enthusiastic as I'd ever been about riding a race.

I'd now had several schooling sessions with Julia de Morlay and for the first time in my riding career, felt that I was in control of my horse rather than the other way round. Julia had been right when she'd said I would feel glued on once I got my irons back. Riding without stirrups had taught me more about balance and grip than I could ever have imagined.

Jane had managed to enter my old hunter chaser in a very uncompetitive field, and despite sending the horse off with the obvious handicap of having me on board, was quite sanguine about our chances. She had owners visiting the yard, and couldn't come to watch, but she wished me luck.

Almost the first person I saw as I walked from the car-park behind the old Victorian stands at Ludlow was Connor.

'How are you?' he said in answer to my greeting.

'Having serious bowel trouble.'

'That should help with the weight,' he laughed.

I nodded. 'Yes. But why are you here? Is your nap running?'

'It is,' he answered, with a hint of nervousness.

'And who's the lucky selection today?'

'You are.'

I felt as if a bomb had dropped right on my head, and stopped in my tracks.

'What?' I spluttered.

'Only kiddin',' Connor said hastily when he saw my reaction. 'Mine goes in the race before.'

'Which is it?'

'If you haven't phoned, I'm not tellin' you.'

'The price on the boards'll show it anyway,' I said, annoyed and still quivering from the shock he'd administered. 'So, why have you come?'

'I just wanted to see it run. And yours as well, of course,' he added unconvincingly.

I watched Connor's selection win comfortably, on a television in the weighing room. No one should have been surprised. It was running way below its class, but I couldn't stop myself from thinking of Toby. I prided myself on being a good judge of character, and when he'd told me he had no more interest in tipping, I'd believed him. Now, I wasn't so sure.

After that I concentrated entirely on my own race. The Shropshire course, laid on gravel, was riding well that day, with just enough cut to please my old boy.

He was a very experienced and safe jumper and needed encouragement, rather than instructions, from his jockey. Nevertheless, the benefits of Julia's merciless criticism bore spectacular fruit as I found I was giving him some real help over each fence. We had only one difference of opinion over where we should take off, and even though Baltimore had the final say, I never looked like falling off.

At the end of the three miles, I felt as if I'd won the Derby, not a fifteen hundred quid hunter-chase. As I pranced into the winner's enclosure to collect my pot, it was the first time I'd finished a race less exhausted than my horse.

I rang Matt on my way home. 'How did you get on with Griffiths?' I asked first.

'Bastard wasn't there. He'd had to go to some crisis meeting at the plant which makes these injector things in Germany. Never had the bloody manners to tell me, though.'

I judged this wasn't the best moment to crow about my minor victory on Baltimore. 'Did you see Dysart, then?'

'No, he was with Griffiths.' After a short pause he went on reluctantly, 'How did you get on, by the way?'

'We won.' I tried not to sound too triumphant.

'Bloody hell!'

'Sorry,' I said with a tentative laugh.

Matt had the good grace to laugh with me. 'Well done. I suppose I'll have to get you a drink, though God knows, you must have been up against some terrible horses, and even worse jockeys.'

'You'll eat your words,' I retorted.

'I'll eat your old trainers if you ever resemble a jockey.'

'We'll see,' I said, laughing, and put the phone down.

During the night, a few faxes spewed out of my machine bearing congratulations on my modest victory and soon after eight in the morning I received the first of half a dozen phone calls.

One was from Toby. It was the first I'd heard from him in over a week.

'Well done,' he said. 'He wouldn't have been my nap.'

'Toby, I hope you haven't been napping anything since you agreed to quit?' I was thinking of Harry Chapman's icy appraisal of Toby's greed.

'Why? Who have you been talking to?'

'Harry Chapman.'

'Look, I don't know what's been happening but if Connor's doing the business – and from what I've heard, he's on the same kind of run as I had – it's got nothing to do with me.'

'I believe you, thousands wouldn't.'

'Well, that's their problem.'

'Where are you now?' I asked.

'In London – at the flat.'

'Is that wise?'

'Of course.'

It shouldn't have made any difference to me what happened to Toby, and yet I did feel somehow responsible for his safety. I also had absolutely no doubt that, having paid Toby a handsome sum, the bookies would be furious if they thought he was turning them over. 'It's up to you, but just be careful.'

'Yes, of course.'

He rang off, leaving me wondering why I'd bothered. But he was after all my trainer's son.

The next day I sat waiting in the reception area of the Jockey Club. Lord Tintern appeared a few minutes after I'd come in and asked to see him. Although he didn't look pleased to be interrupted without an appointment, he took me through to the meeting room where he had first briefed me two weeks before.

'I have to tell you, Gerald, I think you were right,' I started.

'About what?' he asked.

'About some kind of connection between Toby and Connor. The only thing is, I don't think either of them is aware of it.'

'If they're working together, then of course they are.'

'What I mean is, I think someone else is pulling the strings.'

'Don't be absurd! If they've somehow contrived to influence the results of races, they'd both know how it was being done. At the same time, it seems they've sometimes tipped the right horses, which have won fair and square – like Sox O'Dee on Saturday.'

'The steward took a blood test from him. Jane told me so.'

'Yes, I know.'

'We asked to see the results of dope tests on any of

Toby's winning naps that had been tested. That was a couple of weeks ago and we haven't received them yet.'

'I've got them here,' Tintern said, leafing through some papers in a file he'd brought with him. 'They were all negative. See for yourself.' He thrust a list of incomprehensible data at me. 'And if you're trying to suggest that these animals have been systematically drugged, then I'm afraid you're wasting your time. Whatever the answer is, that's not it. Frankly, I'm sure Toby's still directly and wittingly involved, and I was hoping you'd be able to tell me by now why he'd stopped naming horses himself.'

'I can tell you that,' I said, ignoring Harry Chapman's warning. 'He's selling his naps to a consortium of bookmakers who are rewarding him better than his phone service.'

Tintern looked annoyed. 'I don't think that would stop Toby from continuing to earn a bit on the side, though.'

I couldn't see any benefit in arguing about it, although I was almost certain that Toby, acquisitive as he was, was equally keen to avoid risking his own skin.

'These bookmakers must really be starting to feel the pinch by now,' Tintern went on. 'So keep your ear to the ground. The last thing we want, for the good of racing, is a string of bankrupt bookmakers.'

'Presumably, if all the bookies went bust, the punters would just have to use the Tote, like the Pari-Mutuel in France?'

Tintern grunted. 'Frankly, life would be a lot simpler

if they did. I've been helping in the preparation of a Green Paper to go before Parliament with proposals that all betting in this country is channelled through the Tote, with the high street bookmakers simply acting as their agents.'

I nodded. 'I heard the idea at your lunch party last week. I should think the bookies will fight it tooth and nail?'

'Well,' Tintern said mildly, 'they can try, but the time might come when they'll be delighted to be guaranteed a profit for their business.'

I left him, I thought, reasonably confident that Matt and I would get to the bottom of it. On my way out I asked the receptionist, using Lord Tintern as my authority, to send us a list of all the personnel at the Equine Forensic Laboratory at Newmarket.

Armed with a digital camera and a conventional one with black-and-white film, I drove out of London and headed for Worcester, where Connor's selection was running in the last race.

My mind was seething with the ramifications of the bizarre events spawned by Toby's three weeks of spectacular success.

I felt as if I were gazing at one of those jumbled pictograms that appear in the Sunday magazines from time to time, from which, by looking at it for hours through squinting eyes, one is supposed to be able to extract a view of a totally unexpected three-dimensional object. I found that I kept snatching glimpses of a hard-edged image, but the moment I lost concentration, the picture melted into invisibility once more. But I was at least encouraged to believe that these rudimentary glimpses were leading me in the right direction.

Chapter Twelve

'There was something on Teletext this morning about Salmon Leisure's share price,' Matt said. 'Anything in the business sections?'

The day after I'd seen Tintern at Portman Square, Matt and I had set off in good time to go racing at Cheltenham. Emma had come with us and Matt drove while she and I looked through the papers.

I leafed through to the back of the *Telegraph*. 'You're right! They've dropped from four-thirty-seven to two-eighty-two in the last ten days. And no one's likely to come to the rescue as long as they're losing money.'

'They're certainly going to have to do something. If Connor's naps keep coming up, there's going to be absolute carnage. What do they say about that?' Matt asked.

I turned to the racing pages, read a few lines and laughed. 'They hate to admit it, but now Connor's named nine out of ten, they can't pretend it isn't happening.' I read on a bit. 'They don't like it. They're as good as saying they can smell a very large rat. And they almost sound sorry for the bookies.'

'Hypocrites!' Emma said. 'They're jealous, that's all. Though God knows why they should take the bookies' side – they've been winning since time began, and now at last the tables have turned, they're whinging like spoiled brats. Anyway, what are you two looking for today?'

'Same as yesterday. I'm going to photograph everyone in sight, anywhere near the horse, around the paddock and down at the start.'

'What's the horse called again?'

'Free Willy.'

'Oh, dear,' she groaned. 'Why do people do things like that?'

I laughed. 'It's quite a good horse.'

About thirty seconds after the start, Free Willy looked like the right name for the horse. 'Free' was what he was as soon as he had deposited his jockey at the second fence and, to the delight of the bookmakers, galloped home alone.

After we'd left Cheltenham two hours later, I wanted to get straight back to London to start processing the films in Catherine's dark room. Matt dropped me at Swindon station and took Emma on to Ivydene.

Once I was in London, I settled down in semi-darkness in Notting Hill to develop all the shots we had taken over the last few days. Once I'd got that going, I transferred all the digital shots on to our computer and started to sort through the prints for any matches from the five napped races we'd already covered. I reckoned I had five hours' work ahead of me to do the job thoroughly, and Matt and I had both accepted that this was our only jumping off point – until something better presented itself.

Rerunning the videotapes of the races hadn't given us the spread or depth of coverage we needed, which was why we'd chosen this old-fashioned, laborious, but ultimately reliable way of surveying the crowds in particular locations.

I stopped occasionally to pour myself a drink or make a sandwich, and thought jealously of Matt taking Emma home.

A little before nine, I was making good progress and thinking of talking to Emma myself, when the phone rang.

I picked it up almost unconsciously as I concentrated on rinsing off a batch of prints.

'Hello.'

'Oh, hello.' A soft, attractive female voice, which I didn't recognise at once. 'I'm sorry to ring now, but I was looking for Matt.'

'I'm his business partner. Can I help you?'

'Oh, hi, Simon. It's Sara here.'

I stopped what I was doing and tried to concentrate. 'Sara, I'm sorry, I didn't recognise your voice. I'm afraid Matt's not here. I can give you his number in Henley, he should be back there later.'

'I don't need to talk to Matt necessarily. Either of you will do. Can I come round?'

'Sure. Do you have the address?'

'Yes.'

'If you haven't eaten, I'll buy you dinner, if you like?'

'Thanks. I'll be there in about twenty minutes.'

When she'd rung off, I tried Matt's number myself but only got the answerphone. Similarly on his mobile. I reluctantly dialled Ivydene, and found myself talking to Gerald Tintern.

'Emma's gone off to dinner with that partner of yours,' he answered my query with some satisfaction. 'I don't know if I'll be around when she gets back, of course, but I could leave a message for her?'

'No,' I said, 'it's not important.'

It was half an hour before the door bell rang. I went to open it and found Sara standing there.

Her blue eyes shone beneath her bob of windblown black hair. A wry, conspiratorial smile dimpled her cheeks and made me suddenly aware of her attractions. I had to remind myself that she was the first girl in recent history that my partner had visibly fancied. As I gave her a welcoming kiss, I tried to think of Emma.

I waved her through the door and down to our office. 'Can I get you something from the company drinks cupboard?'

'If there's anything in it.'

There wasn't a lot, but we finished off a bottle of Chardonnay while Sara leaned back in the only comfortable chair and told me, with more than a hint of nervousness, why she'd come.

'Harry's going crazy. McDonagh's skinning us alive and Harry's convinced that Toby's the cause of it all. He thinks he's behind McDonagh. You know Harry bought Toby off the tipping line?'

'Yes.'

'Well, he's hopping mad now – thinking he's been conned.'

'But I told him Toby wouldn't dream of double-dealing. For a start he's far too much of a coward. But do you know if Harry's contacted Toby yet anyway?'

'No – I'm not sure I know where he is. Do you?'

'Not any more,' I said, trying to dismiss the sudden thought that she'd been sent by Chapman to get a fix on Toby.

'That's just as well,' Sara said, to my relief, and I decided it was time to go out to eat.

Over a quick dinner in a small, old-fashioned Italian restaurant, Sara carried on questioning me, but now it was about Matt. She was a good-looking girl, but any temptation I might have felt was easily dispelled by her obvious reciprocation of Matt's interest; I just hoped he was behaving as well as I was.

I dropped her back at her flat in Fulham, and said goodbye with no more than a fleeting kiss on the cheek. Feeling virtuous and frustrated, I went back to my job in the dark room, and spent the next few hours wondering about Toby and Harry Chapman.

Shortly after midnight, when I was thinking about packing up, the phone rang again. This time it was Matt.

'Hi,' he said, 'just checking in to let you know your girlfriend has been watered and fed.'

'So has yours,' I replied gleefully.

'What?' he asked sharply.

'Sara came round with some fresh news. We couldn't track you down. Your mobile was switched off,' I added starchily. 'It's lucky it wasn't anything urgent.'

When the empty 6.30 Intercity pulled out of Paddington next morning, I was on it. Matt had arranged with David Dysart that we would be at Wessex Biotech at 8.30 for a demonstration of his Powderjet injection system. He had insisted that we should have a proper look at the equipment we were supposed to be investigating.

Matt was waiting for me at Bristol Parkway. Quietly, and without embellishment or omission, I filled him in on exactly what Sara had told me the previous evening, and how she had spent most of dinner asking about him.

'Did she say what Chapman and his friends were going to do?'

'No, I don't suppose she knows. Anyway, there's not a lot they *can* do, is there?'

'If they're desperate enough, they'll do anything. This isn't some tin pot little business we're talking about. They turn over hundreds of millions a year.'

'I've told Toby to let us know if they start giving him a hard time,' I said. 'But I think Chapman's a bit above ordering beatings up. Did you discuss any of this with Tintern last night?'

'No. As far as I can tell, all he wants is to find out what Toby and Connor have been up to.'

I wasn't so sure, but I was also aware that my distrust of Lord Tintern was due, as much as anything else, to his attitude to me personally.

★ ★ ★

David Dysart was buzzing like a dynamo when we were shown into his office – a room with two glass walls set at right angles to each other, overlooking the birch woods that clung to the hillside where the building stood. This gave the impression we were meeting in a forest clearing as the morning sun slanted between the leafless trees.

'Thank you for coming,' Dysart said, watching his secretary pour coffee for us. 'I've got one of our development people coming in to demonstrate – ah, here he is. I think you've already met Brian?' he added with a faint grin.

'Morning.' Brian held out his hand which we shook in turn. He seemed to bear us no grudge from our last visit. 'David's asked me to show you precisely what you've been looking for, what it does and how it does it – up to a point,' he added with a chuckle.

He led us across the room to a table in front of one of the glass walls. On it was a white plastic object about the length and girth of half a cucumber. One end was flat and slightly concave.

Brian picked it up. 'This is the dermal version of our Powderjet system. If we place this flat and on an area of skin, reasonably free from hair, the Powderjet can fire particles of drugs – molecules, peptides, proteins or genes – into the skin. And it can do it to varying depths, depending on where the drug is needed.'

'How do you mean, fire?' Matt asked.

Brian unscrewed the round end of the object. 'See here? This is a cylinder of highly compressed helium.

When it's released, it blows through this drug cassette, accelerating the particles through the end at a supersonic speed, peppering the skin rather like a shot gun.'

'And the person feels no pain?'

'They feel nothing.' He deconstructed the compact piece of equipment to show us the various components, impressive in their apparent simplicity.

I turned to Dysart, who hadn't tried to interrupt or override anything Brian had said. 'When does it come on stream?'

'The Department of Health have a few more trials of their own to complete, then we launch into the private and public health services.'

'What about the veterinary profession?'

'We haven't really looked at that yet because animals don't suffer from the psychological trauma of anticipation and can easily tolerate the actual pain of an injection.'

Matt nodded smugly at me. 'That's what I was talking about.'

'But surely,' I pursued, 'it must be quicker and more convenient not having to jab great needles in? And, anyway, some animals do mind; I've had horses that hated it when you got the needle out.'

'Our view is that the gain is unlikely to justify the cost,' Dysart said. 'Besides, it would mean shaving a patch of skin, which would offset the time gain.'

'Most animals have a few bare patches – a horse on the underside of its loins, for instance.'

Dysart smiled. 'No doubt once the vets have seen it in action, they'll draw their own conclusions. Certainly, there's no reason why it shouldn't be applied to animals if it was thought appropriate.'

'As it is, though,' Matt asked, 'it's got no competition?'

'As far as we know. We're the only people who have made public what it will do; though, of course, the precise mechanics of it and the physical chemistry involved in particleising the drugs are what we called you in to protect. They're subject to various patents being granted, and there are just a few more hurdles to jump yet.'

'Could a rival work it all out from one sample?'

Dysart shrugged. 'Not easily, but it's possible – enough to worry the shit out of us.'

'What's the most critical element of the equipment?' I asked.

'Probably the gas projection system,' Dysart said thoughtfully.

'And who was responsible for that?'

'Most of the development work was done by Michael Taylor. He came to us from a French company, actually, specialising in highly sophisticated compressed gas weapons. He's the real brains behind the technology.'

'What do you actually use as a propellant, then?'

'Very densely compressed helium,' Dysart said, picking up the sample Griffiths had shown us and opening it up again. 'It comes in these custom-made canisters.' He indicated what looked like a shiny metal miniature Calorgas bottle.

Matt nodded. 'I can see how tempting it might be for the competition to find a short cut.'

'That's why I wanted you to see this at first hand.' Dysart waved the sample at us. 'I should have arranged it when I originally instructed you, but to be honest, at that time I was doubtful that these prototypes had left the building. I'm still doubtful, because I can't identify even a potential culprit from among the people who would have access to them.'

Matt and I nodded together.

'I'm sorry we haven't got further. We'll give the project absolute priority, but it may mean having to interview all relevant staff in some depth.'

Dysart nodded. 'All right, but be careful. You know how Brian here took umbrage at your. questions – though I'm sure he's not holding it against you.'

Brian smiled. 'Not at all. Is there anything else I can tell you now about the Powderjet?'

'Not as far as I'm concerned,' I said, looking at Matt.

He shook his head. 'No, I'm clear.'

'Right then,' the ungainly young scientist said. 'I've got other things to get on with. I'll leave you with David.'

When he'd gone, Dysart invited us to sit at the table by the window while he topped up our coffee.

'Is there anything else I can tell you?'

'Yes,' I said. 'I just wanted to confirm that it was through our meeting at Lord Tintern's party that you got on to us?'

'Yes. I believe I told you the other day on the phone: I met you at Lord Tintern's, and you subsequently sent us your sales package.'

'Yes. You did tell me, but I wondered how you originally met Lord Tintern?'

Dysart gave me a quick look of surprise, but evidently made up his mind to answer what he clearly thought was an irrelevant question.

'The research to develop this piece of kit was very expensive. It's the sort of project that has to be funded with real venture capital. Your friend Lord Tintern has a reputation for providing seed money for high-risk projects. I cold called him, and he did it for me, and went on to introduce other investors.'

'Does he have much to do with the company now?'

'Not a lot. He's a non-exec director. He turns up for most board meetings and AGMs, and a few internal presentations we've had. But, really, other than giving some financial advice, he's never got more closely involved. Why do you ask?'

'Just curious,' I said. It's incredible what a small world this is.

' "Just curious" indeed,' Matt said as we drove from the sylvan valley where Dysart's building nestled. 'What were you getting at?'

'I'm not sure, but I wouldn't put it past Tintern to try and sell the idea to some other larger company, now he knows the thing works.'

'There's no way he'd do that,' Matt scoffed. 'He stands to make far more from his holding in Biotech. And anyway, I'd say he's totally honest. He's a member of the House of Lords, for God's sake.'

'Membership of the House of Lords hardly precludes

members from any wrong-doing,' I said drily.

'Maybe not, but there's no doubt you resent him personally simply because he doesn't think you're good enough for Emma. Your name cropped up yesterday evening and, frankly, I can see his point. I mean, she's quite a catch.'

'Good God!' I said. 'You sound like Mrs Bennett. And besides, if this business of ours ever takes off, *I'll* probably be quite a catch too.'

'It's going to be hard to get it off the ground if you keep slipping off for riding lessons at the drop of a hat,' Matt said stiffly.

I didn't speak for a few moments. Instead I picked up the mobile and dialled Connor's tipping line. When I'd heard what he had to say and he'd earned his thirty pence from me, I put it down.

'We may as well go to Chepstow, now we're here. Connor's nap's running in the second race.'

We repeated the exercise with the camera among a Saturday crowd which huddled in a damp west wind and managed to get a comprehensive set of shots covering everyone who came near the horse that had been favoured with Connor's fancy.

Matt dropped me off at The Coach House with a curt good night. I decided I would go on up to London early next morning and took the opportunity to catch up with post, e-mails and phone messages that had accumulated.

For once I went to bed early and was happily dozing off in front of an old film when the telephone jerked me back to reality.

'Hello, Simon,' a well-known voice said anxiously. 'It's Toby.' He didn't need to tell me that something was worrying him.

'What is it?' I asked.

'Can you come round?'

'Where are you?'

'At my flat.'

I weighed up the concern in his voice and balanced it with my own comfort, but couldn't face moving. 'Toby, what is it?'

'I just need to talk to someone.'

'I'll be round first thing tomorrow.'

Toby sounded relieved. 'Thanks.' He rang off.

I ordered an alarm call for 6.30 next morning and sank back on my pillows. But when I tapped the play button on the VCR remote, somehow the black and white movie had lost its interest for me.

I thought of Toby, and of Connor.

I thought of the legion of starry-eyed punters who pursued their dreams through the utterances of an obscure Irishman.

I got out of bed, wrapped a dressing-gown round myself and went downstairs. I poured myself a whisky and sat down at the battered pine boards of my kitchen table.

Then, as if an outside force was guiding my arm, my hand found the phone and punched in Emma's mobile number.

'Hello,' I said when she answered.

'Hello, Si,' she murmured back. 'Where have you been? I haven't seen you for weeks.'

'It's only two days.'

'Two days too much. What are you up to? I'm already in bed.'

'I couldn't sleep,' I said. 'I thought you might like to come over and play Scrabble?'

'Which version?'

'Which do you want?'

'*Not* the one with letters and a board.'

'Suits me.'

Chapter Thirteen

When the phone chirruped at me next morning, my first instinct was to thump it. But I prised my eyes open and shook my head clear enough to remember my alarm call and my date with Toby. A quick shot of adrenaline jerked me wide awake. I picked up the phone and cut the call.

'What's going on?' a sleepy voice asked through the duvet.

I was already out of bed, stepping into rumpled Levi's I'd discarded a few hours before.

'I've got to go to London.'

'Oh, God!' Emma groaned and instantly fell back to sleep.

I sighed and in the half-dark delved into a chest of drawers for a clean shirt. I was thoughtful enough not to turn on the light, though I doubted that Emma would have noticed if I had.

Downstairs, I rang Matt. He answered as if he'd been at his desk for hours.

'Toby called last night,' I said. 'He wants me to go to his flat.'

'Are you on your way?'

'Yes.'

'I'll meet you at the office in twenty minutes.' He rang off.

The traffic on the motorway and in West London was sparse at 7.30 on a Sunday morning. Matt and I were swinging into Park Lane just thirty-two minutes after we'd left our office.

A couple of minutes later, we were standing in the pillared portico of the handsome, Neo-Gothic building that contained Toby's lavishly appointed London apartment.

I pushed the bell button labelled 'T. Brown, Esq.', gazed into a CCTV lens, smiled for the videotape and waited. When there was no answering squawk from the small speaker set in the wall, I tried again, twice. Still nothing.

Matt had stepped back on to the cobbled street and was looking up at the windows of Toby's second-floor flat. 'All the curtains are drawn,' he said. He flipped out his mobile and dialled Toby's number.

I watched his face while he listened, until he shook his head. 'Not even an answerphone.'

I pushed the button marked 'Porter'.

This time, with a gruff, resentful edge, we were answered. 'Hello. Who is it?'

'Simon Jeffries and Matt James. We came a couple of weeks ago.'

'Morning, sir.' The change in tone reflected, no doubt, his appreciation of the fifty-pound note Matt had pressed into his hand when he'd come to bug the phones. 'I'll open the door and come up to meet you.'

A long blast on a buzzer indicated that the door's lock had been released remotely and I pushed it open. Matt and I stepped into a lavishly furnished hall, rich with the woollen scent of new-laid Wilton and bright with gleaming brass door fittings.

The porter, unshaven and tieless, appeared through an arch at the back of the hall.

'Morning, gentlemen. What can I do for you?'

Matt curtly put a finger to his lips. The man grinned back obsequiously and gestured at the door through which he had come. I nodded. He led us into the stale tobacco ambience of his small panelled office, and closed the door.

I remembered the man's name. 'Good morning, Mr Tilbury. We were wondering if you'd seen or heard Mr Brown this morning?'

'It's not yet eight. I've not been up long, there's not much call to be on Sunday.'

'All right, but Mr Brown's not answering his door now and we had an appointment with him. We need to see if he's okay.'

Tilbury looked worried. 'Have you tried ringing him?'

'We tried, but there was no answer.'

'I can't just let people into my clients' apartments without their say-so . . .'

I was already pulling a wallet from my pocket. 'Mr Brown wouldn't have asked me to come if he didn't think it was urgent.'

'No, sir, I suppose not,' Tilbury said with half an eye on the fifty-pound note I was fingering.

'And if you can't let us in,' I advised, 'we'll have to call the police.'

'That won't be necessary, sir,' Tilbury said quickly. I guessed a combination of the money and the possibility that his precious clients might be disrupted by police sirens wailing in the mews had convinced him that letting us into Toby's flat was his best option.

We followed him up the broad shallow stairs to the second floor and a tall, dark oak-panelled entrance with oversized architrave and a carved tympanum above. He unlocked and swung open the heavy door. He stood back while I went in first, followed by Matt.

I stopped a moment to listen. Matt moved up silently beside me, sharp as a fox. I tried to catch his eye but it was occupied.

We were in a small, hexagonal ante-chamber, along with a pair of throne-like oak chairs and a large oriental carved wooden tiger on a gilt plinth. There were five other doors, all closed except the largest, opposite us.

The only sound came from Tilbury's heavy breathing. I advanced a few steps across a Chinese silk rug until I was standing in the open doorway. It gave into the biggest room in the flat, a room on a grand scale with the proportions and feel of a Tudor banqueting hall. A vaulted ceiling of moulded plaster was supported by three pairs of ornate double hammer beams.

From the farthest beam dangled something long and bulky wrapped in a robe of figured silk which fluttered as it swung gently in the draught from the open door.

I didn't want to focus but gazed with horrified fascination until I knew beyond any doubt what we'd found. Unlike Matt, I wasn't used to such sights. I had to swallow back the vomit welling up from my tightening guts.

I looked away, ashamed and unexpectedly saddened. I glanced at Matt who offered a characteristic display of zero emotion.

But he must surely have realised that this stiffening vessel of a spent human life meant we had comprehensively failed to grasp the seriousness of our Jockey Club brief.

Hanging from a hempen noose looped around his neck, a look of puzzled disbelief on his once handsome face, was Toby Brown.

I tried not to retch as I stared with horror into eyes that were wide open and quite inert in waxy lifeless features.

A few paces behind me, I heard an ugly spluttering sound. Tilbury was being sick.

'For God's sake!' Matt hissed in disgust.

'I know how he feels,' I admitted. 'I wonder what the hell's happened here?'

'He's topped himself by the look of it,' Matt said, nodding at a small ornate chair which lay on its side, with one leg splintered, below the velvet-slippered feet of the dangling corpse.

'But, Matt, he can't have done. He rang me last night. He sounded a bit worried but . . .'

'People do this kind of thing when they're worried.'

'But why did he ring me?' I couldn't reconcile Toby's

normal abrasive self-confidence with this ultimate act of despair.

'Simon, don't you think he might have wanted to be found fairly quickly? Or maybe he didn't even want to succeed. Or maybe he was a gasper, and lost that chair by mistake.'

'For God's sake, Matt! Don't joke about it, the guy's dead.'

'Well, it happens,' he justified. 'Or he might have had pressures we don't even know about. For some people, the smallest problem can grow out of all proportion – so they take their own lives while the balance of their mind is impaired. That's how they put it, isn't it?'

This didn't seem to me to be the right time to be arguing about the cause of death. I guessed we might do better by leaving that to the experts.

I pulled my mobile phone from my pocket. 'I'm calling the police. In the meantime we'd better not touch anything.'

'I think,' Matt said, producing a handkerchief, 'I'll just remove our bugs first.'

He carefully extracted the two miniature microphones secreted by the phones in the drawing room and bedroom. I picked up the phone to dial 999 and turned away from the mortal remains of Toby Brown to see Tilbury hunched in a chair, his head between his knees. 'Look, Mr Tilbury, you'd better get to the door and make sure no one wanders in. I'm just calling the police.'

Tilbury didn't move; the emergency services exchange answered after six rings. I told them I wanted the police. When I heard the emotionless, efficient tones of a police switchboard operator I told her what we had found, and where.

Within two minutes, sirens were echoing up the narrow cobbled street. Tilbury, still groaning, was spurred into action by a hammering on the main door of the building. He lolloped out of the flat and down the stairs to open it before it was knocked down.

Two uniformed men, a sergeant and a constable, came into the room and took in the scene at a glance.

I'd seen them arrive out of the window and was watching a second car slither noisily to a halt in the mews outside. Matt was sitting, almost languidly, in a gilt and brocade Empire chair.

'Right, gentlemen,' the sergeant rasped. 'Which of you found him?'

'We both did,' I replied.

'How did you get in here?'

'The caretaker – the man who opened the door to you – brought us up and let us in.'

'Why would he do that?'

'Toby . . .' I stopped and nodded awkwardly at the swaying body '. . . rang me last night and asked me to come here this morning. When I arrived and couldn't get an answer, I asked the caretaker to help.'

The younger man was walking round Toby's oscillating corpse, taking conspicuous care not to touch or disturb anything while he murmured in jargon and acronyms over his radio.

Outside, the mews was already filling up with ancillary vehicles. I guessed that sudden deaths in wealthy

167

areas always attracted more press and professional nosy-parkers than in council estates.

Within minutes, it seemed, the large flat was full of pathologists, scene-of-crime investigators, doctors, ambulance men, and two detectives in conspicuously casual clothing. One, in jeans, a brown suede jacket and a crew-cut, came over to me, flashed a warrant-card and put it back in his pocket before I'd had a chance to read a word on it. 'DI Wyndham,' he said. 'I understand you found the deceased?'

'Yes, with my colleague, Major James.'

'Colleague? Were you here on some kind of business or are you a friend of the deceased?'

'Toby,' I said. 'His name was Toby Brown, and I suppose I was a friend.'

'Known him long?'

'About twenty-five years.'

'I see. I wonder if you'd mind coming into another room with me where we can get a bit of privacy?'

And not be overheard by Matt so that we could make our stories tally, I thought.

'By all means,' I agreed calmly.

He led me into the hexagonal hall and opened three of the doors that gave off it before he pushed one wider and went in to what I guessed was Toby's bedroom – very opulently furnished with a vast French half-tester draped in maroon velvet and topped with a carved gilt coronet.

DI Wyndham forgot himself enough to open his eyes in doubtful and faintly censorious wonder before he sharply brought his facial features under control.

'Right, it's a bit of a tart's parlour but it'll do,' he said, closing the door behind me. He waved me expansively at a deep-buttoned chaise-longue while he pulled a notebook and Biro from his pocket.

'So,' he said, setting his jaw, 'you came to see the deceased, your friend Toby, this morning. Why was that?'

'He rang me and asked me to.'

'What time?'

'Just after ten last night.'

'Do you know why he wanted to see you?'

I shook my head. 'Not for sure. You may have heard of him – he was a very successful racing tipster. Until the other day he was fronting a telephone service which had been having a fantastic winning run.'

Recognition dawned on the policeman's face. 'Right,' he said, nodding his head. 'I've read about him – just recently. Are you in that business too?' he asked with sudden sharpness.

'Not on the tipping side, no. I own a couple of horses and occasionally I ride them, as an amateur.'

'And what reason *might* he have had for asking you to come here?'

I opened my hands, palms up, in a gesture of bewilderment. 'I don't know. He'd just done a deal with a consortium of bookmakers to supply information exclusively to them, and I dare say they were expecting him to carry on in the same spectacular way.' I shook my head again. 'I don't know what you know about racing, but you can take it from me – statistically, there was no way he could have kept up for long what he'd been doing for the last few weeks.'

'So he was under pressure, you think?'

'I don't know that for sure, but it's possible. He didn't tell me what the trouble was when he rang – just that he wanted to see me. He sounded agitated about something, but that was all. If I'd known he was in such a state, I'd have driven up last night.'

Wyndham looked at me for a while, either making a shrewd assessment of my qualities as a witness or at least giving a good impression that he was.

'Do they know how long he's been dead?' I went on.

'About an hour, maybe a little longer. What time did you get here?'

I shrugged. 'Seven forty-five?'

The detective looked at me sharply, sensing evasion. 'Come on, you can do better than that.'

'It was about three minutes before I dialled 999.'

'Right.' He nodded and scribbled in his notebook. 'Now, I'll need a few details and we'll be in touch to get a full statement.'

'Has anyone been in touch with Toby's family yet?' I asked.

'No, not yet.'

'I know his mother very well. I think it might be best if I broke the news to her first.'

The policeman nodded. 'Yes, that would be better, but I must ask you at this stage to inform her only that her son has met with a fatal accident.'

'I'm not going to lie to her.'

'I'm not asking you to, sir. But as we haven't ascertained precisely the circumstances of his death . . .'

'All right,' I interrupted. 'I'll go right away. How can

I get in touch with you if I need to know more?'

'Here's my number.' He scribbled in his notebook, tore out a sheet and thrust it at me.

I took it. 'How long will all these people be here, then?'

The Detective Inspector glanced around. 'Not much longer. But before you go,' he held up a hand in the time-honoured way, 'your details, please. And I must ask you to give a set of fingerprints to forensics – just so that you can be eliminated.'

We walked through to the drawing room where I introduced him to Matt, and they disappeared back into the bedroom.

While I was rolling my prints on to a card, Mr Tilbury was brought up by the uniformed constable and sat, upright now but ashen-faced, on one of Toby's baronial chairs.

The other plain-clothes man was rifling through the bookshelves and the contents of a writing desk, while Toby's body was lowered from where it hung and placed on a stretcher by two ambulance men. One of them covered the silk-gowned body with a grey blanket, from which the velvet monogrammed slippers protruded bizarrely.

Matt emerged from a brief interview with Wyndham as Toby's body was carried from his exotic home for the final time. We went out behind the corpse and sat in my car and watched while it was loaded into an ambulance.

As the official vehicles began to disperse, I picked up the phone and dialled the number at Wetherdown.

'Morning, Jane. How are you?'

'I'm fine,' she said in her usual breezy manner. 'What on earth are you doing ringing at this time on a Sunday morning?'

'I'm sorry, Jane, I've got some bad news.'

There was a brief pause. In an entirely different voice she asked, 'Toby?'

'Yes, I'm afraid he's been in an accident.'

'Accident?' she whispered. 'How bad?'

I knew she wouldn't forgive me for prevaricating.

'I'm sorry, Jane. He's dead.'

I heard her gasp. 'Oh my God!' Then I could almost hear her trying to pull herself together. 'Are you sure?'

'Yes.'

'What happened?'

'The police haven't said yet.'

'But, I mean, was it a car crash or what?'

I couldn't believe how measured her tones were. I guessed something in the human body just takes over in times of such immense shock.

'No,' I answered quickly, 'no, it was some kind of domestic accident. But, Jane, I'm coming down to see you.'

I heard a few dry sobs. 'You're in London now – at Toby's?'

'Yes. He rang me late last night and asked me to meet him here. Matt and I found him, but I'll tell you all about that when I come. I'm only ringing you now because I wanted to let you know before the press find out.'

'The press? Oh, God,' she moaned.

'Look, Jane, they're bound to be interested.'

'I suppose so.' She sniffed. 'Thanks so much for ringing. Come as soon as you can, please, Simon.'

'I will.'

On our way out of London, I called Emma. She was just waking up at my house. As concisely as possible, I told her what had happened.

'I'll go and see Jane now,' she offered without hesitation.

'That would be really kind. I should think she'll need some support.'

'It's no problem. I certainly don't feel like going back to Ivydene now.'

'You should be careful,' Matt said when I'd rung off. 'Emma'll have moved in to your place before you know it.'

'So?' I said. 'That could save me a lot of time and petrol.'

As we turned off the M4 on to the Oxford Road, fifteen minutes from Wetherdown, I started to worry.

'What on earth are we going to tell Jane?'

'I'll ring that detective and see if they've got a result yet,' Matt suggested.

'They won't know any more by now.'

'They might,' he insisted.

I handed him the piece of paper on which the policeman had written his number, and he dialled it.

'DI Wyndham? It's Matthew James here. We'll be seeing Mrs Brown shortly. Can you tell us yet what you think happened?'

He listened for a few moments, nodding his head. 'I see . . . And you're sure about that? . . . Okay, thank you. We'll tell her.'

He clicked off the phone, turned to me and pulled a gloomy face. 'They're convinced it was suicide, but they won't be releasing a statement for the time being. It seems the press haven't picked it up yet.'

'I was really hoping it wasn't suicide,' I said, disappointed and not at all looking forward to telling this to Jane.

'They found no sign that anyone else had been in the flat.'

'But how did Toby get up to that beam?'

'He only had to stand on the chair and chuck the rope over, didn't he?'

I thought about Toby, tormented to the point where his life seemed intolerable, and wondered what any of us could have done to help him.

Nothing was going to make it any easier to tell his mother, I thought, as I turned through the gates of Wetherdown.

'No,' Jane said firmly. 'No way.' She looked at me defiantly.

I turned and walked across her drawing room to take refuge in staring at the view through the bay window.

Matt, tactfully, hadn't entered the conversation. He sat in the chair to which Jane had waved him, with his head tilted back and his eyes half closed. Emma, who had been doing her best to comfort Jane for the last half hour, sat forward on a sofa with her chin in her hands.

Jane was on her feet, aiming sporadic, angry thrusts with a poker at the fire which blazed in the large iron grate.

I turned back to look at her. 'Jane, I'm sorry to be the one telling you this, but I'm only passing on what the police think. And I have to be frank – when we walked into the flat this morning, it was the first thing we thought,' I said, trying to convince her despite myself.

Jane pulled herself up to her full five feet seven, standing a couple of paces in front of the fire. 'Toby wouldn't have taken his own life for anything. He was far too confident of his own abilities – and too fond of himself, for that matter. He was well able to handle any crisis that came along – emotional, financial or . . . sexual.' She faltered a moment and looked at me with an unfamiliar, hunted expression in her eyes.

'You must know, Simon, there were aspects of his private life of which I did not approve . . .' Her voice tailed off as she seemed to be struggling with her conscience. She sat down heavily in an armchair by the fire where she gazed into the flames for a few moments.

When she was ready, she took a deep breath and turned to look at me. 'I presume you knew that he was gay?' She glanced at the two other people in the room, then quickly turned her face to the glowing logs once more.

Emma, Matt and I didn't speak for a moment. Not because we were shocked but because it had obviously taken such a lot for his mother to admit to Toby's homosexuality.

'No,' I said eventually. 'I didn't know – not for sure. He never said or implied anything about it to me.' I slowed down to choose my words carefully. 'I wouldn't deny, though, that the possibility had occurred to me. I don't remember his ever being involved with a woman.'

Emma nodded. 'He must have been very discreet.'

When Jane looked up at us, tears glistened in her eyes. 'Can you imagine how much he suffered, pretending to us – to all his friends? I think he was terrified of its getting out – even in this day and age, when most people don't seem to care about that sort of thing. Of course, he knew I knew, but we never said so openly. And I believe he tended to go for chaps a long way from his own social milieu.

'I may not have approved of those aspects of his life-style,' she went on, speaking more firmly now, 'but, God knows, I loved him and knew him very well. And I can tell you categorically that whatever else he might have done, Toby did *not* commit suicide.'

She breathed in deeply through her nose and squared her jaw. 'He must have been murdered. And if the police aren't going to treat it as murder, then you two are going to have to.'

Neither Matt nor I spoke as the gold carriage clock on the mantelpiece ticked on another ten seconds.

Jane looked sharply at each of us in turn. 'Well? I'm asking for your help – for your professional services.' Her voice was rising. 'I'm instructing your company to find out who murdered my son.'

I looked at Matt. His eyes swivelled from Jane to me. Almost imperceptibly, he shook his head.

I looked at Emma. She gave no indication of her opinion.

I took a deep breath. 'I'll do what I can, Jane, but it won't be on a professional basis. I'll do it for you.'

I saw her face almost sag with relief. I hadn't realised how badly she needed my support, or how much she'd had to force herself to keep strong, to convince me that she wasn't becoming hysterical.

'Thank you, Simon. You're a good friend.'

Chapter Fourteen

We drove several miles across the wet and windswept downs in silence but as we dropped into the Thames Valley, Matt spoke. 'I'm not promising anything, but if the Jockey Club decides to retain us, I'm prepared to treat Toby's death as murder, as part of that investigation.'

I glanced at him gratefully. 'Thanks. I think I'm going to need all the help I can get.'

'Let's get on with it then, at least until Tintern takes us off the case,' Matt said, resigned to losing the rest of his Sunday, though probably glad of the action. 'But this has all turned a bit nasty,' he added impassively. 'I wonder why Toby did it?'

'Why are you so sure he took his own life?'

'That's obviously what the police think. I hardly knew him, but I wouldn't be surprised if he was involved with a lot of fairly unsavoury people. Or maybe his new bosses had seen through him or found him out, and he couldn't face the consequences. You knew him better than I did but how well was that? Did you have any real idea how he ran his private life?'

I shook my head with a sigh. 'No, of course not. He talked to me about horses, and sometimes pictures and furniture, occasionally about his mother, but never anything about his private life.'

'So you really can't say, one way or the other, if there might have been good reason for him to top himself?'

We talked around Toby's death for half an hour. As we reached the edge of London, I dialled the number at his flat. No one answered, not even a machine. I guessed the police had already taken away the answer-phone tape for analysis. Fortunately, we didn't need it; we had our recorder in the basement.

We drove on to Hay's Mews and, after a few minutes, raised Mr Tilbury from his lair again. He was still looking queasy and deeply shocked. The police had gone, he said, but he wouldn't show us up to the flat this time – simply handed over his key with a request that we give it back on the way out.

The police had tidied away most of the mess they'd made in the course of their investigations, but the broken chair was still propped against a table, with a single, dusty footprint on its brocade upholstered seat.

Elsewhere, on the furniture, windows and doors, the forensic team's powder still lingered.

'I should think the police have helped themselves to any interesting paperwork,' I said.

'They could have missed something.'

But, after a thorough search, we found nothing significant. It was only after we'd given up and I was in Toby's bathroom that I noticed one curious item on the wall.

It was a regimental photograph – the sort of group shot that hangs above thousands of loos, only ever gazed at for a few brief minutes by male visitors. I saw that it had been taken thirty-five years before and scanned the names underneath. In the third row, fourth from the right, was Major Gervaise Brown. My eyes flicked back to the faces, and I found Toby's father. There was a marked similarity between him and his son but, if pressed, I'd have said Toby was more like Jane.

I went back to the list of names. Sitting behind Major Brown was Captain The Hon. Gerald Birt, Emma's father – young, determined, and easily recognisable. Fascinated, I studied the rest of the names and faces for a while, but found no others that meant anything to me.

In the mews outside, Matt got into the car beside me.

'Right. Where now?'

'I thought we might go and pay a call on Mrs Hackney.'

'Toby's cleaner? The one I met when I delivered the wine?'

I nodded. 'That's her.'

'Okay,' he said. 'Jane gave you her number didn't she?'

For answer, I pulled my notebook from a pocket and passed it to him.

'I'll get it,' he said, 'but you speak to her. You're better at that sort of thing.'

★ ★ ★

''Ullo?' a sleepy, female voice answered.

'Mrs Hackney?'

'That's right.'

'My name's Simon Jeffries. I'm a friend of Toby Brown's.'

'Oh, yes.' Her voice suggested that she had, at least, heard of me.

'Sorry to have woken you.'

'What's the time?'

'It's eleven-thirty.'

'Oh, gawd!' she wailed. 'I was up 'alf the night with me sister at the 'ospital. Didn't get back till five in the mornin'.'

'Then I'm very sorry to trouble you, but I wanted to come round and see you – it's to do with Mr Brown.'

'What about him?'

'He's had an accident and we'd like to talk to you.'

There was a moment's silence before she answered. 'Why? What happened?'

'I'll tell you when I see you.'

'Oright then. 'Ow long'll you be?'

'Fifteen minutes.'

There was another long pause. 'Is Mr Brown oright? Can I speak to 'im?'

'No, I'm afraid you can't. They took him off in an ambulance,' I added, glad to have lied only by omission.

'That's lucky,' Matt said when I'd finished. 'It sounds as if the police haven't been to see her yet.'

'Maybe they don't even know about her. Perhaps

182

Toby paid her in cash. He was passionate about evading tax where he could.'

'I should think Tilbury would have told them. Anyway, let's hope we get there first.'

Matt read the map and directed me to Mrs Hackney's address in a block of council flats near Victoria station. Although it was only a few hundred yards from several famous London landmarks, it was a grimy, disintegrating monument to shoddy sixties architecture.

'I'll mind the car,' Matt said.

Inside the block, the lift to the seventh floor wasn't working. I took the faintly urine-scented staircase, and was grateful for a life that had spared me living conditions like these.

Blowing a little, I pressed the bell push and was answered by a five-note chime. This prepared me for the unsophisticated but well-polished ambience of the small flat into which I was invited a few moments later.

Mrs Hackney was a homely, grey-haired figure of about sixty, dressed in a powder blue track-suit and a pair of pink fluffy slippers. From the look of concern on her face, I guessed she was very fond of her eccentric boss.

I accepted her offer of a cup of tea, and looked around the cheap, cherished souvenirs and mementoes strewn around the surfaces of her living room where she had left me on a wood-framed sofa. There were plates and mugs depicting the marriage of Prince Charles and Lady Diana; a poorly painted Swiss weather house, in which both man and wife lurked indecisively in their doorways. A vase of silk lilies and a real four-trumpeted amaryllis sat on the two low tables in the room.

Mrs Hackney moved the lilies to place my tea, in willow pattern china, within reach.

She proffered biscuits, took a couple herself, and sat down opposite me expectantly.

I composed my face into a sympathetic expression. 'I'm afraid I've come with some very sad news.'

She reacted at once with a collapsing of her face and a visible tensing of her fleshy frame. 'Oh, no? What's happened?'

'Mr Brown was found dead this morning in his flat.'

'Oh my God!' she almost shrieked, and put down her tea cup.

I let her take a moment or two to recover from the shock. She looked around distractedly. When our eyes met again, I saw that hers were wet with tears. 'Poor Toby,' she muttered, though I guessed, knowing Toby, that she hadn't been encouraged to call him that. 'How did it happen? Was it 'is heart?'

'No, it wasn't. It may have been suicide, but we're not sure.'

'Oh, my gawd!' she wailed, even louder, and I regretted that I'd told her so soon. But it was out now, and I had a job to do.

'I'm really sorry to have to tell you, but my partner and I went to the flat this morning and found him hanging from one of those great beams in the drawing room.'

She stared back at me in astonishment. ''Anging? How? Why?'

'The police think it was suicide.'

'Toby – suicide? Never! He'd never do 'isself in, not in hundred years,' she said with utter conviction.

Here was someone else adamant that Toby wouldn't have taken his own life.

'No,' I agreed, 'his mother didn't think so either.'

''Is mother?' Mrs Hackney scoffed. 'I reckon she was 'alf 'is problem!'

'How do you mean?'

She looked at me to see if I was being serious, or just naïve. 'Well, 'e were an iron-'oof, weren't 'e? And I always reckon that takes a bit of living with.'

'Yes, of course, I knew he was gay,' I said, primly. 'But what particular problems did that cause him?'

'The boys,' she sighed. 'Well, not boys, like children or anything – he never went in for that sort of thing – but they was always younger, and never 'ad any money. The times I heard him telling 'em – no, they couldn't 'ave nothing – then giving in. Of course, if he turned the tap off, they just went, didn't they? And that upset him. "They only want me for my money, don't they, Mrs H?" he used to say to me.'

I took the opportunity to push her a little. 'If you don't think Toby took his own life, do you think it is possible any of these boys was responsible? Who was the latest, for instance?'

'Miles? No, it wouldn't have been 'im. He wouldn't 'urt a fly. He was a nice, gentle little chap, and ever so good on the piano. That's what he did, played the piano for them ballerinas to practise to. He seemed to have left Toby, though, but not over money, I don't think. He wasn't the sort to ask.'

'This Miles, did you know his other name or where he lived?'

Mrs Hackney's gaze swept around the small, cluttered room as she grappled to dredge a name from her subconscious, but gave up. 'No, sorry.' She shook her head. 'I think I knew it, but it won't come back. I'm sure he wouldn't have done that anyway. Poor old Toby, he was well upset when Miles went.'

'Perhaps there was another friend, from before that?'

'There were quite a few, I can tell you, and like I said, some of them right little chisellers. There was the one he went into business with . . . talked Toby into that telephone line that brought him all the bother . . .'

'What was he called?' I asked, trying to control my excitement at the promise of so much more useful information.

'Lincoln – Steve Lincoln.' She spat the name out. 'Nasty feller, always trying to squeeze money from Toby. I reckon he was a gambler who believed he could get his hands on inside information. He helped with the tipping line – Steve was part of that, I'm sure. Then they fell out. It was just after that, every blessed nap Toby gave started coming in.'

'Hold on a minute,' I said, sure of the connection now. 'Did Toby call him "Linc"?'

'Yes, that's right.' She nodded her over-permed grey curls.

'I see. Was he still on the scene then, in any other sense?'

'No, I don't think so. Toby'd seen him for what he

was and got rid of 'im by then. Didn't stop him coming round, though, 'specially when the line really hotted up. He reckoned he should have been on a cut, being as 'ow 'e talked Toby into it in the first place.'

'When did he last come, then?'

'I wouldn't know for sure. I only does four days a week there. Toby paid me, mind, like it was a full week, and no tax, and nothing to stop me drawing me Social.'

'All right, but when did you last see him yourself?'

'Let's think.' She adopted her mind-searching posture again, eyes ranging back and forth across the room. 'He certainly come up Friday. Just after dinner, it was, and 'e was well pis— drunk,' she corrected herself. 'Yellin' and shoutin' and telling Toby he knew what had been going on and how he had to have some money. Poor old Toby tried to shut 'im up so I wouldn't hear, then he sent me out to go shopping at Fortnum's for 'im, which 'e often did if he was 'aving a conversation he didn't want me to 'ear.'

'So on Friday, this Steve turned up, still thinking he could ask for money?'

'Yes.'

'And do you know if he got any?'

'I wouldn't know, but I doubt it. One thing Toby could be was stubborn as a mule if the mood took him.'

'Do you know where this chap lives?'

'Nope.' She shook her head decisively. 'His mum had a flat up Kilburn but as far as I can tell, he used to doss down around the place. That's one of the reasons Toby couldn't stand it no more.'

'Never mind, I'll see if I can find him. Now, you said earlier that Toby's line was causing him trouble. What sort of trouble was that?'

'I don't know, really. I don't know much about what went on – only snippets I'd hear. He just seemed worried – not about Steve, but just before he packed it up. He thought the bookies was gunning for 'im. Then I think he agreed with them to stop.'

'Did he tell you that?'

'Well, no, not exactly. But, you know, I was in there quite a bit when he was, and he trusted me not to blabber – and I never did, not till now, when he's gone and you're his friend.'

'Do you know who I am, then?'

'Oh, yes. He mentioned you from time to time – you're not a very good jockey, are you? You was at school with him, wasn't you? There's a picture of you and him, when you was both kids.'

I was amazed that Toby had talked of me to this woman who, by the sound of it, was a close confidante, though she probably didn't know it.

'Yes, we go back a long way,' I agreed. 'I know his mother well, too, and my girlfriend Emma has known him all her life,' I added, wanting to make it clear to her that my concern over Toby's death was sincere. I put my empty tea cup down and got to my feet.

'Thank you so much for helping me. I'll let you know what's going on. Of course, if you think of anything else, just ring me or leave a message and I'll come right round. But I suggest, for the moment, you don't go back to Toby's flat. If he was paying you in cash, without tax, it's probably best not to let the police know, eh?'

She nodded. 'You won't tell them, will you?'

'No, of course not, and you've been a great help to me. I'll make sure my partner and I find out what happened, and we'll let you know, without bringing you into it. Now, I shouldn't take up any more of your time, unless there's anything else you want to tell me?'

She stood up too and started to gather up the tea cups. 'Well,' she said, thinking hard, 'I can't tell you where you can find Steve Lincoln, but I can show you what he looks like, if that's any use?'

'It certainly is.'

She put the tea cups down and opened the door of a small sideboard. From this she took out a large brown envelope and pulled out a few photographs and flipped through them. As far as I could see, they were mostly of Toby with various famous people with whom he'd come into contact over the last few years as he himself had become better known.

'I loved seeing him with celebrities,' Mrs Hackney said fondly. She stopped at one of the photos and handed it to me. It showed three men standing in a row at some kind of ceremony.

'Where was this taken?' I asked.

'When they started the tippin' line. They had a bit of a party for the papers and such.'

One of the men in the shot was Toby, beaming with knowing confidence; one was a top-ranking flat trainer, well-known for turning up at any press event if the envelope of cash on offer was fat enough. I put a finger on the third man. 'I presume that's Steve Lincoln?'

Mrs Hackney nodded. 'That's 'im – nasty little shyster!'

'May I take this and have a copy made?'

'Yes, 'course you can.'

'You've made some headway.' Matt sounded impressed as we headed back through the West End.

'Up to a point,' I qualified. 'Finding Lincoln isn't going to be easy. I don't suppose you fancy cruising the gay bars with his photograph?'

'No more than you. But maybe the other chap will know where to look.'

'You mean Miles, the last boyfriend?'

'Yes. At least we have an idea where he works. There can't be too many professional ballet studios in London.'

'They won't be functioning today, though,' I pointed out. 'I'll start on them tomorrow.'

'Fine.' Matt nodded. 'But we'll have to go back to Toby's now.'

'Why?'

'Because,' he said, about to spell out the obvious, 'we forgot to pick up our tape this morning.'

We pulled up outside the grand front door of the building in Hay's Mews. I rang the caretaker's bell. There was no answer over the intercom, but a few moments later the door was opened by a burly man in a security company uniform who looked out at us blankly.

'Afternoon, gentlemen. What can I do for you?'

'Is Mr Tilbury there?'

'Mr Tilbury's been relieved of his duties for a few days. He's had a bit of a shock recently.'

Of course, we should have known that events would move on even though it was, incredibly, just seven hours since we'd first arrived at this same door that morning.

'We were here earlier,' I pressed, not holding out much hope of gaining access to the flat. 'We found Mr Brown and contacted the police. We're old friends and would like to take a quick look around his flat again.'

'I'm afraid that won't be possible, sir. We've strict instructions not to let anyone unauthorised into the premises for the time being.'

'But we are authorised – by Mr Brown's next-of-kin.'

'Then you'll have a document to that effect?' he asked with exaggerated patience.

'No, of course not. We didn't think it would be necessary. For heaven's sake, this man's taken his own life. His mother wants some of his personal effects. That's not unreasonable is it?'

'I believe the CID have temporarily removed most of that sort of thing, sir. But anyway there'd be nothing I could do, I'm sorry. I suggest Mr Brown's mother contacts the CID at Charing Cross Road. Detective Superintendent Howard is in charge of the case.'

'Let's leave it,' Matt said to me, recognising the blank wall of official obduracy. 'He's not going to budge.'

'Hang on,' I said. 'Is Mr Tilbury in his flat?'

'I couldn't say, sir.'

'Would you mind if one of us just popped down?

There was something I wanted to see him about.'

The man looked doubtful, but his instructions had been to stop anyone from entering Toby's flat, not from visiting the resident caretaker. 'All right,' he said. 'It's through there.' He nodded at the door at the back of the hall which led to the back stairs where we had hidden our recorder.

I found it and concealed it as best I could under my jacket. On the way out, I shook my head at the guard. 'No luck. Never mind, I'll try again another time.'

As soon as we reached my sister's house we went down to the office. We'd decided to listen to the tape there, amplified on good speakers and in the best possible listening conditions, so that we didn't miss any sound or remotely audible nuance.

Matt sat down at the table, pulled the recorder from its leather case and flipped it open.

'Oh, no!' He gave an anguished gasp. 'There's no bloody tape in here!'

My blood froze. Two seconds before, I was certain I'd replaced the last tape; now I just couldn't be sure.

'Oh, God, Matt!' I spluttered and felt my cheeks burn at the stark shame of knowing I might have mucked up a vital source of evidence.

He lifted his head and gave me a withering look. 'Did you put one back in?'

'I'm certain I did.'

I could see him fighting to control his temper. To his credit, he succeeded. He let out a long sigh that made me feel even worse than I already did.

'I don't know what to say, Matt. I guess I was in a hurry, maybe I forgot to replace it. I can't remember.'

He snapped the machine shut. 'Oh, well, there it is. If we haven't got it, we haven't got it. We'd better take a look at our photographs – if you haven't chucked all the film or wiped the discs.'

I couldn't very well object to his jibe and silently got together all the shots, digital and on film, so that we could make an exhaustive analysis of them.

We ate a late lunch of bread and cheese while, still in silence, we carried on processing, examining and sorting the several hundred mug shots we'd accumulated from the most recent race-meetings.

Matt was painstakingly thorough for the first hour while I finished logging the rest and blew up several of them, including a high-resolution scan of the photo Mrs Hackney had given me.

'Okay,' he announced. 'I've identified a dozen people who have been at more than one of the races.'

He had arranged a number of the prints side by side. 'Here's one – at Chepstow, Worcester and Cheltenham.'

I looked at the man – fiftyish and conventionally dressed – and recognised him at once. 'He's an owner, Michael Penruddock. He's always at the races.'

'We can't afford to ignore anyone,' Matt said, resenting my dismissive tone.

'No, of course not, but there are going to be quite a few who crop up more than once.'

'This guy, for instance,' he said, pointing at another.

'He's the Jockey Club starter, attached to all three of those courses.'

Matt went on to point at several others – minor officials, trainers' employees, some of the photographers – who cropped up more than once, but always with complete justification.

But it was while we were both studying one of them that he suddenly thumped the table. 'Look! Isn't that your man Steve Lincoln?'

I picked up the enlargement I'd made a few minutes before and placed it next to the shot Matt had isolated. I swung a big oblong magnifier over them both.

'What do you think?' Matt asked.

'No, that's not him. He's similar, but that's all.'

After an hour, we had re-scrutinised every single shot and still found nothing. But we agreed that finding Lincoln and Miles should be our prime objectives.

I was leafing through *Yellow Pages*, looking for dance rehearsal studios where I might start looking for Miles, when the phone on the table rang.

I picked it up.

'Hello?'

'Tintern here.'

With just the two words he had made it clear he wasn't at all happy.

'Good afternoon, sir.'

'Hardly,' he barked. 'I've just spoken to Emma at Jane's. She told me what happened to Toby. Why the hell didn't you let me know first thing?'

'I was planning to give you a full briefing later this afternoon when we find out more about what happened.'

'That won't be necessary. I've already spoken to Detective Superintendent Howard, who's handling the case. He told me you'd been back to Brown's place this morning without any authority.'

'We had Jane's authority,' I interrupted.

'That's rubbish and you know it! Her son's just committed suicide. Do you imagine she wants all the detritus from that picked over by you and your partner?'

'There is some doubt that it is suicide,' I said.

'That's not what the police think, and I'm afraid I take their view more seriously than yours.'

'That's up to you, sir, of course, but we are also bearing in mind our instructions from you on behalf of the Jockey Club.'

'You can consider those instructions formally rescinded as of now. You'll receive written notification to that effect by fax, first thing tomorrow.'

I felt myself blanch at the news, and the sharpness of his delivery. 'I see,' I gulped. 'We'll forward our account and a final report to the Jockey Club as soon as we've received your written confirmation.' I rammed the phone back into its cradle.

Matt looked at me enquiringly. 'I take it we're off the case?'

'Yes, we're off it,' I said evenly. 'Does that mean you're off Toby's too?'

'I'm sorry, I think it probably does.'

I couldn't argue. Toby and Jane were my friends, not his. And, as he was undoubtedly thinking, we had a business to run.

'Fair enough,' I said quietly. 'But I'm afraid I'm going to have to take some time off to deal with it myself.'

'It can come out of your holiday,' Matt grunted. 'We've got to get to grips with David Dysart's problem, and I could do with some help there.'

'There's nothing our regulars can't do to back you up,' I said truthfully.

'All right,' Matt sighed. 'If you like, I'll complete our report for the Jockey Club, then if you want to stay on in London to follow up this Lincoln character, I'll take the train back.'

'Thanks,' I said, genuinely appreciative given the grossness of my blunder over the tape. Then I thought of another angle. 'I suppose you won't need to keep in touch with Sara now that we're not investigating Chapman?'

'No,' Matt agreed sullenly. 'I don't suppose I will.'

Chapter Fifteen

I started my search next morning among a group of lithe young women at a ballet school in Hammersmith – the nearest I'd found in *Yellow Pages*. I soon discovered it was well-connected with the handful of other classical dance studios in London.

The assistant principal was a former ballerina, brimming with compassion, who evidently assumed my need to contact Miles was a matter of the heart. I would have liked to put her right about my own sexual orientation, but didn't correct the misconception.

While avoiding too much eye-contact, she sympathetically made two phone calls for me to establish where Miles Wheatley, as I discovered his surname was, could be found. He turned out to be quite well-known in the ballet world. I was told that from an early age he had wanted to be a dancer himself, until it had become clear that his stature would always let him down.

A converted Victorian factory in Battersea housed the rehearsal studios of one of London's more avant-garde dance troupes.

When I asked for Miles, my enquiry was once again met with looks of tolerant sympathy, and I was sent along to the studio where he was currently playing accompaniment for the troupe's two leading dancers.

I slipped in and sat on a bench in half-darkness at the back of the room.

While he was still playing, I scrutinised Miles Wheatley from a distance of about thirty feet. He was a small man whose youthful good looks were sharpened by an air of intensity as he played with great skill while always conceding that his function was to accompany.

I'd never paid to see a performance of ballet in my life; I'd always thought it was probably little more than a distraction from good music, presumably evolved for people who found it hard to concentrate on the music alone. But now I watched and listened, transfixed by the stark, graceful and almost violent movements of the company's version of Stravinsky's 'Rite of Spring'.

When the time came for the dancers to take a short break, I was almost tempted to carry on sitting there in the darkness to see more, but someone drew the piano player's attention to me.

He bounded up from his stool and walked quickly across the room to me. His light brown hair flopped in a fringe over his eyes and his mouth quivered into an uncertain smile.

I got to my feet, trying not to look too intimidating.

When I stepped into the light, he looked me up and down and his eyes turned sullen and wary.

'Hello,' I said blandly, offering my hand. 'I'm Simon Jeffries. I wanted to talk to you about Toby Brown.'

The wariness in his eyes became more pronounced. 'What about him?'

'I'm afraid something's happened to him and I need your help.'

The apprehension in his eyes turned to surprise, then fear. 'I don't know what you're talking about.'

'I'm not suggesting you do – please believe me. Look, is it possible to go out somewhere and talk for a few minutes?'

He pursed his lips, looked at me for a few seconds then nodded. 'I'll just tell Madame I'm taking five. She'll forgive me.'

He took me out of the warehouse to a handsome and well-preserved nineteenth-century pub on the opposite side of the road. I bought him the bottle of Grolsch he asked for and myself a pint. There weren't many customers at eleven in the morning, and we found a quiet corner table.

'So,' he said challengingly, 'what's Tobes done now?'

I strained to tell from his voice, his body language, his shifting eyes, whether or not he was acting. If he was, he was very convincing.

Although the morning papers hadn't run the story, I knew that it was already on the front page of the first editions of the *Evening Standard*.

'I found him at his flat yesterday.'

Miles tensed at the word 'found', but said nothing.

'I'm afraid he's dead.'

I watched his fingers suddenly tighten their grip on the frosty beer bottle. 'How?' he whispered.

I had to gulp to get the word out. 'Hanged.'

'Himself?' Miles whispered.

'Well,' I said, 'that's what it looks like, but the police haven't said for certain.'

'What else could it be?'

'Toby's mother doesn't believe he'd commit suicide – she thinks he must have been murdered.'

'But then, why don't the police think it's murder?'

I shrugged. 'They say there was no sign of any intruder.'

'Do they know why he did it?'

'They don't. There was no suicide note, but media reports are hinting it was because he'd been . . . jilted.'

Miles gave a bitter laugh. 'Toby – jilted? That'll be the day!'

'I'd heard it was you who walked out on him?' I said quickly.

'You what? Let me tell you, it was *him* who let me down. Badly. He was going to help me set up my own rehearsal studios . . .' He stopped abruptly, and took another swig from his bottle.

'Well, what happened?'

'It doesn't matter, 'specially not now.' He drained the bottle and plonked it on the table.

'Do you want another?' I offered.

Miles nodded dejectedly.

When he had a fresh bottle in front of him, I tried another angle. 'What about Steve Lincoln? Didn't he chuck Toby?'

Miles looked at me as if I were supremely ignorant. 'Of course not! Everyone knew Steve Lincoln was a right little hustler who only got what he deserved.'

'What did he get?'

'Sweet F A – which was *more* than he deserved, come to think of it.'

'Did you know him?'

'Depends what you mean by know. Toby'd seen him very comfortable for a few months while he was supposed to be helping with the tipping line. Steve said it was his idea, but it's not as though no one else was doing it and all the tips were Toby's. Anyway, when Toby'd had enough of him, he cut off the money, had to change the locks and everything, but Steve seemed to think he should still have some of the profits from the line. Toby had just shut down the one company and started up another. Legally there wasn't a thing Steve could do. Toby was very good at that sort of thing.'

I could imagine he was. And this made sense of the phone calls and squabbles Matt and I had heard through our bug. 'But when did Steve move out of Toby's life?'

'About a month or so ago, when I came on the scene.'

'So it was before Toby started napping all those winners?'

'Yes.'

'Had Steve anything to do with Toby after he'd gone?'

'Yes.' Miles's nostrils quivered in outrage. 'Steve didn't want to let go – Toby was his meal ticket.'

'So, he was very bitter about what Toby had done?'

'Yes.' The little pianist nodded eagerly. 'He started making all sorts of threats.'

'But the locks were changed so Steve couldn't get in unless Toby asked him? Would Toby have invited him in?'

'No way.'

I thought this must be wishful thinking on Miles's part, remembering the conversation between Toby and Steve which the bug had picked up.

'And you? Did you ever go back once you'd split up?' I asked.

Miles took a long swig from his bottle. He put it down and looked at me. 'I don't have to tell you anything. You're not the police – you're just some busybody sticking his nose in. I've got nothing to hide.' He pushed back his chair and stood up. 'Thanks for the drinks.' He turned and headed straight for the door.

I didn't attempt to stop him or call him back. I hadn't any more questions for him anyway.

Half an hour later, I'd found a parking space near Hay's Mews. I went to the front door of Toby's block and rang, not his bell, but the caretaker's flat.

''Allo?'

It was Tilbury.

'Hello, Mr Tilbury. It's Simon Jeffries here. I just called by to see how you are? I know you were very upset and everything and you're having some time off. I just wanted to be sure you were all right for money and so on.'

It wasn't a subtle approach, but I didn't have time to pussy-foot around.

'Come to the side door,' the speaker crackled back at me.

I looked along the building and spotted a small black door, down a few steps and set in a brick wall. 'Right.'

As I reached the door, he opened it before I could knock. He hadn't shaved and looked seedier than ever. He ushered me in quickly and led me along a short corridor where he opened another door into a stuffy sitting room, with a small window set high on one wall and a single-bar electric heater set in front of a cheap wooden-armed easy chair. The contrast with the opulence of the apartments he tended was almost offensive.

'I'm not supposed to talk to anyone,' Tilbury whined.

'Who says?' I asked.

'The police, of course. And they put another security bloke on for a few days – so's I won't get hassled by the press, they said.'

'Were you able to tell them anything useful?'

He glanced at me and pulled a knowing face. I was glad that we had already established our relationship on a business footing.

'I didn't tell 'em nothing. Jus' that you turned up, and we went up and found Mr Brown . . . like we did.'

'Was there anything else you could have told them?'

'You was asking if I was all right for money . . .'

'Yes, of course, you've always been helpful, and this must have been a terrible shock for you.'

'Yer, it was an' all. I could use a monkey.'

'A monkey?' I said, not disguising my surprise that he should be pitching as high as five hundred pounds.

'Oright, then,' he went on quickly, 'a couple of hundred'll do.'

I pulled out my wallet, glad that I'd topped up my float that morning, and extracted ten twenties for him.

'So what could you have told DI Wyndham that you didn't?'

'Like you asked, I didn't tell him about your little tape machine.'

'Thank you,' I said. 'Was there anything else?'

'An' I didn't tell him about the other people who'd been round Saturday night and yesterday morning, before you.'

'What!' I was amazed. It had never occurred to me that he'd been holding anything back from us.

'There was one come round Saturday, about ten.'

Just before Toby had rung to tell me he was worried about something.

'Who was that?'

'One of them,' Tilbury said disdainfully.

'What do you mean, "one of them"?' I asked, though I was fairly sure I knew.

'You know, one of his boy friends. Steve Lincoln's his name.'

'How long did he stay?'

'I don't know, I never saw him leave. I was watching telly.'

'Why didn't you tell the police?'

''Cause when he come, he gives me a score and tells me to keep quiet.'

'But you've just told me.'

'Well, you jus' give me two hundred. You outbid him, didn't yer?'

I nodded. 'So it seems. And you don't know what time he went?'

'No, I jus' said.'

'Would you have heard if he'd left very early next morning?'

'Dunno. Probably. Maybe he was still in the flat next morning.'

'What? When we got there, and when the police were there?'

'Yes.'

'But he can't have been. They searched it. Who else came to see Toby?'

'I'm sorry, Mr Jeffries. You've used up your two hundred quid.'

'All right,' I said impatiently, pulling my wallet out again. 'Another two hundred for everything else you have to tell me. No more doling it out in instalments, or the police'll have you for withholding information.'

''Ere!' Tilbury said with another indignant sniff. 'What do you think I am?'

'I'd rather not say. Just take the money and talk.'

He turned, pulled out a bentwood chair and sat down at the cluttered table. I remained standing but took a few steps back to give him space.

'Well, I didn't, like, see the first bloke on Sunday morning – jus' heard him come and go.'

'What time was that?'

'Early. 'Bout quarter to seven.'

'Weren't you surprised?'

'No. Toby was often up and about early – to go down and see horses on the gallops and that. He made a lot of money, Toby did, but give 'im 'is due, 'e worked bloody 'ard for it.'

'Yes,' I said impatiently. 'But how do you know it wasn't Lincoln leaving from the night before?'

'Because I heard him call Toby's name through the intercom.'

'What did he say?'

'Just spoke his name, saying "goodbye". But it were a toff's voice, like lots of his friends. It wasn't Steve Lincoln, I can tell you that for free.'

'Okay.' I nodded. 'And who was the other person who came?'

'I saw 'im, but I don't know 'im. I didn't 'ear him come, but I seen 'im go. This time I got a bit of a butcher's at him when he went past my door. Shifty-looking cove, 'e was.'

'What was he wearing?'

'Jeans, one of them donkey jackets. Little woolly hat down over 'is ears.'

'Age?'

'I dunno . . . thirty, forty. 'Ard face, and big.'

'Was he . . . one of them?'

'A poof, you mean?'

I nodded.

'No. Well, not like any I seen.'

From my pocket I pulled a packet of photos that I'd printed off the computer. I spread them out on the single table in Tilbury's cramped living room.

'Have a look through this lot and tell me if you can recognise him.'

Tilbury seemed anxious to show that he was earning

his extravagant fee, and diligently worked his way through the fifty mug-shots. I could see him trying hard to recognise one or other of them, but at the bottom of the stack he turned to me, disappointed. 'Sorry, guv. None of these are 'im.'

I was back at Wetherdown in time for supper.

Emma was cooking. Jane had begged her to stay on for a few more days, at least until after Toby's funeral the following Friday.

While Jane was out in her yard for an hour to oversee evening stables, I'd been able to tell Emma what I'd found out, planning to give Jane an edited version later.

And there was another line of enquiry I wanted to follow.

'What's the story on your father and Filumena?' I asked.

'What have they to do with any of this?' Emma asked.

'Nothing as far as I'm aware. I was being curious,' I added, truthfully. 'It's just that he doesn't seem to have friends like most people do, not even one, and no visible woman in his life. And even if he's getting on a bit, I'm sure he likes to get his leg over from time to time.'

'Just the thought of my father getting his leg over, as you so crassly put it, is a bit of a turn off. But as far as Filumena is concerned, I expect you're right. I'd say from the way he treats her, there must be a side to their relationship beyond cooking and cleaning.'

'That's a shame.'

'I couldn't care less, personally.'

'I meant it's a shame because I wanted to ask her if she'd overheard any conversation between your father – sorry, His Lordship – and Toby in the last few weeks.'

'Why?'

'I just wondered if he ever warned Toby that the bookies might start getting heavy. When he told me Toby was his godson, it occurred to me that he actually wanted me to protect Toby in some way.'

Emma looked doubtful. 'I shouldn't think my father takes that relationship very seriously. He's got half a dozen godchildren. His secretary has a sort of standing order to produce cards and presents on birthdays and Christmas – and that's about it.'

'But do you think he might have wanted to warn Toby somehow, when the line really took off and it looked as if he could get into trouble?'

'I suppose it's possible. Anyway, I don't think you'd get much out of Filumena. But I might. I'll see what I can do.'

We sat down with Jane around her kitchen table to eat. She seemed to be coming to terms with her bereavement but was still convinced Toby's death wasn't self-inflicted.

'Is it possible that the chap who went to see him on Saturday night . . . did it?' she asked in a whisper.

I shrugged. 'It's possible, but the police said he'd only been dead an hour or so.'

'But, Simon, do the police know about this visitor?' Jane asked.

'I presume so,' I lied; I'd decided for the time being

not to tell her about the others; I didn't want to stir up her imagination any more. 'But they don't seem interested. They said there was no evidence of a third party being involved.'

Emma stayed with Jane when I went home.

The following morning, I arrived at our office car-park at the same time as Monica. She pumped along on her chubby little legs to keep up with me as we made our way up to the office, and prattled on about her boy friend's misdeeds in a Reading club the night before.

Despite my own preoccupations, I found myself laughing with her, but as soon as we reached the office we were brought down to earth by Matt's grim expression and a curt request for us to get on with it.

When I sat down with him in his room, I almost dared to hope he might still agree to help track down Toby's killer, but after I'd briefed him on everything I'd learned the day before, he came to the rational conclusion that the most obvious thing to do was to pass it on to the police.

'Their resources are infinitely greater than ours – especially as we lost the benefit of our bug,' he added pointedly. 'If you seriously want to find out what happened, let them get on with it.'

'But they were so sure of their opinion.'

'So? Now you've got new information.'

'Why on earth didn't they take the trouble to find it themselves then?'

'As you discovered, old Tilbury was holding out for a

higher bidder, and he knew he wouldn't get anything from the police. I bet you, if you go back, he'll be wanting more from you.'

'You're probably right, but – I don't know. I'd really rather not go to the police; not until it's clearer what happened. I'd much prefer to keep the details of Toby's life under wraps, for Jane's sake.'

'Look, Simon, there's going to be an inquest. It's inevitable that'll produce a mass of sordid detail.'

I thought for a moment. 'Do me a favour, Matt. Would you go and talk to Wyndham and try to establish why they've made so little effort to investigate any other possibilities?'

Chapter Sixteen

The following evening, after a fruitless day spent photographing everyone who had come within spitting distance of Connor's nap at Uttoxeter, I collected Emma from Wetherdown. We drove over to Matt's house in Henley, where he'd invited us to join him and Sara for dinner.

When we arrived Sara was already there, looking a different woman in jeans and jumper. She sat buried in a vast, old-fashioned arm-chair with her shoeless feet tucked up under her in front of a pile of flaming apple logs on a big open grate.

Matt himself was busy in the kitchen. He had produced what smelled like a challenging lamb curry, a suitable dish to counteract the endless wet winter going on outside.

We sat down around an oak refectory table to eat it with some Rioja I'd brought.

'Now you're both here,' Sara said, 'I suppose I'd better tell you what's been going on at the office.'

'I've already heard most of this.' Matt nodded at me with his mouth full. 'But go on, Sara.'

She made a face at his interruption and carried on. 'It's been terrible really, the last few days. Everyone's been on edge and swearing at each other and nobody can decide what to do. I know some of the board want to sell off the Atlantic Hotel chain. There's obviously a punter for it out there because someone's been hoovering up any Salmon Leisure shares that come on the market, but Harry won't even consider it.'

'Do you know why not?' Matt asked.

'I can tell you that.' Emma suddenly joined in the conversation, turning to me. 'I would have twigged ages ago but you never mentioned the firm you've been dealing with was Salmon's. I should think the hotels are far closer to Harry Chapman's heart than the bookies ever were.' She laughed. 'The connection between Harry Chapman and Atlantic Hotels is part of my family history. It's ironic really that Harry should have gone to the Jockey Club for help and ended up with my father organising it.'

'Why's that?'

'It goes back a very long way – it almost amounted to a family feud at the time, though my father would never admit it.'

'How?' Matt asked sharply, leaning forward in his chair.

'The thing is,' Emma paused, 'my great-grandfather, Arthur Birt, actually founded Atlantic Hotels.'

'Good Lord!' I laughed in surprise. 'You never said it was Atlantic Hotels – just that he'd built up a great chain, and your grandfather lost the lot gambling.'

'Yes, that's the point – he lost it all to old Morrie

Salmon. My father never forgave Grandfather, or Salmon's, and it was all made much worse by the fact that my grandfather had a crooked solicitor who led him by the nose and talked him into selling off the hotels, piecemeal, to pay his gambling debts, all to a secretive private company controlled by an old witch called Constance Chapman – Harry's mother.'

'But how did the hotels end up with Salmon's?'

'It's all coming back to me now. Morrie Salmon died without an heir to carry on running the show, and Salmon's was taken over by a gang of young thrusters. They immediately started looking for some major assets to bring into the business. I suppose they wanted somewhere to sink all the money that came flooding in once regulations came off in the sixties. They must have wanted Atlantic Hotels very badly; they had to pay a lot of money for it – old Connie Chapman made sure of that.'

'Was she still there then?'

'Yes, she was over eighty but still in control, and she insisted her son had to be boss of the new group. Salmon's directors agreed and I should think he's been in charge for the last twenty-five years.'

'But Harry ending up boss of Salmon Leisure as well as Atlantic Hotels must have really irked your father?'

'I'm sure it did – privately. After all, Salmon's took all my grandfather's money then used it to buy the hotels *his* father had left him – they were his only assets once all the cash had gone. Since Harry came with the hotels, I'm sure you're right, Sara, he'd far rather lose the bookies.'

Sara nodded. 'Yes, that's why he's desperate to fend off any bid for the group right now, before he's been able to de-merge the hotels. Of course, whoever's bidding would have a pretty good idea of the losses Salmon's are making on their betting business right now.'

'Which means the bidders are either taking a punt that the winning naps will come to an end . . .' Matt looked at me '. . . or else controlling them.'

Sara didn't pick up what he was implying. 'In the meantime,' she said, 'Harry's going absolutely ballistic that these naps of Connor McDonagh's are all coming in. He was positive they'd dry up when we heard that Toby Brown was dead. But he had a meeting with the other big firms again today, and as far as I can tell, they're certain all these horses are being doped somehow. The Jockey Club have told them categorically that all the winners have been drug-tested and passed clear.'

Matt turned his ice-blue eyes on her. 'So how do they think it's being done?'

'They're convinced the dopers are using some new, undetectable masking agent.'

'Well, what are they going to do about it?' I asked.

'They've decided to bribe a stable official to let them have a sample of urine of one of the winning horses to send to the States for analysis. They're convinced the Americans will trace something the Newmarket lab hasn't.'

'What other options are being looked at, then?'

'Just between ourselves, the Tote have shown an interest in buying all five hundred shops.'

'Do you know how much they've offered?' Matt asked.

'Sorry, no.' Sara shook her head. 'But I get the impression it was a pretty derisory sum.'

'When was the offer made, then?'

'Within the last few weeks. As far as I can gather, all the bookies were approached, and simply laughed at the proposal.'

'It sounds,' I said, 'as if the Tote were engaged in what you might call a fishing expedition, just to gauge reaction, and ultimately to judge prices. The chairman of the Tote is very much on record that he thinks all off-course betting should come under his umbrella.'

'Ironically, it was Connor McDonagh who was promoting that idea at lunch the other Sunday, wasn't it?' Emma asked me.

I nodded. 'There's a Green Paper being prepared with proposals to take away the bookies' rights to make their own books and to leave them just as agents for the Tote. The proposers have a couple of Cabinet Ministers on their side and there's a lot of support for it from most branches of racing. There's even a rumour that the government may try to privatise the Tote. But until then, there's no way the Tote could afford to buy these companies on their current profitability.'

'What do you mean, "their current profitability"? They're losing money hand over fist at the moment, which is presumably why the Tote have suddenly decided to come in with another offer.'

'You can't blame them,' I argued. 'It's a heaven-sent opportunity. The way they operate, it wouldn't matter how many tips Connor came up with.'

'The point surely,' Sara said, 'is whether there's a connection between this and Toby's death?'

We all stopped talking for a moment.

'No,' Matt said finally. 'Because the winning naps have just gone on, and the people at the Tote simply recognise an opportunity when they see one. I agree with Simon: they're being pretty naïve because the current position must be very short term.'

'But if it keeps up much longer,' Sara butted in, 'it'll be all over for the bookies anyway. I can tell you, their position is dire.'

'Well,' Emma turned to Matt, 'what do you think happened to Toby?'

He leaned back in his chair with his hands behind his head. 'What's the first thing that comes to mind when someone like Toby is found dead?' He looked around at us all. 'There always has to be a connection with what's called their "life-style". I'm pretty sure this has got nothing whatever to do with racing. I went to see Wyndham this afternoon, and he said they've still no reason to think Toby's death was anything but suicide. I know Jane's convinced otherwise, but that's understandable.'

'All right,' I said. 'But what do *you* think?'

'I agree with the police. If Toby had been murdered by an angry ex-lover or whatever, it would have been a frenzied attack. If he was murdered and the whole thing made to look like suicide, it would have to have been premeditated, and that just doesn't fit.'

I took a deep breath; Jane's instincts carried a lot of

weight with me. 'I still think our priority is to dig into Toby's love life – to find Steve Lincoln.'

'I won't argue with that.' Matt nodded. 'We can carry on looking out for him whenever one of Connor's naps is running – in case he's still mixed up with it.'

I was relieved that I wasn't having to fight Matt every inch of the way and we carried on planning the best approach until soon after eleven when Emma broke things up, saying she wanted to be back at Wetherdown before Jane was up for early stables.

Our first breakthrough came at Hereford, a day later.

The course on the edge of the old city had attracted a good crowd for a Thursday; the West Country people were avid supporters of National Hunt, and the men of mid-Wales, with no course of their own, flocked in by the hundreds.

I was the first to see Lincoln.

He was leaning against the parade-ring rails, his eyes glued to Rowan's Rainbow, Connor's nap. Once again, it was a good horse which would probably have been favourite anyway in a race of this standard.

With my heart thumping and hardly daring to believe that at last we'd found him, I pulled from my pocket a print of the photo Toby's cleaner had given me. I looked at it to double check.

There was no doubt.

I moved quickly to a point where I could watch him unimpeded, afraid he might drop out of sight any moment. Discreetly using my mobile, I alerted Matt.

Between us we shadowed every move Lincoln made,

taking photos whenever we had the chance. When Rowan's Rainbow won, Lincoln did as we had predicted and headed straight for the car-park. Matt stayed with him and watched him get into a well-used red Ford Escort while I started up my car and prepared to follow. I picked up Matt on the way out, with another car and a horse-box between us and the Ford.

Lincoln drove at a sensible speed straight back to London, stopping only once for petrol outside Swindon. He finally came to a halt in a quiet road in West Kensington where, just before seven, he parked and let himself into a rundown red-brick terrace house which had been divided into flats.

After two dragging hours, he reappeared, got back into his car and headed for central London.

We followed, evidently still unnoticed. We passed the Victoria and Albert Museum and managed to tuck in behind him as the lights changed against us when he turned south into Beauchamp Place. He ended up in Wilton Crescent, where he parked and began walking back towards Knightsbridge.

We carried on past him until we found a space for my car. We let him walk by before we opened the doors, chatting inconsequentially, and trailed behind him as he turned east towards Hyde Park Corner.

A double-decker pulled up at a stop beside him. He wavered a moment, as if about to board it. We were still fifty yards from him, too far to sprint without drawing attention to ourselves.

But Lincoln carried on while, with great relief, we stood and observed his reflection in the window of a chemist's shop. He kept on walking for another fifty yards until he stopped outside a large jazz bar that was just beginning to get busy. We turned away as he looked up and down the road, apparently expecting someone.

From the corner of my eye, I saw his gaze fixed beyond us, further down the road. He was standing absolutely still, as if unsure what to do.

'He won't know who you are,' I said to Matt. 'Get into the bar. I'll phone your mobile right now. Keep it on.'

I watched Matt walk in through the double glass doors, laughing into his phone.

Very soon after, Lincoln turned and went in behind him.

'He's followed you in, Matt. You watch him there. I'll stay outside.'

After a few moments, Matt's urgent voice reached me. 'He's walked up to someone at one of the tables. A man. He's got his back to me at the moment, but he's wearing an old cord jacket and jeans.'

'Can you get a look at his face?'

'I'll try.'

Nothing came through for the next thirty seconds, apart from the buzz of the bar.

'Shit,' Matt hissed. 'He's got up – a tall guy, but I still can't see him properly. He's left a packet on the table; Lincoln's just sitting there . . . Tall guy's out . . . he's heading back towards the front of the club. Our man's watched him go . . . he's looking around, not doing anything.'

As he spoke, I caught a glimpse of a man fitting

Matt's description pushing his way out of the bar, through a crowd that had all just arrived together. As I tried discreetly to tail him, he turned sharply east up towards the Lanesborough Hotel, with his left hand raised for a taxi. I broke into a run to catch up with him and get a look at his face, but before I did he'd caught his cab and was in, the taxi pulling away as I reached it.

Sick with frustration, I looked around wildly for another cab to chase him, but there weren't any empty ones in sight.

Angrily, I turned and walked back towards the bar, speaking into my phone. 'Matt, what's happening?'

'Lincoln's on his way out. He's got the packet – shoved inside his jacket. He should be coming out now. Look for him, Simon.'

As he spoke, Lincoln came into view and a siren began to wail – a sound so common in London I didn't give it a thought until I saw Lincoln's reaction.

He had come out looking very pleased with himself; now, suddenly, he was terrified. Before I could register the reason for it, he was gone – straight across the pavement, on to the broad street where three busy lanes of traffic headed out abreast from central London.

The police had spotted their quarry just in time, though. Two of them leaped out of the noisy car and tried to run across the road after him, but Lincoln's route was almost suicidal. His pursuers had to wait, losing a few vital seconds.

Matt appeared by my side and we watched, frustrated, as the two policemen managed to jink across the tide of vehicles and sprinted west towards the Hyde Park Hotel. But by now Lincoln was well out of sight.

'Shit!' Matt snapped. 'They've lost him. Let's get back to his car.'

'I'll call Dougie; he can go and watch the house in West Ken.' Dougie was an ex-soldier, first class in surveillance and one of our regulars on stand-by.

Matt nodded as we turned to retrace our steps to Wilton Crescent where Lincoln's small red Ford was still parked as if nothing had happened.

We spent the next two hours sitting in my car, waiting for him to come back for the Escort, but he didn't appear. Bitter at our failure, having got so close, we gave up just before eleven. Without any real hope of its producing anything, we took a note of the car's registration number and headed home.

'Lincoln must have been set up,' Matt muttered as we left London behind at Chiswick.

I nodded. 'Either that or the police were already following one of them. I wonder what was in that package?'

'Money or dope.' Matt shrugged. 'I'd bet money.'

Chapter Seventeen

I couldn't justify it, but I felt sure we'd achieved something. It was just possible that what we'd witnessed in Knightsbridge was connected in some way with Toby.

The very fact that Lincoln had taken the trouble to go all the way to Hereford to watch the race before coming back to London to pick up whatever was in that package encouraged us to think the two events must be related.

I called Emma and, although it would be well after midnight by the time I got there, arranged to go and see her at Wetherdown. On the way, Matt and I went to the office to have a closer look at all the shots we'd taken at the races that afternoon.

There were still a few cars in the car-park, and scattered lights showed in the glass and steel building where people were working late. After the noise of the wind and the incessant rumble of traffic on the motorway there was an air of cloistered calm and gentle warmth in the ultra-modern block.

Up on the fourth floor, in the far corner of the

building, the deep silence helped me to channel my mind into an hour's concentration.

I made large prints of everything that had come back on disc and spread them out across the broad ash table under a strong light in my office.

Within the first few minutes, I matched one of them and recognised another face I hadn't picked out before. It belonged to one of the official photographers. There were sometimes one or two down at the start but we hadn't taken a lot of notice of them and, anyway, they were hard to identify, usually obscured by their cameras or bending over their kit bags.

I was suddenly certain that this man had been photographing down at the start of every single race we had covered. With the diverse geographical spread of all the courses involved, it was beyond the realms of chance it could be mere coincidence.

Then, looking harder at him, trying in some way to get to know him from this scanty photographic evidence, I knew I had seen this man somewhere before, maybe in some other context. But, try as I might, I couldn't think where.

Jane had been making arrangements for Toby's funeral which had been fixed for the following day. It was obvious that the emotion this aroused had for the time being overwhelmed her. She had been in bed an hour or so by the time I got to Wetherdown around one. It seemed that Emma had been shouldering a lot of the job herself, and she was very glad to see me.

The funeral was being held in the village church.

Toby was to be buried in the ancient graveyard there, alongside his father.

'What's happening afterwards?' I asked Emma as she bustled around, cooking me a very late supper.

'Jane's laying on a massive reception here. She thinks hundreds of people will turn up and expect a drink or three afterwards.'

'That's normal enough,' I said. 'I hope everyone comes back and has a party after I've fallen off for the last time.'

'Simon! Don't say things like that. Do you know, if you hurt yourself now, I'd be miserable.' Emma widened her green-blue eyes and pulled a doleful face. 'In fact, I think I'm going to ban you from riding any more.'

I laughed. 'It's okay – I'm improving all the time. I've had a lot of sessions with Julia de Morlay, and she says my jumping's much better.'

'I hope that doesn't mean you're thinking about riding Nester again?'

'I don't know,' I replied evasively. 'Anyway, we were talking about poor old Toby's funeral. Who does Jane think will turn up?'

'Obviously most of the racing world, and her family and Toby's father's relations.'

'Are there many of them?'

'Not really. But what's worrying her is the gay contingent. She has simply no idea who or how many of them will come.'

'My God!' I gasped as the thought hit me. 'Lincoln . . .'

'He won't turn up here tomorrow, will he?'

I shrugged. 'We'll just have to wait and see. But, as a matter of fact, this wake of Toby's might give us an opportunity to check out a few other people.'

Emma turned back to the tagliatelle she was cooking. 'Well, I'm glad it's going to make someone happy.'

'Come on,' I protested. 'That's not fair. We're doing this for Jane, remember?'

Despite the lack of sleep and the tension of the last twenty-four hours, I was buzzing with adrenaline as I drove over to Reading through a drizzling, dark predawn. I had arranged to meet Matt at seven.

In the office, Monica primed us with coffee while we pored over all the shots again and Matt agreed with my findings. We couldn't do Toby's funeral and the races, so we allocated Larry to the job of checking out the day's nap, focusing on the photographers and Lincoln, if he showed up. There'd been no sign of him at the flat, and Dougie had reported that his car had been clamped, apparently abandoned.

The sky was clearing as we drove back over the chalk downs to East Ilsley for Toby's final send-off.

As Jane had anticipated, the crowd of mourners was too big to squeeze into the church and the late arrivals found themselves outside in, fortunately, mild, early-spring sunshine, listening to the service through loudspeakers.

Toby's uncle, Frank Gurney, had arrived from France first thing that morning. He came prepared with a moving eulogy, stressing Toby's skills, talents and enthusiasm.

I had seen photographs of Frank but this was the first time I'd seen him in the flesh. As I listened to the well-chosen words of his affectionate, unsentimental address, I couldn't stop myself from thinking of Emma telling me of her conviction that he and her mother had once been lovers.

Frank was impressive in an understated way. His deep voice was quiet; his well-preserved six-foot frame clad in unostentatious, high-quality Savile Row tailoring. His thick sandy grey hair was cut to a fashionable length and his tanned skin showed few direct blemishes or signs of strain. As he spoke, his candid blue eyes moved around the congregation in the crowded pews, coming to rest more than once on Emma, sitting between me and Jane.

Afterwards, back at Wetherdown, where every room on the ground floor had been cleared and opened up to accommodate around three hundred mourners, I searched for Steve Lincoln. I found Miles Wheatley first. He looked as if he'd been crying.

'Hello, Miles,' I said, as kindly as I could.

He looked up guardedly. 'Hi. Sorry, I must look a bit of a sight.'

'I'm sure we all do,' I said. 'A lot of people were very fond of Toby.'

'Not many of us here, though,' he said.

'No,' I agreed. 'Most of these people are from racing. That chap over there, for instance,' I said conversationally, pointing out Connor McDonagh, 'is the man who's taken over as the infallible tipster since Toby died.'

This didn't appear to mean much to Miles who glanced at Connor and shook his head.

'No sign of Steve Lincoln,' I remarked.

'Thank God!' Miles spat.

'Do you think he might have had something to do with Toby's death?'

'I'm sure of it.'

'Why?' I looked at him hard.

Miles thought for a moment. 'I don't really know, but I'm sure he was part of it. He's just that sort of person.'

I spent a few more minutes trying to prise out more information but finally gave up and excused myself when I saw Frank Gurney standing a few feet away.

I caught his eye. 'I'm Simon Jeffries – a friend of the family's. Aren't you Jane's brother, Frank?'

'That's right,' he said affably. 'And I know who you are. Amongst other things, you own one of Jane's star chasers, Better By Far.'

'I'm afraid you're not completely up to date. I had to move him.'

'Why was that? Not paying your bills on time?' he laughed.

'No. Gerald Tintern sent Purple Silk to the yard and that produced a conflict of interests.'

There was a momentary stillness in Frank's lively eyes. 'Did it indeed?' he said. 'Tintern getting his own way as much as he ever did, then?'

'I haven't known him long enough to say,' I answered innocently.

'I have,' Frank said, but in a way that made it clear that he wasn't going to elucidate – not then, anyway. 'By the way, I wanted to talk to you in rather more detail about what Toby was up to. I gather you found him?'

'That's right.'

'I didn't want to discuss it with Jane. I thought it would only upset her.'

'I'd be glad to,' I said.

'Let's go to the office; it's the only place that won't be crawling with people.'

In the comparative quiet of the small, book-lined room, Frank listened with complete attention and few interruptions to my resumé of everything Matt and I had unearthed so far.

When I'd finished, he nodded slowly. 'I'm not surprised Jane's reluctant to talk about it; coming to terms with your own son's homosexuality must be awfully difficult, especially as he seems to have been involved with some fairly tacky characters.' He pursed his lips and shook his head. 'And there's a nice irony in the fact that it was Harry Chapman who paid him to close his line, when Gerald Tintern had asked you to investigate it.'

'Emma told me there wasn't much love lost between them,' I remarked.

'You can say that again! I've known Gerald for forty years and I can tell you that his prime motive for building up the King George Hotel Group was to get his own back on Salmon's for taking Atlantic Hotels from his father.'

'He doesn't seem to have made a bad job of it,' I said. 'And you're a shareholder, aren't you?'

'That's right. I'm not complaining. But Gerald still hasn't got the London flagship hotel he's always wanted – a Ritz or a Dorchester – to give the King George Group the same status as Atlantic, and he won't be happy until he has.'

'That's interesting,' I said, making a connection. 'The other day I bumped into a property agent who deals with him. I got the distinct impression that something big was due to happen, something that would make Gerald very happy, apparently.'

'You must mean Daniel Dunne?'

'That's right.'

'Very indiscreet of him.'

'Why? What's happening?'

'It's just that Gerald is close to securing a very large site in Buckingham Gate.'

'Do many people know about it?'

'I very much doubt it. I'm certainly not supposed to. Gerald's a naturally secretive operator; it's the sort of thing he likes doing best. He's bought almost all the freeholds and leases that make up the block through a series of different property companies and Jersey investment trusts, and left them occupied by tenants who are still trading – at least for the time being. I should think he's moving very cautiously now so the last few leaseholders won't twig what's going on and hold the whole deal to ransom.'

Frank nodded knowingly.

I sensed his disapproval. 'Isn't this an official King George Hotel deal, then?'

'No. Or at least, not yet. Gerald certainly doesn't know that I know about his activities. But whether he's intending to put the site together on his own account then sell it on to the group, or planning to set up his own hotel there, I couldn't say.'

'How do you know about it then?'

'He's borrowed a lot of money to do the deal, using his King George shares as collateral, and it just so happens that Alec Denaro, the chairman of the bank who's lent him most, is a very old friend of mine. In fact, although Gerald's probably forgotten it, I introduced them.'

I was surprised by the equanimity with which Frank seemed to accept the position. I thought of Lord Tintern, in the next room, doling out words of wisdom to everyone around him. 'But doesn't that concern you?'

'Not unduly,' Frank said. 'What he's doing isn't illegal or strictly speaking even unethical. I've got nothing to complain of in Gerald's performance so far; I backed him when he started in the fifties, and he's done me very well. My original investment has appreciated several hundred times over.

'Now,' he said with a change of tone, 'I've probably told you more than I should have and ought to get back and support my sister. Please be discreet but feel free to get in touch any time if you think I might be able to help somehow. I'd dearly like to see Toby's death properly resolved, for Jane's sake.'

★ ★ ★

Later, I said goodbye to Jane and promised I'd come round again soon to see her. Emma was staying to the bitter end. I kissed her goodbye, resigned to another night on my own.

Matt and I had arranged to meet up with Larry and get reports from Dougie in London. As we drove back to Reading, I thought of Frank and realised that the reason he'd looked so familiar was that there were mannerisms and physical features in him I'd already seen in Emma. I thought that perhaps her theory about her parentage had some basis in fact after all.

Back in the office, Jason greeted us gloomily. He had already logged all the reports that had come in and there had been no sign of Lincoln all day, or indeed any other visitors to the scruffy little flat in West Kensington.

Larry had been more successful at the races. His trip to Ascot had thrown up sightings of the photographer and the same suspicious character I'd spotted at Plumpton and Hereford.

Obeying orders, Larry had done nothing about the photographer, but had tailed the other man back through the race-course after Connor's nap had run. But once he had disappeared into an office at the back of the stand, Larry had lost him – at least, he didn't reappear inside the next hour – and when finally Larry had knocked on the door, there had been no reply. He discovered afterwards that the office interconnected with several others and anyone entering could easily have left by a different exit.

We arranged that the next day we would all be on duty, wherever that might be, to monitor this man and the photographer.

On my way home, I found myself thinking back over everything Frank had told me about Gerald Tintern, and his almost obsessive ambition to own a major London hotel. I decided to take a detour by Buckingham Gate.

The site Frank had described was directly opposite the southern entrance to the palace. It was a long Victorian terrace of shops and offices that didn't look as if they had seen a paint brush in years. Most of the shops were closed and unoccupied; only three were still operating. One was a newsagent, one a launderette, and the other a bookmaker. Above the window, on a familiar dark blue sign, was the name 'Salmon Racing'.

I sat and stared at it for a few minutes before I drove on, turned into the Mall in front of Buckingham Palace, and headed straight for Hanover Square and Harry Chapman's office.

Chapter Eighteen

In the morning I arrived at our office just before nine. Matt was already there with Sara. As it was a Saturday, neither Jason nor Monica was in and I had the impression Sara and Matt had been taking advantage of the empty office. I evidently didn't hide my surprise well enough.

'What's the matter with you?' Matt asked brusquely.

'I just didn't expect to see Sara.'

'Sorry,' she said with wide-eyed self-deprecation.

'Listen to what she's been telling me,' Matt said.

'Salmon's have formally announced that Atlantic Hotels is for sale,' she said. 'I think it's just a smokescreen to show the licensing authorities they're doing something to secure their position but everyone's screaming at the Jockey Club for not pulling their fingers out, and telling them they should bring the police in. But the Jockey Club say they haven't got a single scrap of evidence of any criminal activity. And listen to this – you know I told you the bookies were going to get one of Connor's winners dope-tested over in the States?'

I nodded keenly.

'They managed to get hold of a urine sample from that horse Free Willy that Connor napped at Cheltenham last Friday – the one that dumped its rider,' she said.

'A sample of urine from a Free Willy? Sounds right,' I laughed.

'For God's sake, Simon,' Matt snapped. 'Try to be serious for a few minutes.'

'Matt,' Sara protested, 'don't be such a miserable git. Anyway,' she turned back to me, 'they couriered the sample to the lab in Florida, and the result came back yesterday. Apparently the horse was clean as a whistle.'

'I never really thought it wouldn't be,' I said.

'But listen to this,' she went on excitedly. 'They also sent a sample from another runner – the second favourite, I think – and it was stuffed full of Demosedan!'

'Bloody hell!' I stared at her. 'Wasn't it masked?'

'No, not as far as we know, but the animal was passed totally clean in the post-race test at Newmarket.'

'I don't believe it!' I gasped.

'It's true,' Matt said. 'Sara saw the American result for herself.' Matt turned to me. 'What does Demosedan do?'

'It's a serious sedative. Just half a cc in a muscle would slow a horse right down. And it only takes a couple of minutes to work.' I put a hand to my forehead, trying to make sense of what had been happening. 'So the winner hadn't been doped, and another horse had. But they don't always test the winners, so why did they choose Free Willy and this other horse?'

'We've been over this already,' Matt said tetchily.

'We've established no common factor between all the naps, including Jockey Club stewards, local stewards and stipes, who do the choosing. It's got to be the lab, yet we ran a check on everybody there after they sent us the personnel list, didn't we?'

Matt opened up the file he'd been building on the Jockey Club case and leafed through the stack of notes and print-outs that had accumulated in it. 'We asked the Jockey Club to verify security clearance on all parties who might have been involved in monitoring and checking, yes,' he confirmed, 'and all staff at the Equine Forensic Lab were cleared.'

'We'll have to check them individually.'

'Agreed, but we won't get anywhere with that today. The place isn't open on Saturdays.'

I turned to Sara. 'What are the chances that either the wrong sample was sent to the States, or that the American lab got it wrong?'

'As far as I can tell, absolutely negligible. You've got to work on the basis that this horse and some of the other runners in the races where the naps won were well and truly doped. But you've been thinking along doping lines for some time, haven't you?'

'For want of any other logical explanation, yes. But we were always stuck with the problem of how they weren't caught by the Forensic Lab. Maybe we should go and see them again.'

'Our first priority's to get our hands on this photographer and see if he's noticed anything,' Matt said.

I nodded, and picked up the phone to dial Connor McDonagh's line.

Three minutes later, I put the phone down with a satisfied smile. 'Good news. We've only got to go to Newbury – Tahiti Bride in the novice hurdle. We'd better get hold of Dougie and Jack. We'll need a couple of fresh faces.'

There was no sign of either target until Tahiti Bride's race. Matt spotted the photographer first and, almost immediately afterwards, the man Larry had lost at Ascot, both down by the two-mile hurdle start.

Whatever the photographer was doing, it looked to us from where we stood in the stands as if the other man was following him. Matt pointed him out to Dougie and Jack who made their way down to the side of the track so that they wouldn't lose sight of him.

There was a slight mist across the course, and soon after the start the runners disappeared from sight on the far side. When they came back into view, I could see Tahiti Bride's colours leading the pack towards the second last flight. A minute later, she hurtled past the post to huge applause. Matt and I walked briskly from the Members' stand to the unsaddling enclosure, when Dougie's voice crackled over my radio.

'The camera man's heading for the car-park, and so's the other.'

Matt grabbed the radio. 'Dougie – stop the second man! Any way you like, but just get him off the scent. And tell Jack to follow the photographer. We're coming through to the car-park.'

A moment later we had the photographer, his tail and Dougie in sight, but from the way he was moving, it looked as if the photographer already sensed that something was wrong. His pace had increased until he was almost running. He was heading straight towards us as we turned and ambled slowly in the same direction.

We could hear his breathing, the irregular rhythm of an anxious man, as he gained on us. A few moments later he brushed right by Matt, who tripped him, so that he fell out of sight between two cars. He hit the ground hard and was grunting with pain.

Matt swiftly leaned down and grabbed the camera, but the man threw out a hand and grasped the leather strap. For an instant he must have thought he had it but then the buckle gave way under the strain and Matt ran off into the crowd.

I turned on my heel and walked briskly back to my car. I got in and drove for the exit where Matt was waiting. We'd seen no sign of the photographer by the time we passed through the gates and were heading back towards the A4. I hoped Dougie was still on to him.

Matt chucked the photographic bag on the rear seat and pulled out his own radio.

'Jack? How are you doing?'

'Okay. I stopped yer man.' Jack's unruffled cockney voice echoed over the short waves. ''E wasn't happy. Turns out 'e's with Jockey Club security.'

'Shit!' Matt spat out the word with feeling. 'Why didn't we think of that! Jack, does he know who you are or who you're working for?'

'No way,' Jack chuckled. ''E just knows some

drunken geezer barged into 'im and sort of fell on top of 'im. There's no sign of our camera man now.'

'What about Dougie?'

'Nor 'im.'

We didn't hear anything from either man during the half an hour it took us to get back to our office. When we arrived there, the first thing I did was to open up the back of the camera to take out the film.

There wasn't one.

'He must have taken it out already,' Matt said, 'I'll look in the bag.'

He tipped the contents of the large canvas hold-all on to a table. Frustratingly, there was no film there either. We'd been assuming that this would give us some clue to what had been going on.

I picked up the camera – a Leica with the massive 800mm lens I had seen through my binoculars. I opened the back again to inspect it more closely.

Where the film should have been, there was a miniature compressed gas canister.

I showed Matt. 'What the hell do you suppose this is?'

'I don't know,' he admitted. 'Maybe it's something to do with the motordrive.' He turned back to the pile of objects that had come out of the bag. 'There are four more of them here . . . and what are these?' He had picked up and opened a small plain tin with a screw lid, like an old-fashioned lozenge tin. He tipped it over on the table and poured out a dozen metal pellets, about ten millimetres in diameter, each with a small pointed glass capsule on the front.

I stared at them, then back at the camera in my hand. Slowly I turned it over to remove the cap over the long lens, and revealed not a glass lens, but a flat, matt black metal disc, in the centre of which was a circular aperture, about ten millimetres across.

'Good God!' I held it for Matt to see. 'This isn't a camera, it's some kind of gun – for firing these little capsules.' I nodded at the pellets.

Matt took the weapon. After five minutes of fiddling about with it, replacing what turned out to be a spent cylinder with a fresh one, he looked through what was obviously a sighting aperture and fired a capsule somewhere into the bushes below the window of my office.

'I guess the sights have been adjusted to perform at an optimum distance, maybe ten yards or so, which is as close as he could reasonably expect to get to the runners at the start. How big a target area would he have?'

'I don't know for certain,' I admitted. 'I'm not a vet, but generally if you are giving a horse a booster, it has to be in a vein. Otherwise something like dope can go into any muscle, though they tend to do it in the quarters.'

Matt picked up another of the pellets. 'These little capsules would be more or less invisible, I suppose. I presume they just break off and release whatever's in them straight into the blood stream, and from there it would take just a few seconds to get to the heart.'

I shrugged. This was uncharted territory for me. 'Sounds right. I guess we and the Jockey Club man must have got on to the photographer at just about the same time.'

Matt nodded. 'And Lincoln was there already – or was he part of it?'

'There was no sign of him at Newbury today and Larry hasn't called in with a sighting in London, has he?'

When Matt had gone back to Henley to meet up with Sara, I rang Wetherdown. Frank Gurney answered.

'It's Simon here. How's Jane?'

'So-so. I'm taking her out to dinner later. I think she'd benefit from seeing a few other people around.'

'I was going to come over to see her and pick up Emma.'

'The lovely Emma has gone back to Ivydene.'

I thought I could detect a hint of wistfulness in his voice. 'I'll go there, then,' I said. 'Give Jane my love.'

'I will. And, Simon, we ought to talk again – sometime in the next few days?'

'Whenever you like.'

'Okay. I'm not going back to France for a while so if nothing else comes up in the meantime, let's be in touch next week.'

I put the phone down with a feeling that Frank was a man who didn't waste people's time. Anything he wanted to tell me would be enlightening.

Before I drove into Ivydene, I phoned Emma to let her know I was coming.

'Good,' she said. 'My father's here, and he's not in a good mood.'

That much was obvious the moment I walked into the big black-and-white tiled hall of Lord Tintern's house. He cornered me there before I'd even seen Emma.

'I'd like a word with you,' he said without a glimmer of his normal charm, and opened the door to his study.

I could, I supposed, have refused to go, but I thought I might as well hear what he had to say now and get it over with.

Inside the room he made no attempt to offer me a seat and came straight to the point. 'Did you or did you not receive a fax from Portman Square at the beginning of the week?'

'Confirming your instruction to cease our investigations?'

He nodded curtly.

'Yes, we did.'

'Then why have you ignored it?' he rasped.

'We haven't,' I said simply. 'We sent a final report and account and, as far as we're concerned, we aren't acting for the Jockey Club in any capacity at all.'

'Why, then, were you interfering with a Jockey Club official going about his business at Newbury today?'

I was annoyed that he'd already worked that out, but there didn't seem to be any point in denying it was us. 'We've been instructed by another client to examine the circumstances surrounding Toby's death,' I said calmly. 'We had no idea the man you're talking about was one of your people. We'd never seen him before.'

'You'd never seen him before because he's newly appointed. I deliberately wanted a new face to handle this because you people got nowhere and this absurd string of winners hasn't dried up. I've come in for some very sharp criticism for hiring you and your gung-ho partner. And now, just when one of our own people looks as though he's getting somewhere, you stick your oar in and we lose our suspect.' He glared at me. 'Am I right?'

'Up to a point,' I said. 'But do you think the people responsible will still try to carry on what they were doing?' I was fishing; I wanted to know just how much Tintern's appointee had discovered.

'Maybe not,' he said, 'for the moment, but we need to produce a culprit and thanks to you, that's going to be very difficult.'

'I can only say I'm sorry if we've hampered your investigations, but I think you'll find we did nothing we weren't entitled to.'

'I wouldn't be so sure. Somebody assaulted our man, and I strongly suspect you had other people out on the course where they shouldn't have been.' He paused. When he started to speak again, his manner was milder. 'Now listen, Simon. I don't want you interfering in Jockey Club business, but if you do find out anything at all connected to this tipping business, let me know. We really do need to get to the bottom of it.'

'Of course,' I agreed. 'And I may well need your help. For instance, do you happen to know much about the personnel at the Equine Forensic Lab?'

'I remember distinctly giving you all relevant information about that. There's a man called Rupert Greeves who's responsible for security there. He'd have told us long ago if we had anything to worry about there.'

To my relief, at that moment Emma burst into the study.

She ignored the annoyance in Tintern's face. 'Sorry, Dad.' I could hear her forcing out the word. 'I've got to drag Simon off or we'll be late for dinner.'

I shrugged my shoulders and gratefully followed her from the room.

'Late?' I asked, once we were in my car and driving away from the house. 'Where are we going?'

'Who cares?'

I looked at her; she was on the verge of tears. 'What's the matter?'

'I don't know.' She shook her head.

I put a hand on her shoulder and gave her a squeeze. 'It's seeing Frank again, isn't it?'

'Yes,' she murmured. 'I'm sure he knows who I am.'

'Maybe you should face him with it.'

'I couldn't. Suppose I'm wrong?'

'But if you want to know the truth it might be your only course. After all, unless your mother told Gerald about her affair there's no reason for him to assume you're not his daughter.'

'I think he knows bloody well I'm not his. And for some reason, he seems to want me to know it too.'

'Look, Emma, let's get this business of Toby out of the way then we'll deal with your problem, I promise. But in the meantime don't let yourself get uptight about it; that'll only make it worse for you.'

'You're right,' she sniffed, 'but seeing Frank again . . .'

'I understand.' I nodded gently. 'But let's concentrate on Toby first, for Jane's sake.'

Chapter Nineteen

By the following morning there had still been no sign of Lincoln at the West London flat. The photographer, though, had been trailed by Jack and Dougie to a small house on the edge of Windsor.

'I've told them to leave it for the time being,' Matt said. 'Now we know where to get him when we want him.'

'Have they found out anything else about him?'

'They've checked with the electoral list. The house is registered to someone called Frederick Tresidder, and a neighbour's confirmed it. I suppose that must be him. He lives there with his wife apparently.'

'That sounds a bit too cosy and suburban,' I said, trying to reconcile it to the bizarre contraption he'd been carrying at the races.

We agreed then that our first move that morning should be to pay a visit to Connor McDonagh's house to try to establish once and for all just how much he knew about what was going on and to see if he could be persuaded to co-operate with us.

I drove the five or six miles over the downs in bright,

crisp sunshine, feeling patches of ice beneath my wheels in some of the narrower lanes. I met Matt at the crossroads in East Garston and we drove on up the side of the valley in my car to Connor's place. It was a large Victorian house, handsome in the bright winter sun against a backdrop of artfully sited cedars and beeches.

In all the time I'd known Connor, I'd visited his home perhaps four or five times for drinks parties and once for dinner.

We'd always got on well enough and I'd decided to risk showing up with Matt unannounced.

Although Connor wasn't a notably sociable man, he liked animals, and the grounds of his house provided living space for an eclectic collection of domestic fowl, dogs, cats and goats. A pair of timber gates, lined with chicken wire, were closed across the entrance.

Matt jumped out of the car and opened them to let us in, taking care to close them once I was through.

We parked on a wide area of gravel in front of the house and walked to the short flight of steps that led up to a colonnaded porch.

Our footsteps made a loud crunching sound in the still, cold air which gave a deserted feeling to the isolated place.

I pushed a big china button beside the front door and heard the distant sound of an electric bell. But no one came to the door. I tried again, and backed it up with a few resonant raps of a large brass knocker.

This time we heard distinct sounds of activity and relaxed while we waited for the door to be opened.

Still no one came.

'Maybe he hasn't heard us. Let's just go in,' Matt suggested.

I didn't want to abuse my scant friendship with Connor. 'We'll give it a little longer.'

Matt raised his eyebrows in an impatient expression which changed to alertness, then alarm as a door was banged at the back of the house, and we heard the sound of a car being started.

We both stiffened.

'Something's going on.' As he spoke, a small red Peugeot shot into sight from the side of the house.

I couldn't see clearly, but whoever was driving, it wasn't Connor. We leaped down the steps from the porch and raced across the lawn towards the gate at the end of the drive.

For an agonised second, I thought the car was going straight through it, but at the last moment the brake lights came on and it shuddered to a halt.

A man in jeans, black donkey jacket and a woollen watch cap jumped out and sprinted away across the broad lawn towards a fence which separated it from a dense wood of young ash and birch. He leaped over it like a steeple-chaser, half a dozen strides ahead of Matt. I took a few paces after them before some instinct told me not to follow but to get inside the house.

I ran back up the steps and tried the handle to the front door. It was locked and immovable. I didn't waste any more time on it but instead ran down the steps and round to the rear where Matt's quarry must have left by a back door.

I found it and pushed through into a dark, narrow

passage, stopping for a moment to listen for any noises.

After a few seconds of silence broken only by the raucous calls of the crows outside, I heard a faint but distinctly human moan.

I advanced quietly to the door in front of me and pushed it open. Beyond was a gloomy hall. Through another door, I heard a second moan, sharper than the first.

Nervously, wishing Matt were with me, I edged cautiously into a small sitting room which, by my fleeting assessment, was Connor's everyday snug. He was in there, half lying across a canary-coloured sofa. His eyes were open, but rolling wildly so they showed almost all white.

I couldn't begin to guess what had been going on, but it was clear that Connor's condition was more than serious. His breathing was coming fast and stertorous from his heaving chest. He was motioning to me with his left arm.

'Connor!' I crouched down on one knee by his head. 'What happened?'

He shook his head, closing his rolling eyes in pain and resignation. 'Gone,' he whispered.

'Yes,' I said. 'He's gone.'

'No . . . no.' The words were little more than an expulsion of air. With a visibly supreme effort he tried to speak again. But it was too much for him.

I remembered that Connor was a diabetic, but I knew next to nothing about the condition, other than that in extreme cases the need for a significant infusion of insulin could be critical.

'Do you need insulin? Have you got any, anywhere?' I asked urgently.

His only reply was a faint shake of his head.

I straightened my legs and looked around the room until I found a phone. I grabbed the receiver and lifted it.

The line was dead. I jabbed the button, but still nothing.

I ran from the room. Using my skimpy knowledge of the house I found his study, and another useless telephone. The man in the donkey jacket must have cut the line outside. I ran back to the snug where Connor had stopped writhing. His chest moved only faintly. 'Have you got a mobile phone?' I asked. 'I've got to get you an ambulance.'

I could just detect a shake of the head.

I raced outside and round the house to the Audi, pulling my own phone from the arm rest.

Fumbling with panic, I pressed in nine nine nine; I had to do it twice more to get through.

Finally I was able to blurt out to someone what had happened. A woman's calm voice asked me to tell her again, and to give precise details of the victim's condition and the location of the incident.

I clicked off the phone, shaking but confident that help was on the way. Still clutching it like a life belt, I ran round the house, through the back door and into the room where Connor lay.

With intense relief, I saw that his eyes were still open. I detected a faint effort to turn them towards me as I came in. I squatted down beside him again.

'There's an ambulance coming.'

He didn't give any perceptible reaction.

'What happened?'

This time Connor blinked with the strain of getting the words out. 'The naps,' he gasped.

'He was asking you how they won?'

Connor barely nodded.

'What did you tell him?' I asked, breathless myself now.

He closed his eyes and lay very still. It was thirty seconds before I realised he'd stopped breathing.

I simply hadn't known that his condition was so serious. In a haze of guilt, I wondered if an ambulance was coming from Newbury or if the operator had contacted the doctor in Lambourn, who would take half the time to arrive. I guessed that was more likely, and set about trying to revive Connor, pumping at his chest for all I was worth.

I knew it wasn't working; I thought about applying my mouth to his pale, open lips, but couldn't bring myself to do it. I stood up and gazed down at him with horrified fascination. I thought of the doctor, or an ambulance, already on their way, arriving pointlessly, too late.

What was I going to tell them?

Should I phone the police?

I couldn't decide; instead, I went out to look for Matt. There was no sign of him, or any sound from the woods where he'd plunged after the intruder. Without thinking about it, I ran to the end of the drive where the Peugeot had been abandoned, and drove the car back behind the house to make way for the ambulance when it arrived.

In the silence after I'd switched off the motor, I steeled myself to go back inside the house and see if, against all likelihood, Connor had revived in some way.

I put my head through the door of the snug and saw no sign of life in the sprawled body.

Shaking, I forced myself to walk across the hall to Connor's study which looked out across the front lawn. I didn't know what I was looking for, but felt intuitively that there must be more of a link between Connor and Toby than just their spectacular success as tipsters.

I made myself rummage through the papers on his desk and in the drawers, but my mind kept returning to the body lying on the floor, ten yards away.

I felt guiltily certain there must have been more I could have done to help him.

Maybe, I thought, I should have tried to get him into my car as soon as I'd found him, and driven him straight to the village.

But I hadn't wanted to move him; I hadn't known what to do. And it was too late now.

I carried on fumbling through the uninformative contents of the desk and was slipping some bank statements, showing a healthy but not especially large balance, back into their folder, when an ambulance turned into the drive, hurtled up to the house and slithered to a halt across the sea of gravel.

Two men in green uniforms leaped out carrying medical bags.

Although there was no hurry now, I ran to the front

door and beckoned them into the room where Connor's body lay.

I waved them at it and they clustered around, assessing the position at once, immediately applying standard revival procedures.

As they did it, I wondered how warm the pale flesh was now. Had there been sufficient time for the body to cool?

Perhaps it had only been four or five minutes; I had no idea. I'd lost all sense of time in the stark surrealism of this second death, occurring exactly a week after Toby's.

Meanwhile, the paramedics heaved and pumped, grunting words of encouragement at Connor's body, until one of them turned to me with an implicit shrug.

'I'm afraid he's already gone. Do you know when he stopped breathing?'

'I'm not sure,' I lied, not wanting to get involved in long, drawn out explanations. 'That's how I found him; there was nothing I could do, so I dialled nine nine nine.'

'We'll take him back to hospital so they can have a look at him. Are you all right to make your own way there?'

'Me? Why do you want me to come?' I realised that I'd spoken a little more hastily than I should have done.

'You found the gentleman. You called us; now he's dead. They'll need to know how he was when you came. Perhaps you'd better come with us.'

'No, that's okay. I've got my own transport. I ought to secure this place first.'

The younger of the two men had brushed past me from the room, I guessed to fetch a stretcher.

'Ought I to tell the police as well?'

'Oh, yes, sir. We'll have to put in a report, too.'

As I watched the ambulance disappear into the lane at the end of the drive, I picked up the sounds of human presence in the woods across the lawn. A moment later, Matt was clambering over the fence, tugging a belt wrapped around the wrists of the man who'd leaped from the Peugeot twenty-five minutes earlier. The small, hard-looking individual had lost his woollen hat. His mousy hair was cut short, with long sideburns. I guessed he was about forty but his face was bruised and his mouth swollen so it was hard to tell. There was a trickle of blood over his temple and his narrow tawny eyes slid resentfully from side to side.

Matt only spoke when he was standing in front of me. 'Was that Connor in the ambulance?'

'Yes.' I nodded.

'What's happened to him?'

'He's dead.'

I noticed the sudden look of alarm on the prisoner's face.

'How?' Matt asked. 'This little shit says he hardly touched him.'

I shrugged a shoulder. 'Connor was a diabetic.'

Matt turned on his scowling prisoner. 'What did you do to him, you little bastard?'

'I din' touch the wanker. I tol' you – he had some kind of fit.' The man rubbed the side of his face. 'And

I'll report you to the police for what you done,' he growled.

Matt gave him a sideways glance. 'Oh, really?' As he spoke, he threw a fist so hard and fast into the side of the man's head that he buckled to the ground, unconscious for a few seconds.

I looked sharply at Matt, not hiding my disapproval. 'Why did you do that?'

He shrugged, as if he'd just brushed a speck of dust from his jacket. 'Well, if he's going to report us,' he tried to justify his action, 'he may as well have something to tell them. And when he comes round, it'll be easier to find out what he was really doing here.'

We found a coal cellar below Connor's house. Access to it was by a flight of outside stone steps at the back of the building. I went down to open the heavy door and held it while Matt bundled our prisoner down. Once he was in I banged it shut behind us.

There was a single, naked electric bulb hanging in the dank space, just enough to light the way to the heap of coal in the far corner below the chute.

Matt picked up a billhook he found beside a pile of chopped wood. He crouched next to the man and pressed it into his neck.

'Now, let me tell you,' he said in an icy voice that it would have been impossible to take lightly, 'we're a very long way from anyone here, and any sounds you or I make aren't going to be heard by anybody else. If I chop your fingers off, one at a time, the only living creatures who'll hear are a few sparrows outside, and maybe some of the rats that live down here. Now, I don't want to have to hurt you, but if you waste my time or lie to me, I'll have no choice and no one to stop me.' He paused for a few seconds. 'Understand?'

The bowed head nodded twice.

'Good. So, let's have some answers. What's your name?'

'China,' the man grunted.

'China? China what?'

'Smith.'

Matt abandoned that line. 'Who asked you to go to McDonagh's?'

'I don't know. There's a geezer I do a bit of work for – he tells me to go down and put a bit of pressure on McDonagh to stop tipping 'orses.'

'And this geezer didn't tell you who had asked him?'

'Nah, but it's got to be fuckin' obvious, 'asn't it? Everyone knows the bookies've been doing their bollocks over him and the last one.'

'The last one?' Matt asked. 'Toby Brown?'

'Of course.'

'Did someone ask you to go and see Toby, too?'

'Yeah, but I never killed him,' China said quickly. 'I went round his place Sunday morning. He was brown bread when I got there.'

'How did you get in then?'

'Whoever done it must have left in a hurry; the front door was on the latch, and the door of Toby's flat was still open.'

'How was he killed?'

''Anged wasn't he? Like it said in the papers. But I

told my punter I done it, so's I got my wages.'

'So the bookies, if they're your clients, think you did it, and that you made it look like suicide?'

'That's right.'

'They must be very pleased with you. Why do you suppose they wanted to kill Toby when he'd already stopped publishing his naps?'

'I dunno. And they weren't too happy about it, I can tell yer. I wasn't paid to kill him, just duff 'im up.'

'Why?' Matt pushed the billhook a little harder into the sinewy neck.

'I 'eard they done a deal with him to stop, and they reckoned he was taking the piss and just tellin' the Paddy what to put. But when the winners still keep on coming after he's dead, they knows they was wrong.'

'And why didn't they want you to duff up McDonagh?'

'They just said to find out what was happening, like, but when I gets here, he's out the back, messing around by the dog kennels. When he sees me, he does a runner, right down through the woods then back to the house and bangs hisself in.' China shrugged. 'I just gets in by the khazi window and finds him on the floor, groanin' and pantin' like a dog. I can see he's in a bad way, and I want to get out, so I tell 'im I come from some people who want to know who's tellin' 'im which 'orses to tip. But he just stares at me, like, splutterin' about some dope he needs, but I can't 'ear for sure, then you people turn up.'

'And now he's dead. I suppose if you're lucky, the coroner'll find he died of insulin deprivation.'

'Looks like it,' the man muttered, more confident now, sensing that we had no interest in dealing with the police.

'All right,' Matt said, suddenly sounding reasonable. 'You can go.'

'What? Just like that?'

'Yes,' he said, and walked over to open the cellar door.

China Smith, if that was his name, had no intention of waiting to see if Matt was going to change his mind. He was up the stone stairs and in his car inside half a minute.

'What do you make of that?' I asked Matt as we locked up Connor's house and walked away. 'Do you think it's Chapman's consortium?'

'That seems most likely.'

I agreed. 'I could see Chapman doing something like that, and it makes sense of Toby's death.'

'No, it doesn't. China Smith said he found him dead and I believe it. The way Toby was presented was far too convincing to have been done by a hoodlum like that. And there are still too many other things that don't add up. We may know how those horses were being doped, but we don't know who was organising it.'

'I'll have to get over to the hospital,' I said, 'or they'll be wondering where I am. I'll drop you at your car and meet you in London later.'

A policeman was waiting to see me outside the mortuary at Newbury hospital where Connor's body had been temporarily housed. He was a nervous young constable, manifestly overawed to be dealing with the death of a local celebrity.

I told him the dead man had been a friend of mine and I'd simply dropped in to see him when I'd found him in the last stages of some kind of attack, and though I knew he suffered from diabetes, I hadn't known how badly. 'As soon as I saw him,' I said helplessly, 'I realised roughly what must be happening so I phoned the emergency services.'

It took twenty minutes to marshal these facts into a format acceptable to the procedure-conscious constable, but to my intense relief he took it all at face value and didn't probe for any inconsistencies he could have spotted.

I signed the statement in which I was glad to see I hadn't had to tell any lies, though there were plenty of omissions.

Later I arrived at the house in Notting Hill to find Matt already there and on the phone. 'That was Jack,' he said as he put it down. 'He says the photographer has just driven away from his house in Windsor and he's tailing him.'

This meant that Tresidder hadn't been to the races, which in turn suggested we now possessed the only example of the 'camera' air gun.

Matt and I sat in our basement office trying to work out a strategy to consolidate the knowledge we had pulled together so far.

I phoned a racing service to find that Connor's nap had won again.

Matt grunted. 'What are the chances the horse Connor napped today would have won without any outside help?'

'From the indifferent way the other seven horses ran, no worse than evens. But then Connor and Toby only ever picked horses that had a chance. Even if they weren't in good form at the time, they'd always shown at some point that they had the ability to win, if they could produce it on the day.'

We carried on reviewing every fact that we'd found and kept coming up against dead ends.

After an hour, Matt stopped pacing up and down the room. 'This is hopeless. Even the police are coy about following up what happened to Toby.'

'Enough people turned up at his flat that morning,' I agreed. 'But the police don't seem to have talked to any of them.'

'We've got to see Wyndham again,' Matt said decisively.

'We'd be wasting our time. Why would he tell us anything else?'

'Let's at least bloody well try!' he snapped.

'All right,' I relented. 'But where do we find him on a Sunday?'

Matt picked up a phone and dialled a number.

'DI Wyndham, please,' he asked when his call was answered. 'Yes, this is Major James of Thames Valley Technical Protection Services.' He added two telephone numbers where he could be contacted and rang off.

'Not there, then?' I asked.

'No – at least they say not, but they also say they'll contact Wyndham and let him know I rang.'

'Why did you bother with all the "Major James" stuff?'

'Policemen are like soldiers – they react instinctively to rank. Both forces attract people who like order and hierarchy.'

DI Wyndham hadn't struck me as a lover of rigid discipline and chains of command, but half an hour later I found myself talking to him on the phone in our office.

He sounded a lot friendlier than last time I'd spoken to him. When I asked him if he was prepared to talk to us again, he sounded quite happy at the prospect and suggested we should meet right away on the main concourse of Paddington station.

'Why here?' Matt asked once we'd made contact under the departures board.

'I've got a train to catch,' Wyndham said. His hair had been cut even shorter since we'd last seen him and he looked like a stocky version of Vinnie Jones in a black leather bomber jacket and jeans.

He led us to a small bar beside platform one. 'Well, what do you gentlemen want to talk to me about?' he asked.

'Are you here officially or not?' Matt asked.

'As a matter of fact, I was having a day off, going down to see my sister, when the Duty Sergeant phoned me. So, here I am. I expect you want to know if we've changed our minds about your friend's suicide?'

'What we want to know,' Matt said quietly, 'is why you decided against any more enquiries? You know as well as we do Toby could have been murdered.'

'There was no prima facie evidence of murder, and the powers that be aren't interested in pursuing marginal cases these days.'

'But surely,' I protested, 'there must have been other lines you could have followed before you gave up?'

'Maybe. My Sergeant reckoned it might be worth checking out more background, but there weren't any real leads and, frankly, in my boss's opinion it was a cut and dried case.'

'Did the forensic report throw anything up?'

Wyndham didn't answer at once. 'Not as far as I'm aware.'

Matt glanced up and down the platform, then turned back to him. 'Look, Inspector, we think we've spoken to a man who might well have been involved in this. He's admitted to us that he was in Toby's flat that morning, though he says Toby was dead when he got there. I don't know if that's true. I think it probably is, but he could tell you a lot more.'

'I told you, we've closed the case already. New fish to fry.'

'But who should we tell, then?'

Wyndham shrugged. 'If someone decides to re-open the case, I'll let you know.'

'But, for heaven's sake, there hasn't even been an inquest yet!'

'The inquest'll only find what we've told the coroner's court.'

'Is there really nothing else you can do?'

'Sorry, lads, I'd love to help but there it is. And I've got to go now.'

We watched as Wyndham caught his train.

'Well,' Matt said, 'what the hell do you suppose is going on?'

'God knows. The police must have their own agenda and priorities.'

'I don't think it's as simple as that.' Matt shook his head. 'But I dare say we shall see.'

While he was speaking, my mobile rang.

'Hello, Simon?' The voice was vaguely familiar. 'It's Richard Simpson here. Jane Brown gave me your number.'

I searched my memory for a lead on the name.

He obviously sensed it. 'I'm Jane's vet,' he prompted.

My immediate reaction was that one of my horses had had an accident. 'There's not a problem with old Baltimore is there?'

'No. It's nothing to do with your horses. It's about Sox O'Dee.'

'What?' I asked, wondering why on earth he should be calling me about one of Tintern's horses.

'Jane suggested I talk to you about it. Are you around later?'

'I'm in London,' I said wearily.

'I know. I'm coming up anyway for the theatre.'

'Fine,' I said. 'Come here, then.' I arranged to meet him at 6.30 and gave him directions to the house in Notting Hill.

Richard Simpson was a slightly dull, but competent and totally dedicated veterinary surgeon. He was the sort of man one could trust implicitly.

He arrived at the house and came in diffidently, almost apologetically. I took his coat, gave him a large drink and sat him down in front of the fire while Matt and I remained standing.

'It was very good of you to take the trouble to call in,' I said.

'No trouble,' he assured us. 'I wanted to see you as soon as possible.'

'So, what's it all about?'

'I think you know – Sox O'Dee should have shown up positive for traces of Dermobian after he won at Towcester the other week.'

'Yes, I saw the girl who does him the next day. She was in a terrible state, and told me all about it.'

'Well,' Richard went on, 'I phoned the Jockey Club yesterday. He was tested and has been given the all clear.' He paused to weigh his words. 'There is no way that horse could not show positive.' He stared at us, both calmly nodding our heads. 'But, for God's sake,' he blurted with an unexpected display of passion, 'this means that someone is fiddling with the urine samples! Either they swapped his sample on its way to the lab, or someone in the lab fixed it. Don't you see the implications?'

'Yes, of course,' I said, understanding his reaction to our complacency. 'It's happened before.' I explained what Sara had told us about the bookmakers sending a sample to the States.

'But why on earth hasn't all this come out yet?' the vet protested.

'It will, very likely any moment now, especially since the second winning tipster has gone.'

'Gone?' Simpson stared at me. 'What? You mean Connor McDonagh?'

I nodded. 'I'm amazed it hasn't filtered out already. We went to see Connor this morning and found him in the throes of a diabetic attack. And now he's dead.'

Chapter Twenty

Matt had already gone out for a run round Hyde Park when I came down to the kitchen next morning. While I ate fresh croissants with coffee, I made a few personal calls.

It was a little early for Emma, but I caught Derek de Morlay between lots.

'Better By Far worked well,' he said through a mouthful of toast. 'I just wish I could talk you out of this mad scheme to ride him yourself.'

'But didn't Julia tell you how much I've improved?'

'Yes, and I didn't believe her.'

'All right,' I said, not wanting an argument about it now. 'Just give me an update on his gallops.'

However disparaging Derek may have been about me as a jockey, he gave me plenty of encouragement over the condition of my horse, and I was grateful for that.

As for my riding, I didn't need Julia to tell me I'd improved. I could feel that for myself. The hours spent on a horse without my feet in the irons had been well worth the initial discomfort. My balance, the strength in my leg muscles, everything was coming together, and I couldn't wait to put it all to the test on the race-course.

When I put the phone down, I went downstairs to our small office.

The strange piece of equipment we'd acquired from Tresidder at the races two days before was on the table. I picked it up and turned it around, staring at it, when it came to me suddenly that one of David Dysart's technical boffins might be able to throw some light on the way it functioned or how it had been developed.

I picked up the phone and called Wessex Biotech. Dysart was agreeable, and I arranged for Brian Griffiths to come up that evening at five o'clock.

He arrived early and once I'd solicitously settled him in front of the fire in the drawing room, with a Scotch at his elbow, Matt brought Tresidder's contraption up from the office.

'We were wondering if you could have a look at this thing,' he said, pulling the camera from its bag.

Brian took it and turned it over a few times. We didn't prompt him, but allowed him to inspect it in his own time.

He removed the front lens cap and scrutinised the small aperture. 'Ah!' he said quietly.

He undid the back and opened it to reveal the miniature gas cylinder. 'Hmm.' He nodded. 'That looks very familiar. I take it this is designed to fire some kind of small projectile?'

'Yes,' Matt said. 'Dope pellets into horse muscle tissue.'

'Not at any great distance, I wouldn't have thought, though?' Brian suggested.

'No. I expect it's good for about ten to fifteen yards, maximum.'

'Who's been shooting at horses, then?' he asked.

'I'll tell you in a moment, but first – you say the system looks familiar in some way?'

'Oh, yes. I couldn't say for certain, but I'd be surprised if this hadn't been developed by the same people who were responsible for the air-propulsion system in our Powderjets – or at least with help from them.'

'Who was that?' I asked.

'There's one in-house air systems specialist. He did most of the work.'

On a sudden impulse, I picked up Toby's file, lying on the coffee table in front of me, and fished out the best close-up shots of Tresidder. 'You've never seen this man, I suppose?'

Griffiths looked at it and slowly nodded his head in surprise. 'Yes. Have you been following Michael Taylor too, then?'

'No. This is a man called Tresidder.'

'I didn't mean that was Michael Taylor, but I saw him once or twice with Michael in one of the pubs we use near the labs, sometime last year.'

'Okay,' Matt said, on the edge of his seat now. 'Who is Michael Taylor?'

'He's our in-house air-propulsion expert.'

'Is he now?' Matt exclaimed, impressed.

'What do you think the chances are that we'll find

those missing prototypes at Tresidder's place?' I asked both of them.

'Let's assume he's more intelligent than that,' Matt said. 'Anyway, it would have been this man Taylor who'd have done most of the work.'

Griffiths shrugged. 'Not necessarily. He might simply have handed over a couple of prototypes with all the necessary components for air propulsion to someone who had the technical skill to adapt it to this bizarre camera. Do you happen to know,' he went on, 'if there are more than one of these?'

'No, we don't,' I answered. 'But we took that one from Tresidder on Saturday, after he'd used it; he didn't go to the races yesterday, so we think that means he hasn't got another one.'

'What on earth's all this about?' Griffiths asked, utterly bemused.

'I told you those pellets had been aimed at horses?'

He nodded.

'Okay,' Matt went on. 'As far as we can tell, small pellets with breakable snouts were shot at racehorses either at the start of a race or close to it, to deliver some kind of mild sedative – Demosedan, or something like it – just enough to slow them down a little.'

'But surely people would see when the animals were hit?'

'It's not so obvious,' I replied, 'if they're hit as they leave the paddock. Horses often jump and kick as they're set free, and the darts seem to leave no external mark.'

'Hmm,' Brian said, unconvinced. 'I don't know much about racing, but I know that horses fall often enough.'

'Obviously, but good tipsters don't nap dodgy jumpers, and once enough punters had clicked that these horses would always win, they were piling their money on, and so far the bookies and the Jockey Club haven't been able to do a thing about it.'

'Until yesterday,' Matt added drily.

Griffiths left soon after that. He had wanted to take the camera gun with him; we declined, but we didn't stop him taking the helium canister, which was almost certainly the property of Wessex Biotech.

'Emma's on the way over,' I said, walking into Matt's office next morning.

He glanced up. Behind him, the sun was glittering off the wet surface of the motorway and the traffic streamed silently eastward. He looked at his wall clock, which showed 9.30. 'Have you got time for that?' he asked.

'She says she's got something that may be relevant to Toby,' I answered mildly, not feeling I had to justify myself further.

Matt had disappeared by the time Emma arrived. She rushed in to my office and gave me a quick kiss, but she was bursting to tell me her news.

'Dad's called an Extraordinary General Meeting of the shareholders of King George's for tomorrow morning.'

'Has he indeed? What for?'

'He wants the shareholders to authorise a loan which is too big for him to ratify alone, under the Articles of Association of the company. They're holding it in London, at the Belgravia King George.'

'Just remind me who the shareholders are?'

'There are only four: Lord T, Frank Gurney, David Green and me.'

I'd noticed how, increasingly since Frank had arrived for Toby's funeral, Emma chose to refer to her legal father as 'Lord T', or even more scathingly, 'His Lordship'.

'What's the loan for?'

'I've spoken to Frank, but he doesn't know.'

'What about the other shareholder, David Green?'

'Frank came over with his power of attorney.'

'If it came to a vote, that could put you in an interesting position.'

'I've been in a few of those recently,' she said, smiling at me.

I laughed but stuck to the point. 'Why did you think this would interest me?'

She walked towards the window. 'I'm not sure. I just thought it might . . . you know, because of my involvement.'

'Ah, I see.'

'Well, are you interested?'

'I could be,' I said slowly. 'I'd certainly like to know what happens at the EGM.'

'I'll let you know as soon as it finishes.'

I looked at my watch. 'Right. I'm sorry but I've got to get on.'

'Where are you going?'

'Windsor. I want to see if there's anything more to learn about Tresidder.'

'I'll come with you.'

I thought for a moment. 'Why not? I could probably do with some help.'

★ ★ ★

Cherry Tree Close was a quiet and moderately expensive-looking cul-de-sac close to Windsor Great Park and within sight of the mighty Copper Horse that dominated the skyline to the south.

Emma came with me up the short front path to knock on the door. I'd thought this would look less threatening if there was anybody in.

We rang and knocked, but heard nothing from inside. I looked at Emma. 'We'll go next door.'

We walked down the path, along the pavement twenty yards and up the next front path.

This time my knocking produced a small balding man of fifty or so. My immediate impression that he was foreign was confirmed as soon as he opened his mouth.

'Yes? What can I do for you?' He had a strong mid-European accent, perhaps Hungarian.

'My wife and I were wondering if the house next door was to let? We'd heard that it might be.'

'You had? Who from?'

'I can't quite remember. We've been asking around the town, you know, at most of the agents.'

'Well, it might be. I own it but there is still a tenant for the house,' he said. 'Unfortunately, he left this weekend without telling us.'

I nodded sympathetically. 'Where did he go?' I asked, trying to show a polite interest.

'To Spain, I think. He said he owned a house there. He was a freelance photographer, though he said he was in the army before, posted here in Windsor for a while many years ago.'

'Perhaps we could have a look round the house?' I asked tentatively.

I could see he couldn't really be bothered to show us at this stage. I pressed him. 'Just a quick look. If you let me have a key, my wife and I could have a swift glance, so at least we could tell you if it was totally unsuitable?'

He took a deep noisy breath through his pudgy nose, then nodded. 'Okay.' He disappeared, returning with a pair of keys a few minutes later.

'Tell me what you think when you bring them back,' he said, glancing out of the window. 'Your car is the Audi, yeah?'

'That's right.'

' "My wife and I",' Emma giggled as we let ourselves into the house next door.

'But it worked,' I said. 'Let's get stuck in – any papers, objects or anything that might have something to do with his activities round the race-courses.'

'Okay. I'll do upstairs.'

I went into the drawing room and made straight for a small cheap repro bureau.

Most of the drawers were empty. They looked as though they'd simply been tipped out, dust, scraps and all. There were a few bills in the cubby-holes, but nothing of interest.

Next I tried a small chest of drawers, mainly full of dining room utensils which I guessed came with the house. There was nothing to give any clue to the identity of the last occupants. But my eye was caught by something protruding from behind the bureau, where it had evidently slipped to the floor between the back and the wall. I pulled out a framed photograph. The moment I looked at it, I knew I'd seen it before.

It was the same regimental shot we'd found at Toby's flat, including, among the seated officers, Gervaise Brown and The Hon. Gerald Birt. Standing behind them was a Sub-lieutenant Rupert Greeves – another name that rang a bell – and, among the other ranks, a thin, sharp face that stared back at me, very little changed in the thirty-five years since the photo had been taken – that of the recently departed tenant of 9, Cherry Tree Close: Sgt. F.W. Tresidder.

The first time I'd seen our surveillance shot of Tresidder, I'd had a nagging feeling I'd seen that face somewhere before, and now the connection fell into place. Greeves had known Tresidder from his regiment; Tresidder had fired the darts; Greeves worked at the Equine Forensic Lab.

I put the photograph back. I knew I could get Toby's copy from Jane. I carried on searching for another ten minutes until Emma came down with a disappointed expression.

'Did you find anything?' she asked.

I told her about the photo. She saw its significance right away.

'Rather suggestive.'

'Exactly. Right, we'd better take the keys back and tell the man next door that this place is too small for us and our four children.'

Chapter Twenty-One

I watched from my office window as Emma drove her BMW from the car-park. I had a premonition that in the very near future major elements in our lives were going to change irrevocably. In the four weeks since I'd fallen off Better By Far on a soggy Monday at Fontwell Park, it seemed that my life had already moved further than it had in the previous three years.

When I managed to drag my attention back, I contacted Matt to tell him about the photo, and that Tresidder had done a bunk to Spain.

'Shit!' he hissed. 'Another lead dried up.'

''Fraid so. After what happened on Saturday he must have clocked he was being watched and decided to go, especially as he already knew he had that Jockey Club man on to him.'

'Well, we've got the kit, and we've got the photographs of him using it.'

'We still need him too,' I pointed out.

'I know that,' Matt said curtly. 'We're working on it. And we've had a bit of a result at Lincoln's address.'

'What's that?'

'A man turned up there and rang the bell for his flat. No one answered him, but he's been hanging around looking annoyed – as if Lincoln had arranged to be there and let him down.'

'And . . .?' I asked.

'That's it for the moment. The chap hasn't gone yet.'

'I'd better come and join you.'

'Don't bother. There's nothing you can do here. I'll let you know if the position changes and we need any back up.'

Feeling truculent at being left out, I put the phone down and leaned back in my chair for a moment until, decisively, I picked it up again and arranged to have another lesson with Julia de Morlay.

'I'll see you in twenty minutes,' I said as I put the phone down.

Convincing myself that I was getting my priorities right, I left Jason and Monica in charge and drove over the downs to the de Morlays'.

What followed was my best schooling session yet. I jumped Nester over eighteen fences, including three open ditches, and never missed a stride. Instead of sitting up as I approached the take off, I crouched down, keeping my shoulders and hands low, and really felt as if I were helping for a change. It seemed paradoxical that the less I moved, the easier it was, but it worked, and Julia's grin as I trotted back to her after jumping the last fence was almost as big as mine.

I jumped down thinking that, just maybe, riding in the Champion Chase myself wasn't such a crazy idea.

As I left the yard, feeling very pleased with myself, my phone bleeped. It was Jane, wanting to know if Matt and I had found out anything more about Toby.

At once, the guilt that had lurked at the back of my mind as I'd driven to Derek's came back into the forefront. I'd promised Jane I wouldn't let up until we knew for certain what had happened to her son, and here I was, swanning about having riding lessons and schooling horses, which only encouraged fantasies of winning impossible races.

I went straight round to Wetherdown and found her as distraught as she'd been the day Matt and I had told her of Toby's death.

'I'm sorry, Simon,' she said, opening the front door to me. 'Frank's gone to London for a couple of days and I hadn't realised quite how much I'd been leaning on him. The trouble with having a reputation for being a bit of a dragon is that people simply don't believe you when you tell them you can't cope.'

'You don't want to undermine the reign of terror that you wield here,' I joked.

She smiled back tearfully. 'It took a long time to create,' she agreed, leading me into her office where she poured me an early drink to keep her company. 'You said you had some news for me?'

'Yes. We saw the detective who was running the investigation on Sunday evening. I'm not sure if it wasn't just bullshit designed to draw out what we knew, but taking it at face value, he was fairly disgruntled about the fact he'd been pulled off the case before he'd seen the forensic report to establish whether or not

Toby had been killed before he . . .' I was finding it hard to continue.

'Before he was hanged,' Jane finished for me.

'Yes.' I nodded. 'And we also know that at least two, maybe three other people came round to his flat before we got there that morning. Any one of these people could have done it.'

'My God!' Jane said, putting her glass back on the table. 'Who else was there?'

'The last was a man we found when we went to see Connor McDonagh on Sunday morning.'

'Was Connor murdered too, then?' Jane gasped. 'It said on the news that he died of a diabetic attack.'

'That's right, he did, but the man we found had been round to harass him, and we've only got his version of what happened.'

'But who was behind it, Simon? Who would want to kill Toby?'

'I promise I'll tell you, Jane, as soon as we know for sure. Then we'll pass it on to the police, I give you my word.'

She took a deep breath. 'All right. I'm trying very hard not to get hysterical about it but it's getting to be almost more than I can bear, not knowing for certain how my only child was killed.'

'Frank's been helping, hasn't he?'

'Yes, he's been wonderful. Though he was never very keen on Toby, he knows what he meant to me.'

'I understand too, you know,' I said, truthfully.

Jane sighed. 'You're a good friend, Simon, and Frank likes you as well.'

This was a surprise given that he hardly knew me. 'Really?' I asked.

'Yes, and considering you're spending a lot of time with his daughter, that's important,' Jane said with a grin that evidently anticipated a stronger reaction than I gave her.

'You know about that?' I asked.

'I've known for years. Why do you think I've always been so close to Emma? But I didn't think Frank knew, or Emma for that matter, and I didn't want to rock the boat. But for various reasons – physical similarity for a start – Emma worked it out for herself, and when she checked out all the dates, which I'd done too, that confirmed it for her. She told me she'd told you . . .'

'She did, sort of. I didn't realise she'd checked it so thoroughly, though.'

'She's done everything bar having a DNA test, but I'd say it's ten to one she's Frank's daughter.'

'I can't say I'm sorry to hear that.'

'You don't fancy Gerald Tintern as a father-in-law?'

'Who said anything about fathers-in-law?' I said indignantly. 'But since you ask – no.'

'I sense there may be something of a showdown about to take place.'

'You mean, at this meeting of the shareholders of the King George Group?'

'Yes, of course. Gerald doesn't have a controlling interest.'

I nodded. 'And he's a man who likes to get his own way.'

'To put it rather mildly.'

'He certainly won't get his way at this meeting – I wonder how he'll react?'

'Frank will keep him in order, I don't doubt,' Jane said proudly.

As I was nodding my agreement, I remembered my other reason for coming to see her. 'By the way, your late husband was in the same regiment as Gerald, wasn't he?'

'Yes. I thought you knew that?'

'I did, but what I was wondering was if he'd left any records of his time in the army – regimental reports or magazines, anything like that?'

Jane laughed. 'I should say so! There are two trunks full of dreary old publications of one sort or another up in the attic. What on earth do you want to know? I very much doubt you'll find anything detrimental about Gerald.'

'No, it's nothing to do with him.'

'Go up and help yourself by all means,' she offered, and told me where to find the trunks.

Twenty minutes later, sitting in the musty silence of the roof of Wetherdown, I was reading the results of the regiment's annual rifle competition, held thirty years before: winner, for the second year running, Sgt. F.W. Tresidder.

After lunch, I drove out between the impressive gate piers at the end of Jane's drive. As I hadn't had a chance to talk to Derek after my session with Julia that morning, I wanted to know his current view of my plan to ride Nester in the Champion Chase in fifteen days' time. I knew he had no runners that day, but rang to make sure he hadn't decided to go racing anyway. He answered himself and said he was watching it all on television.

When I joined him, we watched a couple of races together, talking in between them about Nester's chances in the Queen Mother Chase, with or without me.

Derek, evidently on the basis of feedback from Julia, seemed less pessimistic about the idea of my riding than he had been. This was a big boost to my confidence because in order to keep his strike rate as high as possible, Derek only sent out horses with the very best possible chance. He never sent anything out 'just for a run' – especially not in a major race at the premier National Hunt meeting.

However, he was still expressing slight doubts and I heard myself practically pleading. I thought he was about to capitulate when the head lad walked in. He looked almost embarrassed to see me. 'Evening, Mr Jeffries.' He nodded and turned to Derek. 'Guv'nor, could you come and have a look at Better By Far?'

Derek was on his feet at once and walking from the room. 'What's wrong?'

'He seems to have a bit of heat in his off fore.'

Derek turned to me as I followed close behind. 'Was that the damaged one?'

'Yes,' I gasped, with a sudden rush of anguish.

We walked briskly across the yard in Indian file to Nester's box and went in. Derek went to the horse's head and stroked him gently down his long dark nose before bending down to feel his lower leg.

He took his time, then looked up to me, with a resigned expression. 'There's definitely heat there. Of course, it may not be the old damage playing up; he may just have bruised his foot. I'll get the vet.'

I knelt down beside my horse and ran a hand softly up and down his leg, from his knee to his toe. I distinctly felt the higher temperature around the once injured bone, and nearly wept. It was in the exact spot that the original trouble had been.

I knew at once what I wanted to do. I quickly got to my feet and ran back to the house to catch Derek before he started dialling.

'Let me get the man who originally cured him to come and see him?'

Derek put the phone down and shrugged. 'He's your horse.'

'Thanks.' I fumbled for my diary to find Esmond Cobbold's address. I dialled the old man's number and listened to it ring a dozen times before, finally, it was answered. There was no mistaking Esmond's wheezy old voice.

'Esmond, it's Simon Jeffries here.'

'How are you, dear boy?'

'I'm fine, thank you. Are you fit?'

'There's nothing wrong with me that a glass or two of good claret doesn't put right.'

'Good, because I'm hoping you'll agree to come down here for a few days.'

'Why is that?'

'Nester's leg is playing up again.'

There was a moment's silence, then a sigh. 'I'm sorry to hear that. I saw you'd run him a couple of times recently.'

'He was perfectly sound after both those races. I rode him out this morning and he was fine, straight as a die, but the head lad checked him this evening and his leg had really heated up.'

'I could deal with it remotely, you know.'

'I'd feel much happier if you could come here. And I've got two bottles of Margaux '76 just waiting to be appreciated.'

There was a chuckle at the other end of the line. 'Devil,' Esmond said. 'Pick me up at Reading at . . .' he paused while he consulted his timetable '. . . six-fifteen.'

I could see this crisis dominating my thoughts and actions until it was resolved – just as other major preoccupations in my life were coming to a head. To myself, I cursed the bad timing. Outwardly, I excused myself from Derek and went to my car. From there I called Matt.

'Do you need me yet?'

I held my breath.

'No, it's okay,' he drawled. 'Everything's under control. We've got our man in sight still.'

'Which man?'

'The one who came to see Lincoln, of course. We think we've seen him before somewhere. I've taken some digital shots and sent them down the line to the office. Could you get in there and see what you think? Or get Monica to e-mail them to wherever you are. Where are you, by the way?'

'I'm at Derek de Morlay's,' I admitted. 'There's a bit of a problem with Nester's leg.'

'For heaven's sake! You're not still wasting time on that, are you?'

'Matt, you know perfectly well that running him in the Champion Chase is a major deal for me.'

I heard a long, self-righteous sigh. 'Just make sure you're ready to run when we need you.'

'Of course,' I said. 'Where are you now, anyway?'

'This chap came by car; he's got one of those small Rovers. He doesn't strike me as very used to London traffic. But he's got to Portman Square – we thought he might be going to the Jockey Club for some reason. He managed to park in the square but so far he's still sitting in his car. He's been there twenty minutes.'

'But isn't anyone waiting to see if Lincoln himself comes back?'

'We checked with the owner of the building who lives on the ground floor. Lincoln was renting the flat. He's gone, paid off two months' rent he owed on Sunday and went with a ruck-sack through the back door, leaving nothing. That's why we're staying with this man. At the moment, he's our best lead to Lincoln.'

I went back into the de Morlays' steamy kitchen where Julia was giving tea to the children.

'I'm off to pick up Esmond. I'll see you later.'

'I'm looking forward to meeting him,' she said. 'I heard all about him from Emma after he'd been down last time.'

I'd arranged that the old healer could stay in the de Morlays' tiny spare room, so that he would be on the spot, and so, frankly, he wouldn't have to rely on me to get him around over the next few days if I suddenly had to take off and do some work with Matt.

I drove to the office first, where Jason was coping with admirable calm. He'd had David Dysart on the phone, demanding a progress report which he'd supplied; he'd had Harry Chapman on too, looking for me. And two more clients to whom we'd quoted for systematic security sweeps had accepted, which meant the speedy recruitment of another highly computer-literate member of staff.

Monica had put on my desk two good clear shots of the man Matt and Larry were chasing.

The first showed him standing outside a run-down red-brick terraced house. I assumed this was where Lincoln had disappeared on Thursday night. Judging from the scale of the building, this man was about five feet ten, dressed in a sheepskin coat and a flat tweed cap. He looked more like a retired civil servant than a conspirator in a horse-doping scandal. The close-up struck me at once as familiar. Narrow dark eyes looked out from under heavy brows on the worried face of a man in his mid-fifties.

With a reference I couldn't quite access nagging at the back of my mind, I logged into all our surveillance shots. It took less than five minutes to find him, with

Tresidder, in one of the first batches I'd taken. But that wasn't the connection that was still buzzing away, unidentified, at the back of my mind.

Feeling I'd done something to earn my keep, I tried to get through to Matt. I couldn't get a reply from his mobile. I looked at my watch and saw with a jolt that it was already 5.50. I ran down to my car and drove through the crawling rush-hour traffic to Reading station. On the way, I tried Matt again. The second time, I got him.

'Bingo!' I crowed.

'You've found him?'

'Yes. With Tresidder at Sandown.'

'Are they talking?'

'Difficult to tell in a still shot. Both their mouths are closed, but the fact is they're standing side by side, and that's way beyond the realms of coincidence, especially in a large crowd like there was that day. There's no doubt they were together.'

'Good!' Matt said. 'I knew he was worth watching. Have you got any idea who he is?'

'I'm sure I've seen him somewhere else, but I just can't place him. What's happened to him now?'

'Nothing much. He hung around Portman Square, got out, had a coffee in the Churchill Hotel, then got back into his car and drove to Victoria. He's booked into a small hotel there and I've left Larry to watch him.'

'What are you going to do now?'

'I've got a meeting with Sara.'

'A "meeting"?' I laughed.

'Yes,' Matt grunted. 'She's giving me an up-date on the state of play at the bookie's.'

'Let me know what she says.'

By this time I was almost at Reading station. I rang off, promising Matt that I'd be on standby.

I parked and walked into the station in time to see the Cardiff train roll in. Esmond clambered down stiffly, clutching a leather Gladstone bag that might have been a hundred years old. He was wearing a dark brown tweed Ulster and a shapeless fishing hat. Once he was down, he turned and gave a hand to a young woman with whom he was carrying on an animated conversation. They were both still laughing when I walked up to greet my old friend.

'Simon!' he exclaimed with a broad smile on his handsome old face. 'Meet Natasha from Cardiff. She's an aromatherapist – we've been exchanging notes.'

On closer inspection the girl looked more like a night club hostess. I grinned at her and at Esmond. 'I hope he hasn't been shocking you,' I said to her, with a slight lift of one eyebrow.

'I've been trying to shock him,' she said with a giggle.

They said goodbye to one another and I carried Esmond's bag to the car while he talked about what an enjoyable journey he'd had. I couldn't help smiling; I hoped I'd still be flirting with girls in trains when I was eighty-five.

Once we were in the car, though, Esmond focused on his mission.

'So, how bad is it?'

'It's difficult to say. There's no visible sign of anything. There's just heat there. But he's obviously feeling it, that's what's worrying me.'

Esmond asked for every detail of the animal's condition, training programme and general performance. He listened to my answers, nodding vaguely from time to time.

'Do you think you can help?' I asked.

'I've no idea,' he said. 'But I'll do my best.'

Esmond had originally come to treat Nester the day after the vet had taken X-rays of the horse's broken pedal bone, when I'd first agreed to take him on from Emma.

The vet's view then was that the only way to save the horse was by drilling a hole through the outside of his hoof and screwing a metal plate to the bone. There would, he said, be no chance of his ever racing again, but at least he would enjoy a comfortable retirement.

Esmond had taken another view – that the leg wouldn't heal on its own simply because of the continual pressure from the horse standing on it. If the horse were human, he'd have been expected to lie on his back for a month.

As it was, after he'd used his own special techniques, he'd dug a small pit in the stable floor by the door and rigged up a harness with an overhead brace, so that Nester could stand on three legs, with his injured foot resting lightly in the hole, on a cushion of foam. Starting with intervals of ten minutes, the harness was winched up to take the weight off Nester's good leg. By the fourth day he was strong enough to stand for two hours without a break.

Esmond had also insisted that the harness was arranged, with a hay net slung over the door, so that Nester had a good view over the top of his stable door and could keep an eye on everything that was going on out in the yard. Few horses would have stood so quietly for so long, but Nester was a perfect patient.

After three weeks on a continuous course of homeopathic bone tablets and twenty-four-hour-a-day observation, he was able to begin putting some weight on the damaged foot. He had developed a lump around his girth, where the sheepskin-covered harness had taken most of the weight, but that had gone down within a few days of its being removed. Within eight weeks of the original operation, with Esmond's meticulous care, Nester had been completely cured.

Half an hour after we'd left Reading station, Esmond was back at work on Nester again.

His method of identifying the epicentre of the trauma in an injured animal who couldn't actually direct him straight to it was to dowse for it, like an ancient diviner of water. From a pocket in his well-worn moleskin waistcoat, he pulled an old gold fob chain, which he wrapped around his wrinkled thumb and dangled over the approximate area of Nester's injury, passing it slowly from side to side.

When the chain started to circle with dramatic suddenness and quite independently of any movement of his hand, Esmond knew he had located the precise spot. He looked up at me. 'It's not the old injury,' he said quietly.

I didn't know whether to be relieved, or worried that something new had happened. 'How bad is it?'

'Not too serious. I'd say it was repairable. My guess is that somehow he's trodden on something sharp.'

Esmond was completely confident now of what he was dealing with and this, he said, made him a much more efficient healer. He asked us to stand quietly as far from the horse as possible while he calmed it, lulling it with his voice and a continual, steady stroking. It seemed that he almost hypnotised it into a state where it was prepared to stand, totally relaxed and oblivious to anything going on around it.

Esmond knelt on one knee and lifted the animal's damaged limb to rest it on the other. 'I need to get all pressure off the joint,' he explained in a whisper, as if the horse had gone to sleep.

He raised the leg very gently with his left hand, checking all the time that Nester was in no discomfort. Then he raised his right hand and held it, palm down, a few inches over the point on the animal's ankle where the chain had spun most vigorously.

Transfixed, I watched him as hundreds of conflicting thoughts raced through my mind. All the time I was dreading the summons that might intrude on the magic at any moment, demanding my presence in the hunt that Matt was conducting in London.

But Esmond stayed where he was, uninterrupted for a quarter of an hour, moving only very slightly now and again to ease the muscles in his old limbs. When he was ready, he took the horse's joint in both hands and started to rub it, gently but firmly, like a physio at a football match. Only then did he glance up and look at any of us.

I felt that the others – Derek, Julia and Sharon, Nester's girl – were as convinced as I that the horse had been positively helped in some way, and yet Esmond had done little more than hold his hand above the animal's limb. The old man gently placed the horse's leg back on the ground, got to his feet with surprising agility and stood back.

'Okay, there you are, old chap,' he said. Taking Nester by his head collar, he led him from the stable and turned to Sharon, who was gazing apprehensively at her charge. 'Could you walk him round the yard for us, please?'

Still doubtful, the girl clipped a rope to the collar and set off at a brisk walk around the quadrangle. The horse moved quite evenly, showing no distress at the pressure on its damaged ankle.

'Good heavens!' Julia gasped.

Esmond raised a hand. 'Don't get too excited. He'll be quite numb, so he may not be feeling it for the moment, but he will again after a while. I imagine it'll take quite a few sessions before it's cured.'

'It's still amazing.'

He shook his head again. 'I haven't achieved anything permanent yet, but given time I might. Then you can make a judgement.'

In the house, over a supper of venison casserole and a bottle of Margaux, I was too nervous about Nester to talk much. But Julia was bursting to know how Esmond achieved the results he did.

He was, as always, frank but vague in his answer. 'To tell you the truth, I don't exactly know, but we all of us possess a personal electromagnetic field. A healer is able to bring his own into harmony with his patient's and stabilise the interrupted flow around the trauma. That lets oxygen reach it more freely and speeds up the healing process. But, quite honestly, like acupuncture, the science of it's still only half understood.'

Derek, by nature more sceptical than his wife, shook his head in unwilling acceptance of the fact that Esmond had achieved the right diagnosis – with his watch chain – and the horse was undoubtedly mending.

I left Esmond with the de Morlays who had already fallen completely under his spell. As I drove down the hill with my headlights reflecting off the rails of their tidy paddocks, I picked up my phone and dialled Ivydene.

Emma answered. 'Hi. What happened to you?'

I told her about Nester, and Esmond's visit.

'Oh, God,' she wailed in sympathy. 'Is he going to be okay?'

'Fingers crossed. Anyway, you can see him tomorrow.'

'No, I can't. There's this King George EGM, and Frank wants me to come up in the morning to talk to him about it over breakfast before we go on to the meeting.'

'Oh, right.'

'But what are you doing now?'

'I thought I might call in at Ivydene for a mug of hot chocolate or something, if His Lordship is out of the way.'

'He is. Do come – but I can't guarantee hot chocolate.'

Chapter Twenty-Two

My mobile started bleeping at me just after seven. I woke and opened my eyes. When I looked around me in a half-sleep, I didn't recognise the curtains, the dressing table, the rug on the floor, or the white broderie anglaise bed-cover. But I did know the mop of auburn hair poking from underneath it beside me.

I picked up my chirruping phone but remembered I was at Ivydene and tried to whisper. It came out as an ugly croak.

'Hello?'

'God, you sound rough!' Matt had obviously been up for some time.

'Morning, Matt,' I managed.

'Right, get into gear. Our man's already up, and it wasn't just to feed his meter. He's gone ten minutes ago, heading north-east – out of London, by the look of it. And I reckon if he's made such an early start, he's got somewhere to go.'

I agreed. 'Okay. I'll stay switched on and aim for the M25. If I haven't heard from you, I'll call you then.'

'Good thinking. Tallyho!' he bellowed in my ear. I

clicked the phone off, shaking my head.

I knew by now that it was best to leave Emma quietly at this stage in the day. I left her a few tender words on the back of an old petrol receipt, pulled on some clothes and set off.

It was a crisp, brightening morning outside and by 7.20 I was heading back over the downs towards the rising sun and London.

I was just half a mile from the junction of the M4 and M25 when the phone on the passenger seat bleeped.

'Yes?'

'Ah, there you are.' The warm resonance of Esmond Cobbold's voice was audible even through the airwaves and the miniature speaker of my phone.

'Hell, Esmond. What's happening?' I asked, trying to refocus my attention.

'I've just had another session with your horse. I wanted to let you know that there are definite signs of improvement.'

Despite the pressures of my current mission, I felt a surge of relief that Esmond, normally restrained in his prognoses, was prepared to say that things were getting better.

'Any idea how long it will be?' I asked, thinking of Nester's truncated training programme.

I could almost hear him shrug his shoulders. 'Impossible to say.'

'Will he be able to run in . . .'

'In the Queen Mum Chase? Maybe. He should be able to canter by tomorrow.'

I thanked Esmond for letting me know there were at least signs of improvement, but when I'd put the phone down, I still couldn't feel happy about it. With a sigh, I was turning my attention to leaving the M4 when my phone bleeped again.

'Hello?'

'Hi, Simon. We're at the bottom of the M11.' Matt's voice carried an undertone of tension. 'Our man's got his foot down. Where are you?'

I told him, and agreed to try to catch him up. 'Anything from the others?'

'Nope. I've called them off and sent them on into London to look round any of the places Lincoln might go, see if they can pick up a lead.'

'Good,' I agreed. 'Do you think this guy's heading for Newmarket?'

'Maybe.'

'If he spent time hanging around Portman Square yesterday, it would have to be a hell of a coincidence if he wasn't waiting to see someone coming or going from the Jockey Club – if he was parked in sight of it?'

Matt agreed.

'Ten to one he's going to Newmarket. I'll see you there.'

Ninety minutes later, I was hammering along the road into Newmarket.

Matt had phoned me to say that he and Larry were sitting in his car outside the Equine Forensic Laboratory.

I found them parked discreetly, a hundred yards from the low building, and stopped a little further up the other side of the quiet road.

I guessed that Matt had a clear view of the main entrance while, through intermittent trees, I could see a side entrance. From the refuse bins by it, I guessed it was the rear door of a small canteen.

I dialled Matt.

'What's your plan?'

'Sit here and wait for the time being.'

'Have you seen anything to tell you why he's gone in there?'

'Nope.'

'Anything on Lincoln?' I asked.

'Not yet. We . . .'

I cut him short. 'He's just come out!' I hissed. 'Can you see him?'

'No. Where?'

I'd spotted our man emerging from the side door. I had recognised him at once from the photograph Matt had sent down the line to the office, and from the earlier shot with Tresidder.

Greeves – Head of Security! That was who he was, one time brother-officer of Lord Tintern, as well as Gervaise Brown and Sgt. Tresidder. Of course, I'd seen the face before: thirty-five years younger in the regimental photograph we'd seen at both Toby's and then at Tresidder's place.

With an abrupt mental somersault, it occurred to me that Toby must have known these people as a child, when his father was still in the army and involved in the regiment's social life. I winced at the prospect that Toby was, after all, the link in the chain between

Tresidder and Greeves, who now seemed as anxious to find Lincoln as we were.

I watched as Greeves walked away from the door. I could see that he was concealing something under his tweed jacket.

He walked swiftly across an expanse of tidily cut grass, fringed with silver birch and tall shrubs. I had a clear view of him now, as he took a manilla envelope from inside his jacket and dumped it into one of the large industrial garbage bins which served the canteen kitchen. He took a quick glance around before he slipped back through the door.

I reconnected with Matt. 'He came out – very suspiciously – and chucked an envelope into the rubbish bins round my side of the building.'

'You're certain it was him?'

'Five ten – ginger tweed jacket, fawn trousers, receding grey hair.'

'That's him. Go in and ask to talk to him. We can watch the exits if he does a runner.'

'Fine, but see if Larry can get round to the wheelybins at the back and find the envelope. It might be important.'

I got out of the car with my heart racing and hurriedly devised a strategy as I crossed the road and walked between the tall iron gates.

Inside, I was greeted by a new receptionist.

'Morning,' I breezed. 'I was here a few weeks ago. Saw a chap . . . I can't remember his name. Fiftyish, grey hair, going a bit thin?' I laughed, praying Dr

Poulton didn't suddenly turn up. The young woman smiled back but offered no help. 'Sort of gingery tweed jacket . . .?'

'That'll be Captain Greeves,' the receptionist said, glad to be of assistance. 'Security.' Her hand hovered over the switchboard. 'Who shall I say?'

'Jeffries,' I answered, suddenly thinking that he might well have seen me before, 'from the BHS.'

She flicked a switch and waited a moment. 'Captain Greeves? Mr Jeffries from the BHS in reception for you . . . All right. I'll tell him.

'He's a bit tied up, he says, but he'll try not to keep you waiting too long.'

Nervously, I hoped that Matt and Larry had all possible exits covered. And I cursed my stupidity for using my own name. Tresidder might well have identified me as one of the people who'd grabbed his converted camera at Newbury the previous Saturday after Tahiti Bride had won.

As I jittered inside, the woman behind the reception desk was staring at me; I made an effort to force a friendly grin and turned away to survey the attractive garden in front of the building.

'Mr Jeffries?'

I spun back to find the man we'd been pursuing looking at me uncertainly but without any apparent suspicion. It seemed he didn't have a clue who I was.

'Captain Greeves.' I held out my hand, which he took automatically. I hoped that the receptionist hadn't spotted that he obviously hadn't met me before. 'I wondered if we could talk, er . . . privately – a security matter?'

'Of course,' he said smoothly. 'There's a meeting room here we can use.' He opened a door into the same room in which I'd talked with Poulton.

He closed the door behind us and waved me to one of the chairs, sitting down opposite me. 'You're from the BHS?' His voice was a sharp, clipped tenor with no regional tinge to it.

'There's no problem there,' I evaded the question. 'What I wanted to ask you about was some dope-testing results. I keep a few horses and my trainer's concerned that she ran one which was inadvertently administered Dermobian just before a race. She was never informed that this had been revealed in a post-race test.'

'Dermobian?' He looked doubtful. 'Are you sure?'

'There's no question about it. Our vet is adamant it should have shown up. He's very concerned and has asked me to look into it.'

I detected a faint reluctance in his reaction. 'I could check it for you, but I can assure you that even a minute trace of Dermobian would be detected. It's a banned substance, and any horse with it would have the race taken off it. What was the horse called, and when did it run?'

'Sox O'Dee, Towcester, the thirteenth of last month.'

The colour on Captain Greeves's face had faded from florid to monochrome as if I'd turned a knob on a television.

'Sox O'Dee?' he said hoarsely, staring at me.

'That's right. And there were one or two other cases where I'd heard a positive test might have been expected.'

His Adam's apple jerked in his throat.

I pressed. 'And runners in other races: Tahiti Bride's last weekend, and before that Free Willy's at Cheltenham and Musicmusic at Sandown. Sergeant Tresidder was at all those meetings, wasn't he?'

He was collapsing before my eyes. His jaw quivered and he didn't even try to answer.

'A man's been murdered, you do know that?' I prompted.

He was on the brink of saying something, but needed another push.

'Do you want to talk about it?' I asked evenly. 'Somewhere else?'

He took a deep noisy breath. 'Who are you exactly?'

'A friend of Toby Brown's. I'm not a policeman – I was working for the Jockey Club. I'm not now.'

I stared at him as frankly as I could and held my breath.

'What do you want?'

'I want to know who killed Toby.'

'What about the other one?'

'You mean Connor McDonagh?'

He nodded.

'The police said he died from a diabetic attack.'

'Do you believe them?'

'I don't know, but McDonagh's not my main concern.'

Greeves took a deep breath. 'I won't talk to you here. Give me ten minutes to sort things out and I'll see you out on the heath,' he said abruptly. 'By the Devil's Dyke.'

'Fine. The people who followed you here from Lincoln's place are outside – they'll be right behind you.'

★ ★ ★

I crouched by the window of Matt's car. 'Did you get the envelope?'

'We did.'

'What was in it?'

'Five sheets of paper, each with a different bar-code photocopied on to it,' Matt said with satisfaction.

I grinned. 'We've got him!'

'Could be.' Matt nodded. 'There's a good chance they're covered with his prints.'

Greeves was waiting for me, a hundred yards from the road. In the lee of the great earthwork thrown up by eighth-century Angles jealous of their fertile land, I saw him, sensibly wrapped up in a big sheepskin coat against the wind whipping across the open landscape. He was standing with his face to the east where a late lot of horses were walking home.

When I was a few yards from him, I called against the wind. 'Captain Greeves.'

He turned, looking pathetically grateful for my use of his obsolete military title. But he only nodded his acknowledgement.

'So,' I said in a businesslike way, 'how much do you want to tell me?'

His gaze followed the retreating race-horses. 'You know about Tresidder – it was his idea.'

'To mask the samples taken from horses he'd drugged?'

'No, not to mask them. Simply to swap them for clean samples.'

'How did you know which ones to swap?'

'The samples come to us in bottles with just a bar-code on. The lab informs the Jockey Club of the bar-code reference of any sample that's shown up positive; it's up to them to identify which horse and which race.'

'Sure, but how did you know the bar-codes?'

Greeves seemed to have an abrupt change of heart about his sudden outburst of honesty. 'Why should I tell you all this?'

'To clear your own conscience, I should think. Why did you do all this in the first place?'

'Why does anyone do anything dishonest?'

'For lots of reasons, but I suppose you mean money?'

Greeves nodded and seemed, I thought, to become more dignified. 'If you don't mind, I'd rather walk while we talk about this.'

'Sure,' I agreed, and we headed north along a track at the foot of the dyke.

Once we had covered half a dozen yards, Greeves heaved a sigh, audible over the wind on this sheltered side of the earthwork. 'I've made a lot of bad decisions,' he said, shaking his head. 'God knows I was doubtful at the time, but somehow you don't imagine how out of hand these things will get. Now I'm being hounded from all sides by people to whom I owe money.'

He took a deep, shaky breath before he went on. 'I made the mistake of marrying for the second time at forty-five. My wife's a lot younger than me, and very ambitious; not that she started very far up the social scale – she even thought marrying a passed over captain was a step up. But she was very attractive and I was flattered, and let myself be pushed into every money-sucking scheme she came up with – holidays in the Caribbean, ski-ing in Switzerland, and now private schools for the two boys. I only had a miserable pension and then, by a miracle, I got the job here.'

He stopped walking; I turned to him. I could see in his eyes the despair of a man who knew he was completely washed up. I nodded to encourage him.

'It's not a bad job,' he went on after a moment, resuming his steady pace along the edge of the dyke. 'Not difficult, not arduous, and not badly paid – considering. Of course, they pay a little over the odds to be sure of getting the right "type" – someone who can talk to the stewards and all the other ridiculous snobs who seem to run everything to do with horses in this country.'

His voice had assumed a bitter note. It sounded as if he might start crying at any moment. I sensed he was making no effort to resist the inevitable.

'How did you know the bar-codes?' I gently pressed.

He sniffed. 'Tresidder gave them to me.'

'How did he get hold of them?'

'I've no idea.'

'Well, how did he get them to you?'

'He either faxed them or sent them in the post.'

'Yes,' I agreed. 'We already have the ones you threw out this morning.'

He spun his head to look at me, appalled at first,

then he seemed resigned to the inevitability of his own disgrace.

'I presume you had a pretty good idea of which horses' samples you were handling?'

'Only because I went to the races once to see what Tresidder was doing.'

'You saw?'

'He was firing sedatives from what looked like a camera with a very long lens, like a lot of the professionals. Of course he had a photographer's badge so he could go where he wanted. In fact, the lens was like the barrel of a gun using compressed gas – but I expect you know that?'

'More or less.' I nodded. 'And you knew what he was trying to do?'

'His job was to dope as many of the fancied horses as he could – anything except the nap. He was very good at it. He never missed.'

'And do you know who he was working for?'

I noticed a microsecond of hesitation before he answered. 'No.'

'Not for Steve Lincoln?'

'Good God, no,' Greeves said with a scorn so heart-felt it seemed to revive his own failing self-esteem.

'What were you doing with Lincoln, then?'

'Being double-crossed, by the look of it.'

I waited; I didn't need to push now.

Greeves sucked in a sharp, resentful breath through his nostrils. 'The little bastard tracked me down. He found me at home – really put the wind up my wife. He told me he'd guessed some horses were being doped – there was no other explanation for the winning naps. He'd already noticed Tresidder was always there with his camera, then he spotted me talking to him.'

'When was that?'

'A week or so before he found me here. It was at Sandown, the day Musicmusic won. Tresidder was furious I'd turned up there.' The self-contempt in his voice was almost painful to hear.

'He was right,' I observed drily. 'It wasn't only Lincoln who spotted you. I photographed you talking to him, though I didn't have a clue who either of you was then.' He didn't look at me. 'What did Lincoln do?' I asked.

'He said he'd already worked out that someone must be switching the samples here and knew it was me. For all I know he was bluffing, but the nasty little shit knows how to needle people. When he said he'd pay for evidence that I'd been asked to swap the samples, I didn't even try to deny what I'd been doing. I still needed more money – what I'd got from Tresidder didn't go anywhere.'

'If Tresidder was paying you to swap samples, why did you stop?'

'He came to see me on Monday in a hell of a hurry. I told him I wouldn't do it any more, not after two people had been killed. I didn't want to be involved in murder as well as everything else.'

'So, what evidence did you have to offer Lincoln?'

'The faxes and notes with the bar-codes.'

'And what did he pay you?'

'I told you – nothing! When he first came to me – ten days ago it must have been, just after Toby Brown killed himself – he said he knew who was telling Tresidder what to do. He said he'd already had two lumps of cash – five thousand a time, I think – and with hard, documentary proof, he could get a hell of a lot more, maybe fifty thousand.'

I tried to keep a grip on the serpentine course of Greeves's revelations.

'Do you think he'd really had some money out of it already?'

Greeves shrugged. 'I don't know. The truth's impossible to discern in a man like that.'

'So, did you give him the evidence he wanted?'

'I only gave him half of each of the bar-codes. I told him he could have the rest once he'd come up with some money. I wouldn't trust him further than I could spit. He hasn't coughed up yet, and I need money tonight. That's why I took the day off and went to London yesterday.'

'Yes,' I said. 'We monitored you waiting outside Lincoln's old address. Then you drove to Portman Square.'

He glanced at me – nervous, like most people, at the idea of having been spied upon. He looked ahead again and his face tightened with shame. 'I nearly caved in; I was on the point of marching into the Jockey Club, putting my cards on the table and pleading for mercy. Then I thought the arrogant bastards would have my guts for garters if it suited them and they couldn't find anyone else to blame. I'd heard they were desperate to produce a culprit and all the bookies are up in arms that nothing's been done.'

'Apart from two dead winning tipsters,' I remarked.

'Well, who do you think killed them?' Greeves almost snapped at me.

'Logic says the bookies, but we've no proof at all.'

'It might help you to bear in mind that whoever is running this scheme still went on with it when they were being blackmailed.'

'Yes, I hadn't overlooked that, or that they must have thought it was Toby until he was dead.'

'If it had started by then. But now it's obvious it's just me and Lincoln.' He turned to look at me, almost elated in defeat. I thought he would not have been a very effective soldier in war conditions.

'Right,' I said, stopping abruptly. 'I have to go. Thank you for what you've told me. I won't be passing any of it on to any official . . .'

'Frankly, I couldn't give a stuff!' The words sounded incongruous in Greeves's tersely accented military English. 'It'll all come out, sooner or later.'

I shrugged. 'Well, if it does, it won't be my doing. If Tresidder gets in touch with you, let me know.' I took out my notebook and scribbled my name and numbers on one of the pages, tore it out and gave it to him.

He shoved it into a pocket without looking at it then turned his back on me and plodded away beside the dyke.

I watched him go and wondered what I should do. After a moment, I turned in the opposite direction and quickly walked back towards my car.

On the way I stopped to speak to Matt, still sitting in his car with Larry.

'What happened?' he asked.

I opened the back door of the car and climbed in. When I'd told him what had been said, as fully as I could remember it, I carried on to my own car.

I drove back on to the M11 behind Matt and noticed that it had just turned twelve. I thought of Captain Greeves: a weak man who knew he had failed at every serious challenge life had presented, while carefully giving the appearance of a man firmly in control of his own destiny.

I would keep my word to him by not telling the authorities about him when the time came – if it ever did. But sooner or later the system would catch up with him.

By the time I reached London forty minutes later, and my phone bleeped at me, my thoughts had moved on. I picked it up.

'Hello?'

'You might be interested to know that Lincoln has just rung me.' Rupert Greeves was the last person I'd expected to call, and when I heard the clipped, clear voice, I couldn't reconcile it with my memory of that hunched figure on the heath. 'He's anxious to have the other half of the bar-codes and says he has money. I don't believe him, but I said I'd meet him at a flat in North London at six this evening to hand them over. I shan't be going, but I thought you might like to.'

'Do you have the address?'

'Sixteen, Mulberry House, Canal Road, W9. I believe it's a council block.'

'Thank you very much,' I said.

The line was already dead.

Chapter Twenty-Three

When we arrived back in London, I told Matt about Greeves's call. He immediately wanted to put two of our men, Dougie and Jack, somewhere near the block of flats to check visitors.

'But it's a big council block,' I said. 'Unless they're inside, it's going to be impossible to know exactly who's coming to see Lincoln.'

'Unless they recognise them.'

'Okay. Let's do it.'

Matt fixed it, and checked with Monica in our Reading office to see if she had found an address for Captain Greeves through our electoral roll access.

He put the phone down with satisfaction. 'He must have been planning to keep the job. He's recently registered in Newmarket – Captain R. Greeves, Mrs Sharon Greeves, and two boys of twelve and ten – as he told you. At least we know where to find him if we need him.'

'What do we do now, sir?' Larry asked.

'I seem to remember you used to be a dab hand at cooking,' Matt said. 'Use your initiative and see if you can knock up something edible for lunch. Sara's on her way over,' he added for my benefit.

'I was wondering what happened at your "meeting" last night,' I said with a laugh.

'It was very productive,' he replied, allowing a faint smile to soften his deadpan expression.

'So, what's going on there now?'

'Sara called me just before we got here. There've been some more developments at Salmon's but she wouldn't tell me over the phone; Harry Chapman thinks their lines are being tapped. She didn't want to take any chances so she fixed herself a long lunch and she's on her way.'

I opened the door to Sara as her taxi pulled away. She came in and sniffed the air. 'That smells good. I'm starving.'

Larry had used his initiative by bringing in a pile of take-aways from the Pizza Express in Notting Hill Gate. He served them up in the kitchen and Sara started bringing us up to date through mouthfuls of *quattro stagione*.

'Harry's been tipped off that a bid for the Atlantic Hotels Division of Salmon Leisure is going to be circulated to all Salmon shareholders.'

'Do you know who the tip came from?' I asked.

'No, Harry wouldn't tell anyone that. But I do know the bid is rumoured to be coming from . . .' she paused '. . . the King George Hotel Group – Lord Tintern's company!' She paused to watch our reaction. 'Well, don't you think that's amazing?'

'Sorry,' Matt said, trying not to smile at her indignation.

This news, momentous as it was, came as no surprise to me or to Matt, it seemed. Harry Chapman's group, in its current state, was a natural target and the King George Hotel Group an obvious predator.

Matt turned to me. 'Did Emma tell you anything about this? She's a shareholder – she must have known.'

'I should think she's probably only just heard herself. Tintern called an EGM of the four King George's shareholders for this morning to get authorisation for some loan – obviously for this deal. But I wonder who leaked it to Chapman?'

'At the office they assume Tintern's just trying to take advantage of Salmon's cash problems after these two consecutive runs of huge losses,' Sara said. 'But if he is, he's too late now Connor McDonagh's died – unless, of course, someone else starts up again. Everyone in the office is expecting another tipster to take over but it hasn't happened yet. Mind you, the punters are still going for it like crazy. Turnover's way up on what it was before this all started; only now, the punters aren't winning all the time, and we're making money again.' She laughed. 'I'm afraid Emma's dad may have missed the boat.'

We sat down to discuss who had most to gain from a take-over of Salmon's by King George, and how we should react to it. Fascinating as this turn of events might be, though, it had no direct bearing on our investigations into Toby's death.

I held up my hand to focus the discussion. 'This may seem like a non-sequitur, but do you think Harry could have been involved in the deaths of either Toby or Connor?' I asked Sara.

Her eyes widened as she absorbed the idea. 'I don't know but it's possible, I suppose. Do you think he sent this guy China to see Connor?'

'China thinks he was sent by the bookies, so Harry must have been involved in some way, but we're not sure if Connor was supposed to be killed or just harassed – or Toby, for that matter.'

As I spoke, the bell on the ground floor rang. I went up again and found Emma on the doorstep, damp from a heavy shower that had just started.

She gave me a lingering kiss on the lips, then slightly spoiled it by swearing at the weather and pushing past me into the narrow hall of the house.

'So?' I asked, ushering her into the office downstairs. 'What happened?'

She saw Larry, Matt and Sara waiting. 'I love an audience.'

'Just to save you from telling us what we already know, I'll tell you what's happened at Sara's office.'

'I should think I can guess some of it. Frank told me he had extracted from Lord T what he was planning to do earlier this morning, and immediately leaked it to Salmon's. He was hoping we might have had a reaction from them by the time we had our meeting.'

'That's not coming until later,' Sara said.

'So Frank's plan worked?'

'If he was trying to evoke a counter bid from Salmon's, yes – like a dream.'

'So, how was your EGM?' I asked.

'Well, it was pretty grim, I can tell you. I almost felt sorry for the old bastard. He assumed it was in the bag, and even if Frank and David weren't going to vote with him, it never occurred to him for a moment that I wouldn't. But Frank was brilliant. He kept so calm. Lord T said it would be madness not to take advantage of Salmon's position, and when Frank pointed out that all these massive winning gambles had come to an end, he said he thought it more than likely they'd start again soon, and it would take a week or so to sort out the formalities of a two hundred and fifty million pound loan. Then Frank, with David Green's proxy, and I voted against raising the loan, and that was that. I thought Dad was going to explode.'

'Look,' Matt said, 'I know this is all very entertaining, but our priority right now is to plan how we're going to tackle Lincoln this evening. We've been wanting to get at him for the last week, and now Greeves has handed him to us, we can't afford to blow it. Tresidder's disappeared to Spain, so Lincoln's our only hope.'

Canal Road was a thoroughfare of over a mile, with a smart end up by the main artery of Maida Vale, and a rough end, where the twenty-storey blocks which had replaced cheap Edwardian housing were already past their use-by-date, just thirty-five years after they'd been built.

Every cost-cutting device known to the LCC architects' and surveyors' departments had been used in these shabby stacks of multiple dwellings and their inbuilt obsolescence was well advanced.

Nobody lived here now from choice, and most of the inhabitants moved in and out like human jetsam on the ebb and flow of a grimy urban estuary.

The police and the social services knew they were fighting a lost battle against benefit fraud, drugs and all the supplementary crimes and deprivation these attracted to this desolate area.

It was four o'clock. I looked at the faded plastic panels, the rusting debris and waste-paper swirling in the damp March wind which eddied around the five bleak tower blocks and thought that a man could get lost in a place like this and not be missed for weeks.

Our cars looked too bright and new for this decaying landscape. We'd left them well secured at the better end of the long, degenerating avenue, and walked singly, in scruffy jeans and jackets, towards the barren hunk of concrete that had been graced with the name 'Mulberry House'.

Emma had come with us in my sister's less than gleaming VW Beetle, which despite its credibility among Catherine's girlfriends in the fashion world, didn't look too much out of place on a North London council estate either.

Matt, using a plan of the estate and his experience of operations like this in Northern Ireland, had already formed an outline strategy for siting us. As we came to the actual place, he fine-tuned our positioning until he was confident that flat 16 was covered by the six of us from every available vantage point.

It was on the fourth floor of the building; Dougie

and Jack had gone in and were stationed on the floor above. I could see Dougie from time to time over the concrete balustrade of a walkway opposite Lincoln's address.

As we waited, the wind dropped and the clouds straggled in thin, ragged pink trails high across the London sky, and the lowered sun lit the towers with a surreal red light, reflecting off the grimy window panes.

By six, the vista had reverted to gloomy mono-chrome, and watching became harder. We moved a little, from one covert spot to another, each doing our best to check the others hadn't attracted any attention.

There was some coming and going around the block; a few men returning from work, many more leaving their homes for an evening's escape into drink, dope or larceny.

We were all connected to Matt and each other with radios open on the same wavelength and exchanged minimal observations on any possibly significant arriv-als, but so far no one had entered or exited Lincoln's lair.

Matt's strategy was to allow twenty minutes after the appointed time of Captain Greeves's arrival for any back-up to arrive.

Six o'clock came and passed. At 6.15 Matt's voice hissed over the radio, 'Start making your way to the target.'

No one had come to the flat; we'd had no sign that Lincoln was in there or that he didn't have a dozen heavies already waiting with him.

I found my blood pumping and suddenly realised

what a buzz I was getting from this. Until then, I'd never really believed Matt when he'd told me how the anticipation of danger could offer such a massive adrenaline rush.

As I made my way to the entrance of the block, I stole a glance across an expanse of rubbish-strewn concrete to where Emma sat in the VW, among the battered Fords and rusting bangers in the car-park.

If she saw me, she did nothing to acknowledge it; I wondered if she was getting the same buzz that I was.

I pulled the collar of my jacket up behind my neck and carried on to the wire-toughened glass doors that swung open into a bare lobby. Inside, three of the four lifts had signs to say they were out of order. Seeing no one else, though aware that Matt wasn't far behind, I took the shallow, gum-spattered concrete steps up to the fourth floor.

I came out into an open walkway where I could feel the crisp night breeze which had sprung up. Lurking in the shadows beyond the door to flat 16, I saw Larry already in place. A moment later, Dougie and Jack slid down the stairs into view. Taking a screw-driver from my pocket, I reached up and removed the wire and glass cover from the bulkhead light. With a sleeve wrapped around my hand, I took out the bulb and placed it on a nearby window sill.

When Matt finally came up the stairs, there were five of us. He stopped in the stairwell, twenty feet away, and whispered to Emma over his radio. She gave the all clear; he nodded at us, and almost soundlessly, lit only by the single remaining bulb in the stairway, we converged on the door of Lincoln's flat.

Larry and Jack were the largest of us. They took a few paces back, ready to charge the door and hammer it with their shoulders.

Before they did, Matt put his fist around the dented aluminium knob, and turned it. Tense but utterly silent, he pushed, and the door opened half an inch.

I saw his mouth turn up in a grin of satisfaction; he wasn't used to finding unlocked doors. With a quick glance at the rest of the team, he pushed the faded blue door wide open into a cramped, rancid hallway, lit only by a sliver of light from beneath one of the three doors that gave on to it.

Matt went in; we followed, until all five of us were crowded into the cramped space.

A sound – a chair scraping on a hard floor – froze us for a few seconds as we waited for the door to open. But the only other noise that followed was the slight cough of a man who had just taken a sharp drag on a cigarette.

We stood motionless, trying to gauge how many people might have been responsible for these sounds. I thought that since Lincoln hadn't even bothered to secure his door, he wasn't expecting trouble and wouldn't have any back-up.

Matt came to the same conclusion. He nudged me and Larry, motioned the others to stay back for the time being, and grasped the handle of the door in front of us.

He opened it and revealed a dirty kitchen, cluttered with fast-food debris and overflowing ashtrays. At the same time, we were hit with the stink of stale fried food and cigarette smoke.

Lincoln looked up from a newspaper, not alarmed in the first instant, as though he'd been expecting his visitor to let himself in. It took him a moment to register who we were; when he did, he was overcome by sudden, uncomprehending fear.

Before he'd recovered his wits, Matt and Larry were on him, pinning his arms over a cheap kitchen chair and taping his wrists behind him.

'What the fuck . . .' Lincoln screamed, before Larry's large fist clamped over his mouth.

'Listen, chum,' Larry hissed calmly, 'if you don't want to get seriously hurt, don't make a bloody sound. All right?'

Lincoln's eyes slid rapidly from me to Matt as he struggled for breath with Larry's hand still clamped over his nose and mouth.

Matt nodded.

Larry relaxed his grip; Lincoln gasped, but didn't yell. 'Where's Greeves?' he asked flatly.

'He's not coming,' Matt snapped.

'What do you want, then?'

Matt drew out the only other chair and sat on the opposite side of the Formica table from Lincoln. He stretched and leaned back. 'Who have you been blackmailing?'

'You're not the filth. I don't know what you're talking about.'

I was struck by the sibilance of his harsh London accent and the startling brightness of his coffee-brown eyes.

'Fine,' Matt said. 'We'll call the police if you'd rather

talk to them. But they've got less leeway than we have in what they can do to you.'

'Who are you then?'

'I'm sure you know who Simon is?'

Lincoln looked at me harder than he had before, and recognition dawned on his face. 'Oh,' he said. 'You knew Toby, didn't you?'

'Yes,' I said. 'I did.'

'So? What do you want?'

'We want to know who killed him.'

Lincoln blinked at my bluntness. 'Well, it wasn't me, all right? So you can piss off!' he snapped unexpectedly with a hiss. 'He behaved like a right bitch to me, but I wouldn't never do anything like that.'

I could see now why Miles had been so disparaging about Lincoln; if ever anyone fitted the description 'rough trade', Steve Lincoln did.

'Like what?' Matt asked.

'Well . . . kill 'im, like.'

'But you went to see him the night before, didn't you?' Matt went on, suddenly leaning forward, right across the table, making Lincoln cower back against Larry. 'And someone saw you leave.'

'I did, I did!' he wailed. 'About one-thirty, after . . .'

Matt cut in as he leaned back again. 'Did he give you any more money?'

'He paid me some of what he owed me, that's all. I was his partner, you know, before they started riggin' the races. And then he gets paid off – bloody millions – and I don't get a sniff of it! He was in a right state when I left him – crying like a baby. But I never killed him,' Lincoln added again hastily.

'Let's go back to my first question then. Who are you blackmailing?'

Lincoln answered by turning his head to one side and sniffing noisily with a pout of his narrow lips.

'Would it help if I told you that we know he gave you a large packet of money at the Jazz Café in Knightsbridge, the Thursday before last.'

Lincoln's eyes flashed. 'That was peanuts. He never left it all 'cause he had the filth on to me; he only put in enough to make sure I'd see some notes in there before they pulled me. But I was too bloody quick for 'em. And he won't try that again. I got something on him now he can't just rub out. I already give half of it to the *News of the World* – in case he does.' He turned to Matt with a malicious, triumphant grin.

'Listen, we're not interested in anyone dumb enough to give you money unless it was them who killed Toby. So, tell us now!' Matt's voice was still quiet but there was a steely edge to it which wasn't lost on Lincoln.

'You didn't see him then?' Lincoln crowed with relief.

Matt didn't register any reaction for a moment. 'Listen, you nasty little piece of shit . . .' He stood and walked round the table, grabbing the collar of the quivering man's shirt at the throat and twisting it as he brought his face close up to Lincoln's. 'If you want to get out of this stinking dump alive, just start telling me what happened.'

I stayed silent, praying that Matt wouldn't lose his cool and blow everything we'd achieved.

But from the look on his victim's face, it seemed as if he was having the right effect.

'Okay, okay,' Lincoln whispered hoarsely as the pressure on his throat increased. When Matt relaxed it a fraction, he went on with a gasp, 'I knew someone was fixing it for Toby's naps and I knew it wasn't him – he hated cheats. You didn't have to be no rocket scientist to work out someone was doping the horses and getting away with it. Either they had a new masking agent,' he paused, 'or someone was swapping the samples. The geezer with the camera stood out like a sore thumb. Who takes pictures of horses with a bloody great zoom lens when they're almost near enough to touch them?' He looked around at us with beady eyes and underlined my discomfiture at having missed such an obvious pointer. Matt and I were supposed to be the smart ones, but this dirty, ignorant little crook had been sharper than the pair of us.

'So, who's the guy you're tumbling?' Matt took an envelope from his jacket and pulled out a photograph which he held in front of Lincoln's nose. 'Is this him?'

Lincoln nodded slowly. 'He's the one.'

'What's he called?' Matt snapped.

'Tresidder,' Lincoln sighed, 'but it's not him who's paying me.'

'No,' Matt agreed. 'What did you organise with Tresidder?'

'Nothin'. But I reckoned he had to be getting the tests rubbished, so I went down to the Equine Forensic place, and when I saw Greeves, I knew I'd seen him talking to Tresidder at the races one time. Then I remembered that poncey photo in Toby's toilet – all them army types – and I knew I had 'em. And despite Greeves's toffee-nosed bullshit I could tell he was boracic.'

'When was that?'

'Just after . . .' Lincoln stopped.

'After what?'

'After Toby died.'

At that moment, Dougie's large, ginger head appeared around the flimsy panel door.

'The girl's just seen someone coming up.'

Matt clicked on his radio. 'Emma? Give me a description.'

'Tall, big anorak, trapper cap, ear-flaps down. Sorry, couldn't get a look at his face.'

'Where is he?'

'Just going up the stairs . . . second floor, now.'

'Okay,' Matt whispered. 'We'll assume he's coming here.' He turned to me. 'You, me and Larry can wait in here. Dougie, close the front door but leave it on the latch, then get ready to get behind him with Jack if he does come in.' While Matt was giving the orders, he deftly taped Lincoln's mouth and bound his wrists and ankles to the chair.

As Dougie silently carried out his instructions, we heard firm, metal-capped footfalls echo along the open landing, incongruous in this place of shuffling trainers. They slowed as their owner checked the numbers of other doors on the landing and finally stopped outside number 16.

There was a brief pause before the handle turned and the door was slowly pushed open.

In the kitchen we saw none of this, but we heard the steps carry on across the rubber-tiled floor of the hall, until the kitchen door, too, was slowly opened.

He saw us the same moment we saw him. He tried to back away, but I could see in his eyes he knew it was a waste of time. Dougie and Jack had already moved in behind him, locking on to each arm with two hands.

Slowly they propelled the tall, lean frame back under the blinding light of the single naked bulb in the grimy kitchen.

Dougie moved round so that he could see our captive.

'Bloody hell!'

I looked at the man and smiled to see him.

'Hello, Gerald,' I said.

Chapter Twenty-Four

Lord Tintern's fury showed only in the slightest twitch of his stony face.

No one moved, apart from Lincoln, wriggling his wrists inside the heavy adhesive tape Larry had used to bind him while we waited to hear what Tintern was going to say next.

'What the hell are you people doing here?' His voice echoed harshly in the bare room. 'I thought I'd made it quite clear you were off the job? Your presence here is utterly out of order. If it prejudices our own enquiries, believe me, you'll pay for it.'

'Just a minute, Lord Tintern,' Matt said quietly. 'Would you mind telling us why *you're* here?'

Tintern turned to look at him with an expression of scorn. 'What on earth do you mean? You must know perfectly well why I'm here. But in case you've just blundered in with half the story, I've come to pick up the bar-codes that Captain Greeves used in order to undermine certain dope tests.'

'Yes – horses running against Connor McDonagh's naps, and Toby's before that.'

'Of course,' Tintern said witheringly. He gave Lincoln a disparaging nod. 'This man offered his service – at a price, needless to say – to acquire evidence that will be vital in bringing the culprits to book. He's been acting on behalf of the Jockey Club so if you people want to retain your licence to operate, I suggest you release him – PDQ!'

Larry looked at Matt who, after a moment, gave a quick nod.

No one spoke while Larry noisily unpeeled the thick plastic tape. When he had finished, Lincoln smirked, stood up and stretched his arms. 'Thanks, Guv,' he grunted at Lord Tintern. 'They scared the shit out of me, I can tell yer. I got to go to the toilet.' He started towards the door into the hall. I instinctively moved to block his way.

'Don't be ridiculous!' Tintern snapped. 'Let him go.'

'Dougie, check the bathroom before he goes in,' Matt ordered. 'He might have a gun in there.'

I took a deep breath and stepped aside to let Lincoln pass and go through one of the doors off the hall. He banged it shut behind him and bolted it.

Dougie stood in front of it, clenching his fists with frustration.

Nobody in the room spoke for the next few moments. If Lord Tintern was feeling the pressure, he gave no sign of it. He stood in the middle of the small, stuffy room, ramrod straight, with a display of authority that defied us to challenge him again.

It was Matt who broke the silence. 'Lord Tintern,' he said with studied calmness, 'I take it you know what's been going on at the Equine Forensic Lab?'

'Yes. I regret to say that someone I placed in a position of trust has let me down. It was because I thought he was totally honest that I recommended Rupert Greeves for the job at the lab, but it seems he couldn't resist the temptation to supplement his income by shamelessly abusing his position.'

'But how did you discover that?'

'When I dispensed with your services, my fellow stewards demanded that one of our internal people was put on the job.' Tintern paused and looked disdainfully at each of us. 'He established very quickly what was going on, despite your interference at Newbury, and was able to put us on the right track.'

'Has he made any progress with finding Toby's murderer?' I asked.

Tintern walked across to the grimy window and wiped it cursorily with one hand. He turned to me with an icy stare. 'The police tell me they've found no evidence or motive to suggest foul play. It's very unfortunate, and of course I'm desolate for Jane, but if you lead the kind of life Toby did, that's the sort of thing you must expect.'

I was working myself up to a reply when there was a clatter from the hall. Matt darted from the kitchen and found Dougie tugging at the bathroom door.

'What's happening?' Matt snapped.

'I think he's gone out of the window!'

'Larry, come and help,' Matt barked. They hurled themselves at the door which caved in flimsily at the first impact of their shoulders.

There was no one inside the narrow bathroom. The single frosted window was open and swinging on its hinges. Larry didn't wait to be told; he carried on through the narrow aperture, though with a lot more difficulty than the slight-framed Lincoln must have had.

I ran out of the flat behind Matt, who was trying to reach Emma on his radio as he went. 'Emma . . . Emma? Come in, for God's sake! Lincoln's done a runner! Have you seen him?' I guessed from the sagging of his shoulders that Emma hadn't. 'Shit!' he confirmed. 'Keep your eyes peeled for him.'

He released the 'talk' button and turned to Dougie and Jack, coming through the doorway of the flat. 'Okay, you two, get after him on foot. We'll back you up by car.'

We all ran to the top of the stairs and were skidding and clattering down the concrete steps, when I stopped, catching Matt's arm. 'Tintern's still in the flat,' I grunted, and ran back up two flights to the fetid apartment and through to the kitchen.

The small room was conspicuously empty now. I pulled out my radio to raise Emma, thinking as I did that she didn't even know who it was she'd watched coming up earlier.

I couldn't get anything back from her. I hunted in the other rooms, drew a blank, and ran out of the flat, this time banging the door shut behind me.

I found Matt three storeys below, leaning over a concrete balustrade with a pair of binoculars in his hands, scouring the ill-lit roads and alleys on the ground. 'I don't know what's happened to Tintern,' I said.

'Don't worry about him – we can always find him.
It's Lincoln we need now.'

Matt and I made our way back to our cars, checking in
with Dougie and Larry who'd fanned out from the
estate but hadn't seen a sign of Lincoln, and I still
couldn't raise Emma.

She got me as I was about to climb into my car. 'Si?
Thank God! I had him – he was ducking south through
the streets, then I lost him down the tube station, I'm
sorry. He hasn't come back out, but I don't know if he
got on to a train or if he's still lurking down there. I've
completely lost him!'

'Okay,' I sighed. 'Don't worry. I'll get Dougie to
meet you at the station.'

Furious and frustrated, Matt started to call in the
others, unwilling to accept that if we'd lost Lincoln in
these circumstances, the chances of finding him again
now were worse than negligible.

'My father?' Emma gasped. 'Not that he . . .' She
stopped abruptly, conscious of what she was saying.
'What on earth was he doing in that horrible, sleazy
place?'

We were in our basement in Notting Hill, holding a
post-mortem on the failure of the operation.

'He's part of it,' I assured her.

'How can you be so certain?' Matt asked. 'I mean,
for a start everything he said was totally plausible. And,
anyway, what was in it for him?'

'I think we ought to ask him that ourselves.'

'Sure,' Matt said sarcastically. 'We could ring him: "Would you mind, Lord Tintern, if we came over and continued the interview we were carrying on earlier in the council flat of a blackmailing rent-boy in one of the nastier regions of North London, just before you legged it?" '

'Emma,' I said, turning to her, 'he doesn't know you were with us this evening. Could you ring him and find out where he is?'

She nodded and picked up the phone. She dialled Tintern's London office and got through to his secretary.

Thirty seconds later, Emma put the phone down triumphantly. 'She doesn't know where he is now, but he's got an appointment with Jane at Wetherdown at nine o'clock tomorrow morning.'

'Good,' I said, 'that gives us time to look in and see how Nester's doing.'

'Simon,' Matt protested, 'you haven't got time to think about horses in the middle of an operation like this.'

'What else can I do? And even when we've resolved this whole thing, Nester's still got to run in the Champion Chase in two weeks.'

Matt shrugged to show his incomprehension of my priorities. 'Just don't blow your chances of talking to Tintern tomorrow. I'd come too, but I think he'd be less evasive if it was just you.'

Esmond Cobbold seemed to have put down roots at the de Morlays'. We found him in the thick of the family, doing magic tricks for the children, having just healed an ailing ferret.

He came out with us to look at Nester. He had completed three sessions with the horse and miraculously, it seemed, the heat had gone from the horse's leg.

'It's perfectly possible, dear boy, that it would have gone anyway. Any little strain could have caused the problem – it may have had absolutely nothing to do with the original damage.'

I thought the old healer was being too modest but it seemed churlish to argue. 'You've still earned that second bottle of Margaux,' I said. 'I'm sure if you hadn't come, the horse would still be hobbling.'

'Barring accidents, he should be all right for the Champion Chase next month.'

'Are you seriously going to ride him yourself?' Emma asked as we drove from the de Morlays' to Wetherdown.

'Yes.'

'Even after last time?'

'You may see some improvement,' I said modestly, not wanting to raise my own hopes too high. 'And, anyway, he's my horse.'

Jane was some way back to normal, though still comparatively muted. She was clearly pleased to see us.

'I'm making some dinner for Frank. There's enough for you two if you haven't eaten?'

I suddenly realised we'd had nothing since Larry's pizzas, which seemed like days ago.

337

While she was cooking, Emma poured us drinks, and I told Jane what had been going on and some of my theories about Toby's death.

When he arrived, Frank seemed pleased to see us, too.

'Hello, Emma!' He kissed her warmly, and his eyes lingered on her proudly. I wondered when the issue of their true relationship was going to be aired openly at last. 'You did brilliantly at the meeting this morning,' he went on. 'You were in a difficult position, and I'm afraid you really wound old Gerald up.'

'You're not a bit afraid,' she laughed. 'And nor am I. Have we had any communication from the board and shareholders of Salmon Leisure?'

'Nothing yet. I wonder how they'll react?'

As they were speaking, an idea began to take form in my mind. It occurred to me that Harry Chapman might benefit from a more intimate knowledge of the share structure of the King George Hotel Group, which I would be happy to provide.

The following morning, I went to Wetherdown early and rode out first lot on Baltimore. I came back with Emma, just in time to see Lord Tintern climb out of his Mercedes.

He showed no pleasure at seeing either of us. I guessed he was wondering how much I'd told Emma about what had happened at Lincoln's sordid flat the evening before.

In the presence of his daughter, his trainer and all the other people milling around the yard, Lord Tintern acted towards me with impressive restraint. He admired Baltimore whom I was putting away. 'That's what you should concentrate on.' He laughed indulgently. 'Stick to riding hunter-chasers. Not too competitive and a lot of fun for an amateur. You ought to sell that good horse of yours back to me. Morally speaking, of course, I don't think you have any alternative.'

'Morally?' I queried, curbing my laughter.

'I sold him on the grounds that he was terminally lame.'

I couldn't suppress the laughter this time. 'Well, now he's very fit and I'm determined to ride him myself in my own colours. Then, of course, I'd consider an offer.'

It was Tintern's turn to laugh. There was a nasty edge to it. 'Ride him yourself? For my own sake, I hope you do.'

I nodded. 'Purple Silk will stand an even better chance of winning, then, won't he?'

Tintern lowered his voice and leaned towards me. 'Now then, Jeffries, you and I must talk in private somewhere. Perhaps Jane will lend us her office for a few minutes before I look at my horses? There's something you should know about Rupert Greeves.'

I winked at Emma, who waited as we walked across the lawn and let ourselves in through a French window to Jane's office.

'So, what should I know about Greeves?' I asked as I closed the door behind us.

'If you're thinking of talking to him again, I'm afraid you'd be wasting your time.'

Inwardly, I groaned. It wouldn't help our case at all if Greeves had disappeared as well, especially with Tresidder already missing and a tricky search ahead for Steve Lincoln.

'Why? Has he left his job?'

'He's left everything – permanently. His wife found him dead in the garage at ten o'clock last night. He was hanging from a cross beam.'

'Good God!' I exclaimed. 'Just like Toby.' And gazed straight at Tintern.

He didn't blink. 'Similar, yes, though Greeves left a note.'

'Unlike Toby,' I added.

Tintern seemed to have a ready answer for every question I put to him. As we talked, I was sure he was involved but knew I still couldn't prove it. So did he.

'Listen,' he said, frowning, 'let me tell you now, once and for all, I don't want to hear that you or your bumptious partner are having anything further to do with this case. I've told you we have our own people on it now and don't want their considerable prowess hampered by a crowd of bungling amateurs. You saw what happened last night when you tried to get too smart – you lost your man. Fortunately, I know where he is and our own people can carry on the investigation despite your interference.'

I was sure he was lying but didn't argue.

'That's fine, Gerald. We're only interested in who killed Toby, so if there's no connection with the doping, I guess we won't need to go down that path any more.'

'Leave that alone too,' he ordered. 'I realise Jane is desperate to exonerate her son, but you'd be doing her a favour in the long run if you could simply persuade her that the truth is he did away with himself, and that's that.'

'Once we know that's true, we'll tell her,' I assured him.

He didn't answer at once, but looked at me speculatively, making no attempt to hide his scorn. 'You really should learn to stop meddling in other people's business,' he hissed with an icy glare.

Tintern's cheek twitched violently as he leaned closer to me. 'I spent ten years and millions of pounds acquiring a premier site in Buckingham Gate. Then you come along and fuck the whole thing up – and for what?' he spat. 'A poxy, tuppenny ha'penny commission from that jumped up oik, Harry Chapman! You bloody fool! Let me tell you, that'll be the hardest commission you'll ever earn. If I were you, I'd take this advice: don't meddle in my business or Toby's death. It could be catching!'

He spun round and marched out of the room by the garden door and across the lawn towards the yard. I watched him go, astonished at his indiscretion.

I wondered how he already knew that it was I who had tipped off Harry Chapman about the Buckingham Gate site.

The branch of Salmon Racing on that site, even under normal conditions, had never reached its target. This was due, Harry had told me, to the high proportion of people living and staying in the vicinity who were visitors or temporary residents with no interest in English racing.

When Salmon's had been approached by a company purporting to be operators of a chain of Bureaux de Change, they had been offered double the value of the eighteen-year lease on the premises.

The shop was a very small component in the whole spread of Salmon's gambling business, and its fate had barely touched on Harry Chapman's attention. However, spurred on by the knowledge that this shop was one of the last pieces in the jigsaw which would become the site of Tintern's biggest London hotel, it hadn't been hard to persuade him to change his mind about disposing of the lease.

Chapter Twenty-Five

When Emma and I arrived back at our offices, a police car was skewed untidily outside, one man sitting in it.

Though my conscience was clear, I took the deferential course of pulling up and getting out of my car to walk over and speak to the driver.

'Excuse me, are you going to be here long?' I asked.

'Do you work here?' he answered.

'Yes.'

'There's another officer in there.' He nodded at the atrium entrance in the middle of the block. 'We're looking for . . .' he consulted a note-book '. . . Thames Valley Technical Pro—'

'That's us,' I interrupted him.

'Who? You and the young lady?' He glanced at Emma.

'No. My business partner's called Matthew James. He should be up there.'

As I spoke, the radio in the car confirmed that the driver's colleague had made contact with Matt.

'The other one's here,' our man said. 'I'll send him up.'

'What's it about?' I asked before heading for the building while Emma parked my car.

'We're following up on an enquiry for Avon police about some stolen property.'

I felt a chill of foreboding. But I could tell that this man wasn't going to tell me any more so made my way with Emma through the post-modern cloisters of hermetically sealed corridors and glass lifts to our offices.

A stolid policeman loomed in our reception area while Monica busied herself at her desk. He seemed less threatening than his colleague, though. It took only one of his politely phrased questions for me to gather that he was seeking information, not treating us as suspects.

'What's going on?' I asked.

Matt turned to me with a faint, confident smile. 'Dysart's supplier has confirmed that the helium canister in the camera can only have come from them, so those prototypes were definitely stolen. But now Taylor, the research guy who dealt with Tresidder, has disappeared too.'

'With the other prototype?'

'Presumably.'

The policeman looked offended at being left out of the conversation. 'Excuse me, sir,' he said to me. 'Could I talk to you separately?'

'Of course,' I agreed, and showed him into my own room.

In fifteen minutes I neither elicited nor offered any more information than I had in the first few seconds of seeing the man. He had none of the details and had come to see us only to establish that we were aware of the identity of the canister.

'A CID officer from Avon will be up to see you later today or tomorrow. Apparently this bit of kit's worth a lot of money.'

I nodded, made polite goodbyes and showed the man out through the reception area where Emma was talking on the phone with great animation.

Matt came in as the policeman left.

'Did he tell you anything?'

I shook my head. 'No.'

Emma finished her phone call. I could see she was anxious to speak to me but restraining herself.

'Something tells me Tintern's been busy,' I said to Matt. 'He's getting rid of witnesses and evidence as fast as he can.'

'Or letting them get rid of themselves,' Matt offered.

'He doesn't know we've got the bar-codes, though.'

'No. He must think Lincoln's still got them.'

Emma was looking at each of us in turn. 'For God's sake, you two. When are you going to tell the police what you know?'

Matt looked at her. 'Wouldn't you mind seeing your father disgraced?'

Emma screwed up the near-perfect symmetry of her face. 'Hasn't Simon told you?'

'Told me what?' he asked sharply.

I looked at Emma. 'I didn't think you'd want me to, until it was confirmed.'

'It has been. That's what I've been trying to tell you! I've just been talking to Frank, and he's had the results of the DNA tests we had done.' She gave a wide, happy smile. 'It's official – he's my real father.'

Matt's jaw dropped a fraction. 'But, how come? I mean, how did this come up after twenty-five years?'

'I'll tell you another time,' she said. 'Let's deal with Tintern first.'

I'd asked Emma if she could find a recording of Lord Tintern's voice, on either video or audio tape. She'd gone one better and helped herself to his Dictaphone.

As we sat in the office and listened to him reciting a list of mundane things to remember, it was almost impossible to reconcile it with his recent activities. I took out that tape, and told Matt and Emma I was going to London to play it to Tilbury, the porter in Toby's block.

I didn't tell them that I was planning to see Harry Chapman first. I didn't want to be committed to a strategy until I was confident that it would work. Besides, I might not manage to achieve it. But I had the information I needed, and an hour's drive in which to make a decision.

I phoned Salmon's as I drove, and Sara put me straight through to Harry. He agreed to see me as soon as I reached Hanover Square.

When I was shown into the cavernous room where Harry worked, I was struck by the contrast between this meeting and our first in that office with Matt.

The chief executive of Salmon Leisure greeted me warmly, as if he were grateful I'd come.

'Drink?' he offered genially.

'No, thanks.' I was far too excited to drink.

'Okay. What's your proposal?'

'First, I have to tell you that Tintern knows it was me who told you about Buckingham Gate.'

'Yes.' Harry nodded. 'I told him.'

I gulped. 'But why?'

'To stop him asking even more questions round the place. I also told him I'd paid you a very fat fee in return. I hope you don't mind? But, if you think about it, it won't do you any long-term harm.'

I sighed, but was inclined to trust his instincts. 'Okay. Now I'll tell you what I had in mind.'

I left Harry cheerfully engaged in bringing about a final act of sabotage and drove to Hay's Mews to find Tilbury.

He was in his small porter's office on the ground floor of the mansion block where Toby had lived. He'd had his week off, the flurry of police and press activity had subsided, and he was back on duty again.

This time, a twenty-pound note was enough to engage his rheumy attention while I produced Tintern's Dictaphone and played it to him.

He was almost certain that the voice was the one he'd heard outside the building, saying goodbye the morning Toby had been found dead.

Satisfied, though aware of the limited value of this evidence, I headed west out of London in the kind of early-spring sunshine I'd almost forgotten existed. Determined to keep faith with what I had set in motion, I arranged to meet Frank and Emma at Wetherdown.

Then I phoned Matt.

'What's new?' I asked.

'We're still looking for Lincoln, and I've put Larry on to tracking Taylor. Nothing on either so far and two plainclothes plods from Bristol were here until a few minutes ago. David Dysart's obviously put a rocket up their Super's backside. They're desperate to get a lead on these prototypes. I had to confirm that at least one of them was partially dismantled to produce the camera-airgun we found on Tresidder.'

'How did you explain Tresidder?'

'I said we were aware through Brian Griffiths that he'd had meetings with Taylor, Dysart's propulsion expert, and that led us to his place in Windsor, where, regrettably, he is no longer to be found. However, I didn't tell them anything about what the gun was being used for, or Tintern, or the Jockey Club investigation into Toby's tipping line. All they're after is Dysart's piece of kit.'

The first of the daffodils bordering the drive at Wetherdown had pushed their way into bloom since the day before. There was no wind shrieking off the downs when I parked and walked from my car and for once the birdsong was audible.

Frank and Emma came out of Jane's front door to greet me. 'We were just going to stroll round to the yard through the garden,' Frank said, inviting me to join them.

'Fine,' I agreed. We set off towards the tranquillity of the hundred-year-old yew alley – a hidden place where time seemed to stand still and the thick, immutable green walls kept the real world at bay.

We sat in a bower there. Frank pulled out his cigar case and lit a richly scented Monte Cristo.

'I thought you'd like to know,' he said, making certain the end of his cigar was glowing evenly, 'I received a fax from Harry Chapman.'

'Good Lord! He was quick off the mark. I wanted to warn you first.'

'No problem, dear boy. But before we discuss his proposition, tell me what you know about Harry and Gerald, and why Harry listens to you?'

I smiled at the way things were working out. 'Have you been to see the property Gerald's buying up in Buckingham Gate?'

'I can't say I've looked at it, no. Why?'

'When I saw there was a Salmon's betting shop on the site and then discovered it was one of the few leases that Tintern hadn't managed to buy, the idea that he might be prepared, even have planned, to buy out the whole Salmon empire first occurred to me. And, of course, the more money Salmon's were losing, the cheaper it would be. It seemed such a crazy idea that I could hardly believe it – I mean, if ever anyone cut a figure of unimpeachable moral authority, it was him. But I went straight round to Harry Chapman's anyway, only to discover that he hadn't got a clue Gerald owned the site all round his, which he'd just agreed to sell to a chain of Bureaux de Change. Naturally, he soon changed his mind.'

Frank smiled widely. 'Gerald must have found that

deeply, deeply irritating. But then, I suppose he's had a lot of other preoccupations. I wonder if he seriously hoped he might see the bookmakers bend to the will of the many and start putting their profits back into racing.' Frank took another long pull on his cigar and exhaled a lazy spiral of blue smoke. 'An absurdly vain hope, I regret, but then, in some ways, Gerald always was an absurdly vain man. I think it must have been Harry's snatching back this shop from under his nose that prompted him to launch his bid for Atlantic Hotels.'

'Yes,' I agreed. 'That's why I did it – to get a reaction. But I thought he would still have found a replacement when Connor died and persevered with the doping.'

'You don't think he killed Connor?'

'No. Harry wouldn't admit it, but I'm almost certain the guy who turned up there was sent by him – or at least on his orders – though not to kill Connor.'

'That sounds more likely, but I think even in his most vindictive fantasies, Gerald must have realised his doping tactic was always risky and hardly likely to be viable in the long term. I think his colleagues in the Jockey Club were getting very close to calling in the police.'

'They probably were, but as Senior Steward, he'd have been difficult to argue with. He's got a lot of very high-level connections, and they'd have been very reluctant to pursue him if there was any doubt about his involvement.'

'So, how much do you know?'

Emma and I spent the next few minutes telling

Frank exactly what we'd been doing over the past forty-eight hours.

'But without this chap Lincoln, or Tresidder, or the scientist, you have no witnesses?' Frank summed up. 'And all the evidence you have is some copies of bar-codes issued by the Jockey Club, and the police have the camera gun. And that's it?'

I nodded. 'We've had the finger-prints on the bar-code papers checked against some of Tintern's that Emma got, and they tally, along with some of Greeves's, but I guess Tintern'll have an answer if we tackle him over it.'

'So there's nothing that really points the finger at him?'

'Apart from Tilbury's identification of his voice. And though it's good enough for me, that won't stand up. And whatever Matt says, we're not likely to get much more, either.'

'I think then, in the interests of justice, we'd better put our faith in Harry Chapman, don't you, Emma?'

He looked at her with pride and affection, and I began to appreciate just how big an event the discovery of an unknown daughter must be for him.

She smiled back, and nodded. 'Let's do it.'

'Fine. I'll ring Chapman and tell him to send us the formal offer.'

I heard my first spring lark next morning, and saw the tiny bird hovering a hundred feet above the dewy turf at the top of the downs.

I had asked Derek de Morlay if I could come out on Nester with the early lot. It was the first time I'd ridden him since Esmond had left, and I was thrilled to find that he was going as well as he ever had.

Esmond had probably been right not to accept all the credit for the recovery, but I couldn't help feeling that, if nothing more, his actions must have worked as a catalyst to the healing process.

With my confidence higher than it had been for years, I drove from Derek's yard to the office, where I was meeting Matt.

'What exactly is the purpose of this meeting with your girl friend's long-lost father?' Matt asked as he dropped into the passenger seat of my car.

'You know that Frank has very long-standing and intricate connections with Tintern. He accepts from what I've told him that there's no chance of getting Tintern to the police with an open and shut case. Either by luck or his own doing, Tintern's effectively got everyone who matters out of the way. Whichever, he's not being pursued over Toby's death, and no official finger has been even vaguely pointed at him over the tipping lines.'

'So, what's Frank's idea?'

'I'll let him tell you himself.'

When we arrived at Wetherdown, I saw Jane briefly on her way out to the yard after breakfast.

'How's Purple Silk?' I asked.

'Never looked better, I'm afraid to say.'

'Nester's looking pretty damned good too,' I grinned. 'As fit as he's ever been.'

'What about his jockey?' Jane made a face of good-natured disparagement.

'His jockey is also in supreme shape, thank you,' I said, mimicking the flourish of a jockey's whip in a finish.

Jane laughed and went on. I was glad to see her looking something like her old self again.

Matt was coming up behind me. 'You can't still be thinking of riding in that race?'

'A man may dream,' I said.

We were at the front door now. I pushed it open and went in to find Emma coming across Jane's dark, creaking hall to meet us. She gave me a kiss on the lips and Matt a dazzling smile.

'Frank's waiting for us in the conservatory,' she said.

Frank looked as if he'd been born ten years after the date given in his passport. He greeted us both with a handshake that felt as if it meant something. 'Good morning.' His deep, quiet voice resonated around the glass walls and roof of the large room. His lively blue eyes appraised us, taking in the manifest tension in Matt.

'First, coffee,' he said. 'I brought my own beans from France,' he added apologetically. 'I hope you won't mind, but I do like my coffee with a bit of bite.'

He poured some for us. I sat at the table and took a sip; I almost had to catch my breath as I swallowed it and the neat caffeine leaped through my system.

Matt carried his to a side table, put it down and remained standing. He seemed anxious to stick to business. 'I gather you've got a plan to deliver Lord Tintern his just desserts?'

Frank raised one eyebrow a fraction as he lowered himself on to a long teak steamer chair. 'Only if you don't have a better one.'

'Let's hear yours first.'

I was grateful for Frank's tolerance.

'The plan's quite simple. Gerald has borrowed a hundred and fifteen million pounds to buy up his Buckingham Gate site, and secured the loan with his shareholding in the King George Hotel Group. Until he's bought the final freehold, and the Salmon's Racing lease in the ground floor, the site is worth a lot less than he paid for it. Most of the properties are derelict with no income. I've arranged that tomorrow the loan will be called in for immediate repayment. The site, as it's currently occupied, would take months to sell, so he'll have no option but to sell his shares in King George.'

Matt stared at him doubtfully. 'But can you do that?'

'You can if the chairman of the bank is one of your oldest friends, and Sir Alec Denaro and I have known each other since we were five. Then, when I put the word around that the site won't be freed up by Salmon's for years, no one else will lend Gerald the money.'

Frank looked at each of us in turn, checking we were taking it all in. He was evidently satisfied now that he had Matt's undivided attention.

'Gerald's been active in extending his interests into a lot of other areas. We've checked his current position as closely as possible and I can tell you that he's put a great deal of venture capital into companies where, if you're lucky, the returns can be enormous. But this hasn't been the case for him. His portfolio isn't broad enough and he's stretched.

'We estimate personal borrowings of over a hundred and thirty million at this point in time. If the Buckingham Gate site is disposed of in a forced sale, with Salmon's still in situ, it won't fetch more than seventy-five million. His shares in the King George Group would realise about thirty-five million and he would be insolvent to the tune of twenty million.'

Matt, I saw, was sitting forward on the edge of his chair, any pretence at lack of interest abandoned. I could tell that he was beginning to see where Frank was taking us.

Matt moved back into the centre of the room. 'So that's it? You think that as it's impossible to get Tintern convicted or punished for murdering Toby Brown, trying to bankrupt him will have to do?'

Frank met his gaze square on. 'Yes. I entirely accept your deduction that it must have been Gerald who visited Toby on Sunday morning before the bookie's man found him dead. But from what Simon's told me, we just don't have enough to tie him to it.'

I nodded. 'Tilbury didn't even see him – only heard him. Let's face it, Matt, it may not be ideal, but this way at least we'll know Tintern's getting what he deserves for what he did.'

'Besides,' Frank intervened, 'are you two sure of what he's done, and why?'

'I am,' I said emphatically. 'We know why he started fixing races, and using Toby as an unsuspecting front, and we know that Steve Lincoln worked out what was going on and decided to blackmail Tintern.'

'Around about the time Toby died,' Frank murmured.

'Maybe Lincoln had got Toby to confront Tintern over whether or not he was behind the doping.'

Frank lowered himself on to his steamer chair and lay back with his eyes tight shut. 'It's very hard to believe,' he said, shaking his head, 'though I think you must be right.' He took a deep breath and opened his eyes. 'But Lincoln then blackmailed him, which must have given Gerald a terrible shock, if he thought he'd killed Toby for nothing.'

'The bookies might have, if he hadn't. They sent China to do it.'

'I think they only sent him after Toby to frighten him. Toby wasn't a hard case, but they thought he was taking their money and carrying on his tipping through Connor.'

'Right, but obviously Tintern thought he'd better nip the blackmail in the bud, and set up Lincoln to be nicked.'

'But how could he risk that?' Emma asked. 'The police would want to know why he was being blackmailed.'

'That's not such a mystery,' Matt said unexpectedly. 'I was doing some research of my own yesterday while Simon was in London. I spoke to Wyndham and asked him to check out what was going on that evening in Knightsbridge. As far as he can tell, that raid was entirely unofficial – a piece of private enterprise which was never recorded, nor would have been.'

'Just two coppers standing by in a patrol car?' I asked.

'Yes.' Matt nodded. 'I shouldn't think it's that difficult or expensive to arrange, and Tintern was probably hoping Lincoln would be frightened off for good by the shock of almost having his collar felt by the police.'

'Okay,' Frank said, holding up both hands. 'I accept that you think you know what happened though you can't prove it. But, as I said, this way at least Tintern gets to pay for what he's done. It won't bring Toby back for Jane, but we'll make sure she knows what we've done, and believe me, that'll help.

'Simon, perhaps you'd be good enough to open the champagne, then?' He nodded at a bottle in a bucket under a palm tree. 'Emma, glasses please.'

When we each had a full glass in our hand Frank raised his a little. 'To justice,' he said. Then, looking at Emma, 'And fatherhood.'

'To justice,' I repeated happily, 'and Better By Far, Champion Chaser.'

Matt looked at me with a cynical grunt. 'To justice, certainly, and possibly fatherhood – but I'm sorry, Simon. I'd like to support you, but I have to say that there isn't a horse in the world that would come in champion with you on its back!'

Chapter Twenty-Six

I understood how Jane felt.

Her son had been found hanging from a beam; she couldn't accept that he might have taken his own life, and yet, apart from myself and a few of her friends, no one seemed to care.

I'd ridden out on Baltimore. The yard at Wetherdown was as busy as usual on a Saturday, with five runners going off to three different courses. Jane was trying to persuade herself that she wanted to go to Chepstow, where she knew she ought to be. But in the meantime, she had agreed to stay back until midday, to talk to a journalist – one whom she trusted enough to report her version of why Lord Tintern's eight horses, including the Champion Chase favourite, were being so abruptly withdrawn from her yard.

I was sitting alone with her in her study.

'Jane, I can imagine what it must be like, believe me, and I wish to God there were some way we could persuade the police to go after Tintern, but we just haven't found anything that categorically proves he did it, and they're adamant it was suicide.'

'It had to be Gerald,' she whispered bleakly. 'Toby was far too proud to have done it himself.'

'I know that's what you think, Jane, and I wish there was something I could say to help, but there just isn't. And at least Tintern's going to suffer, even if it isn't as a direct result of what he did to Toby. You do realise, don't you, that by the time all his guarantees have been called, he'll have lost his shares in King George's? And no one's going to take any pity on him then. He'll pay for what he did.'

'But he'll still be free, that's what irks me,' she said. 'And he won't know the real reason he's lost King George.'

'When he's declared bankrupt, I'll make it my business to let him know how it happened.'

'But how did you do it, Simon?'

'The timing was mostly good luck, but originally it was a chance remark of Frank's that prompted me.'

I explained to her how Tintern had tried to bring Salmon Racing to its knees and, even though he'd failed, bid for it out of desperation when he saw he was going to lose the Buckingham Gate site.

'But then, of course,' I told her, 'it was a crazy idea, and he was too late anyway because the bookies were making money again. I guess you could say they'd outflanked him.'

Jane nodded, even allowing herself a smile. 'Gerald must be seething – at just the thought of losing the hotels, and Purple Silk moving to another yard, so close to the Champion Chase.'

'Why didn't you hang on until after Cheltenham?'

'I couldn't – not once I knew he'd been involved in Toby's death. I made him take all his horses away. I just hope you can beat him on Nester.'

I left Jane with promises ringing in her ears that everything humanly and legally possible would be done to ensure that Better By Far beat Purple Silk in the Champion Chase in ten days' time. But my more immediate, and no less cherished, aim was to see Gerald Tintern pay heavily and promptly for his crimes.

I had marked out Daniel Dunne as a man who would respond better to large quantities of soiled banknotes than anything else.

Having arranged with Frank that such quantities as I might need could be made available, I had phoned Daniel. Without telling him why I wanted it, I'd arranged a meeting late Saturday morning, in his small West End office, a few hundred yards, as it happened, from Toby's last address.

Daniel Dunne's personal tastes were reflected in a display of vast, inept oil paintings of classic horse races that crowded his office walls. The small bronze of a Derby winner on his desk confirmed it.

'Hello,' he said, getting up from behind it to welcome me warily. 'I hope you haven't come here to try and sell me a horse.'

'I don't think I've got any fast enough for you,' I said, nodding at the pictures.

He gave a disappointed laugh. 'I'd always be interested in a nice inside deal. So, what can I do for you?' He waved vaguely at a faux-Chippendale chair.

I concluded that Tintern, for his own reasons, had not yet told Dunne I was responsible for Harry Chapman's volte-face.

'You've occasionally had to acquire properties for our mutual friend Gerald Tintern, haven't you?' I said, sitting down.

Dunne was instantly on his guard. 'I've acted for him once or twice, in sensitive situations.'

'Like when he's been building up a holding in a block?'

'How the hell do you know?'

'I can tell you that Tintern won't be in a position to complete on anything as from tomorrow. But I've come here to tell you there's still a way you could earn a commission.'

Dunne's cheek twitched in a way that reminded me of Tintern. 'Really? How?'

'What I want to know is which of the fourteen freeholds in that block Tintern hasn't bought yet.'

'Why should I tell you that?'

'Because if there are any left, he won't be buying them, and with Harry Chapman sitting on his lease for eighteen years, the block's worth bugger all to any developer.'

'Have you got a punter?'

'Yes, if there's one of the freeholds left which could create a bit of leverage.'

'As it happens, there is one left,' he said quietly, 'and I'm just on the point of getting the old bastard who owns it to sell. He's wound me up on the price as far as he could, not because he knew Tintern's filling a gap but because he's one of those canny old boys who can just smell how keen you are, however well you fake it.'

I had to fake hard myself, to disguise my relief there was still one part of the deal that would escape receivers if Tintern's loans were called in.

'Well, if you want a buyer,' I said calmly, as if there were some question about it, 'who'll pay you another five percent over the top, in readies, I've got one.'

The tension in Jane's cramped office was almost tangible.

Four days after my meeting with Daniel Dunne, we were waiting for the phone call that would confirm that the deal was done – or, at least, was so far down the line that it was irrevocable.

The phone tinkled, and I answered it.

'Hello, Simon. Harry here. Just to let you know we've bought that little property you recommended. I haven't had a look at it, but my surveyor tells me it's a terrible place and will probably fall down in a few years anyway. And your Mr Dunne was in for a good cut.'

'I know, Harry, but you understand as well as I do it was money well spent.'

'I do indeed. And I was phoning to say thank you. We'll be in touch.'

I put the phone down with a satisfied grin.

'Well done,' Frank said. 'That'll really sting Gerald when he finds out.'

'What exactly have you done now?' Jane asked, pleased that Tintern seemed to be getting what he deserved, but confused by the details.

'Let me tell you,' I said. 'Tintern had marked out a major hotel site which he'd been buying up for years. By promising to grease the palm of a chap called Daniel Dunne, I discovered that of the fourteen freehold premises on the block, Tintern had acquired all bar one. Most of those freeholds had various commercial tenancy agreements within them, and he'd bought out nearly all the commercial leaseholders, letting some hang on under licence until he'd got a full house. As it happens, the building of which Salmon's shop occupies the ground floor was the only freehold he hadn't got. Until yesterday he thought he had it, and even though Salmon's had backed out of their agreement to sell him their lease, I'm sure he thought that once he'd got the freehold, sooner or later he'd get them out somehow.'

'Or maybe,' Frank said, 'he was sure he was going to buy out the whole Salmon group anyway.'

'Exactly,' I agreed, wondering if Jane was following, or cared anyway. I went on. 'Daniel Dunne was on a percentage of the whole deal when it was complete, but after I convinced him that would never happen, he switched horses like a circus rider. Yuri Ashkenazy, the old boy who owned the last of the freeholds, of which the Salmon's shop occupied only the ground floor, had owned the property since the fifties, when he'd operated a small jeweller's there. When he retired, he granted Salmon's a lease and himself lived in the top three floors of the building, resisting all efforts to buy it until now. His health is failing, though, and his daughter in Portsmouth has insisted that if he wants care, he will have to move to pay for it.

'But that hasn't stopped him stringing along the Jersey property company who seemed so anxious to acquire the impractical building that they were prepared to offer almost double the price Dunne had originally put on it.

'When his tenants on the ground floor came to him with an offer a good ten percent higher than the Jersey company's bid, on condition he exchanged and completed within a week of the offer, Dunne told him the original bidders wouldn't go any higher, and Ashkenazy's just signed a deal with Salmon Racing.'

'Lord T must be fuming!'

It was nearly a week later, and Matt had picked me up from home at nine in the morning to drive us to the first day of the Cheltenham Festival to watch the Champion Hurdle. He was looking at me now with an odd grin. 'I'm sure he's fuming – he was arrested yesterday.'

'What!' I gaped at him. 'Tintern arrested? What are you talking about?'

'The police went round to Ivydene yesterday; they took him away plus the contents of his study.'

I was still finding it hard to believe.

'Jason rang me from the office half an hour ago. The police from Bristol phoned, wanting to talk to us. They've caught Taylor . . .'

'Who is Taylor?' I asked with my mind still in turmoil at the news.

'David Dysart's research scientist, the one who went missing. They caught him flying back in from Spain yesterday – to collect his dog, of all things – and he totally broke down; definitely not one of life's born villains. He gave them the whole story about Tintern becoming a shareholder in Powderjet and then offering Taylor money and a research company of his own if he would create an air gun from a camera. I suppose the whole scam hinged on the fact that Tintern had free access to the bar-codes that were used to identify the runners, and that he could easily authorise a photographer's badge; he thought it was his chance to cripple the bookmakers.'

I shook my head in amazement. 'Quite a nice idea. Especially Tintern using a good tipping service to make the selections for him. It must have been strange for poor old Toby not having a clue why he was tipping so many winners.' I noticed that Matt was heading into the centre of Cheltenham. 'Why aren't we taking our usual route to the race-course? We don't want to get snarled up in the town with the rest of the punters.'

'No choice, I'm afraid,' he said airily. 'We've got to go and see Inspector Wyndham; he's at the local nick.'

'Why on earth didn't you say so earlier?'

'Because I didn't want to spoil your day sooner than was necessary.'

The detective was waiting for us in a room in the County Police HQ in Lansdown Road. He looked even closer shorn and meaner than last time. But I could see that under the hard exterior, he was very pleased with himself.

'Morning, gentlemen,' he said. 'I thought you were

never coming. I guessed you'd rather see me here than have to talk to me at the races tomorrow – it's a big day for you, I gather?' He looked at me.

'Maybe.'

'Right, I thought I'd tell you myself what's been going on, and I need you to corroborate some of it. I told you when I saw you at Paddington if anything new came up that justified it, we would re-open the case. As you've no doubt heard, Lord Tintern was arrested at his home yesterday evening. One of the parties to this doping scam – a man called Taylor – has spelled the whole thing out. Did you two know anything about this, by the way?'

'I expect the CID in Bristol have told you they came and spoke to us about some missing prototypes which Taylor had developed,' Matt said blandly. 'We'd been asked by Wessex Biotech to find them. At least David Dysart will be a satisfied customer now,' he added smugly.

'We didn't do much,' I put in.

'It was because we found Tresidder that Taylor got out,' Matt reminded me.

'Yes,' I conceded, but turned to Wyndham. 'How come you're involved? You didn't have anything to do with the prototype enquiry, did you?'

'No. But after he got nicked for the theft of Biotech's property – and he's already been charged with conspiracy to defraud for that – I was offered the chance to talk to him a little more about the late Toby Brown. As a result of further enquiries, I was able to pull him for the doping scam.'

'But I thought you'd been told to forget Toby's death?'

'That was before Lord Tintern got pulled on this other matter; it's amazing how quickly influence can dry up at times like these,' he grinned.

'Okay, but what prompted you to go after him over Toby?'

'When the CID from Bristol went round to Ivydene to pick him up, they collected every document they could find on the premises. One of these was a note written by Toby, addressed to his mother, telling her why he was going to commit suicide.'

I looked at Matt, who nodded, unsurprised.

'I always thought it was the most likely scenario,' he said.

I sat back and sighed. 'So, what happened?'

'Tintern admitted he'd been round to Toby's that morning.' I tried to look surprised while Wyndham went on. 'And the night before.'

Now I *was* surprised.

'Apparently Toby had rung him and asked him to come; said he wanted to talk to him about a very delicate matter.'

'Did Tintern tell you all this?' Matt looked puzzled.

'No. He told us some of it, but on the strength of what Toby wrote, we've also been out and picked up a nasty little character called Steve Lincoln – I believe you know him, too?'

We nodded.

'Why didn't you mention him before?' Wyndham growled.

'At that stage, we couldn't see why you seemed so reluctant to investigate Toby's death. If you'd shown more interest, maybe we would have done.'

'Did you know he was round at Toby's too, the night before?'

'Yes,' Matt said.

'He said if we didn't charge him, he'd tell us what we needed to know. He hadn't got anything out of the blackmail apart from a few quid Tintern used as a decoy. And we'll need a rock solid case against someone like him.' Wyndham shrugged pragmatically.

'Lincoln said that he and Toby had been arguing. Toby was still infatuated with him, apparently.' Wyndham wrinkled his nose. 'No accounting for taste! Anyway, Lincoln told Toby it wasn't his brilliant judgement that was picking all these winners, it was because Tintern was doping the opposition. Toby wouldn't believe him, and rang Tintern to come up so he could tackle him about it, face to face. Lincoln was still there, hiding in another room, when Tintern showed up, so he heard everything – like Toby saying he knew exactly what Tintern was up to, and how he was trying to bring the bookies to their knees. Tintern denied it at first, but finally said the bookies had been robbing racing for years and they deserved it. Then Toby started getting hysterical and screamed that no matter what Tintern thought of the bookies, what he was doing was out and out criminal fraud and he was a disgrace to racing.

'This didn't cut much ice with Tintern. He kept very calm, Lincoln said. He agreed that he had made sure that all the naps had won, but said that Toby would never prove a thing and if he ever mentioned it to anyone, he'd send everything he knew about him and his rent boys and gay junkie friends to the papers, then Toby would stop being everyone's favourite, cuddly television racing personality overnight. He said that if Toby's father were still alive, he'd be utterly ashamed of him.'

I winced, imagining the hurt Toby must have felt.

The detective sniffed. 'Tintern didn't say much more after that and left, but Lincoln had already sussed out most of what was happening anyway. And he'd seen some photograph Toby had in his toilet. It showed Toby's dad in his regiment, as well as Tresidder, Greeves – the chap in Newmarket who topped himself – and, would you believe it . . .'

'Yes, I would,' I said. 'We've got it. Lord Tintern's in the photograph too when he was mere Captain The Hon. Gerald Birt. So what did Lincoln do?'

'He stayed on and told Toby if he didn't give him any money, he'd get it out of Tintern. He told Toby exactly what he thought of him, and said if Tintern did give a story to the papers, he'd be selling his part of it too for the right money.'

'What did Toby do?' I asked, beginning almost to feel sorry for him.

'Blubbered like a baby, according to Lincoln. From the letter he wrote his mother, he must have been in a shocking state.'

'Are you telling me you've taken all Lincoln's statement at face value?' Matt said scornfully. 'I'm amazed you're treating him as a reliable source.'

'And you would be right, Major,' Wyndham gave

him a deferential smile, 'if we hadn't had Mr Brown's letter and another very strong piece of evidence to corroborate it.'

Matt looked back at him warily.

'When we'd seen this document,' Wyndham went on, 'we went back to his flat and interviewed some of his neighbours again, to check that Tintern really had been back like Lincoln said. The first person I saw was a lady in the flat below, an American lady in fact, with an eleven-year-old son who's a bit of a liability by the sound of it. A few weeks ago, the inquisitive little bugger found a tape recorder in the building, hidden behind a fire hose under the back stairs.' His eyes rested keenly on Matt, who didn't even blink. 'He didn't think he could get away with pinching the whole thing – but he helped himself to the tape. Trouble was, it was a DAT-cassette, and he didn't have any equipment to play it on. When he told his mum, he owned up to her where he'd got it and went to show her but by that time the machine had gone too; that was the day after Toby died.'

He cocked his head to one side. He knew he wasn't going to get an answer from us yet, but it was clear where his suspicions lay.

'How extraordinary,' Matt drawled, making no impression on the policeman. 'What was on the tape?'

'Enough.' He looked at each of us in turn. 'Someone had obviously secured a radio mike somewhere in Toby's flat and installed a sound reactive recorder to pick it up. Now, who do you suppose would want to do that?'

I looked at Matt, shrugging my shoulders. I was delighted I'd been acquitted of having made a crass error, and I knew that there was nothing Wyndham could do to prove we had anything to do with it. I also thought it wouldn't have suited him anyway, it would only have made things awkward for him if we owned up.

'Well,' Wyndham said, 'whoever it was did us a great favour. The whole of the conversation between Lincoln and Toby, then Toby and Tintern, more or less as Lincoln reported, was recorded in digital stereo; then we heard what Lincoln didn't tell us which was that he wasn't having anything more to do with Toby. Called him a sad old slag who wouldn't know how to turn on a jelly fish.' Wyndham pursed his lips in disapproval and shook his head in disbelief. 'After Lincoln left, Toby was sobbing his heart out. Then he put on some loud heavy music, and that used up the rest of the tape.'

Wyndham sat back, glad to have got it all off his chest.

I resisted the temptation to take some of the credit for the tape, and looked at Matt. He didn't react.

'When did Tintern find the letter?' he asked Wyndham.

'He said he went back on Sunday morning to talk something over with Toby. He found him hanging, and, on top of the bureau, a letter, just folded, with "Mrs Jane Brown" written on the outside.'

'Why didn't he bring it straight to you?' Matt asked.

'Because it contained a clear account of what had happened, fully implicating him in the doping scam, that's why.'

'So why didn't he destroy it there and then?'

'Because if we ever tried to pin Toby's death on him, it would prove that he didn't do it.'

As he spoke, I thought about Tintern leaving, as Tilbury had told me, pretending to talk to Toby through the intercom for the benefit of anyone witnessing his visit. 'He must have been quite happy to see Toby dead, though, if he thought he might have told you lot about him?'

'Yes, and it must have come as a very nasty shock when he got the first demand from Lincoln a day or two later.'

'Have you got this letter of Toby's?' Matt asked.

'We've got a copy. We've already given the original to Mrs Brown, with our undertaking that we won't divulge the contents to any third party. The fact is, she didn't know it, but we've spoken to Toby's doctor who told us he was undergoing treatment for clinical depression. Did you know that?'

'No,' I replied honestly. 'I didn't, though now you tell me, I can believe it.'

'He had some pills, but apparently he got sick of taking them, wanted to tough it out on his own, then found he couldn't and everything got too much for him. You'd be surprised how common it is.'

'I saw it in the army,' Matt agreed. 'If they were the volatile type, some of the hardest men would crumble.'

'Who broke the news to Mrs Brown?' I asked.

'I went with a WPC, on the way here. It was a blow to her, of course, but I think she'll find it easier knowing exactly what happened.'

'We'll go and see her after this. In the meantime, I

suppose we ought to congratulate you. We never thought Tintern would get caught for the doping, not once Taylor and Tresidder had gone.'

'I always knew there was more to Toby Brown's death than we'd found. And it's good to get rich, pompous bastards like Tintern from time to time – shows how impartial we are. Now, Major, last time we met you started telling me about a man who might have had something to do with all this.'

I guessed he was talking about Matt's reference to China Smith – Harry's man. We certainly didn't want to bring Harry into the game now.

I glanced at Matt. 'Who was that?' I asked. 'I didn't know what you were talking about.'

'We'd never find him again anyway,' Matt dismissed the lead. 'Nothing was stolen, was it?'

'No,' Wyndham grunted cynically, 'but I still need a full statement about this bloke, anyone else you spoke to and every single thing you know about it all.' He started opening a file and pulling out statement forms.

'What? Now?' I groaned.

Wyndham turned his stony gaze on each of us in turn. There was a cold, heartless glint in his grey eyes. He took a long breath through quivering nostrils while I wondered if he even had the right to hold us here, if we didn't want to stay.

Suddenly, his face creased into an indulgent smile. 'Go on then. I fancy a day at the races, and I don't want to spoil your big day. I'll see you Thursday morning, nine o'clock – if you can still remember anything then.'

Frank Gurney seemed to be making a habit of producing bottles of very expensive champagne and finding excuses to drink them. We had several when we arrived back at Wetherdown that evening.

We were gathered, once again, in the large, comfortable drawing room at Wetherdown. All of us except Frank were sitting on Jane's deep, yielding sofas. A large fire of massive logs helped to dispel thoughts of the harsh mid-March gales thrashing across the downs and encouraged us to relax after the six most frenetic weeks most of us had ever lived through.

Emma was wallowing in the security of her new-found identity as Frank's daughter.

Matt was delighted that two of our company's biggest investigations so far had – somewhat tortuously – found their way to satisfactory conclusions; but when he told me that he had a thousand pounds at five to one on Better By Far to win the Champion Chase, I was suddenly hit by the reality of what was happening next day and couldn't touch another drop of champagne.

Jane was doing her best to join in.

'Poor Toby,' she said. 'Whatever the doctor says I still hold Gerald totally responsible. If he hadn't set up this whole mad scheme, Toby wouldn't have been driven to the edge. Do the police think Gerald'll go to prison?' she asked Matt.

'Yes. They've already accumulated a very strong case against him.'

Frank handed Jane a foaming glass.

'Is he really going to go bust?' she asked him.

'Probably. With luck he'll be a couple of years in jail,

and come out absolutely broke, with no friends . . .'

'And no family,' Emma added, with feeling.

'You know, what puzzles Harry most,' Sara said, 'is that Tintern had all these horses doped and he never had any money on the winners – not even his own horse. It seems so bizarre to go to all that trouble, and not even have a bet.'

'Not really,' I said. 'That wasn't his purpose. He was simply obsessed with doing down the bookies – all of them, and especially Salmon's, and his thousand or so wasn't going to make the vital difference; he wanted the whole country to be punting against them, and he nearly pulled it off for a few weeks.'

'I wonder if he'll see the race tomorrow?' Jane asked.

Frank gave her an enigmatic grin. 'He no longer has any interest in the horse. But if he runs well, I think you'll have him back in your yard for next year – in fact, any day now.'

Jane looked at him, puzzled for a moment. 'Why? Haven't the receivers or someone like that taken over all Gerald's assets?'

'I offered him a fair price; the receiver won't object.'

'Oh, no,' I groaned. 'Not again. Does that mean I still can't send Nester back to Jane?'

Frank paused from opening the bottle he had in his hand. 'That depends,' he said, glancing round the room with a smile, 'on what our relationship is this time next year. It's up to you.'

I glanced at Emma, who wouldn't meet my eye.

'Well,' I said, easily. 'It doesn't really matter. Nester's very happy where he is now.'

TIP OFF

★ ★ ★

Eighteen nerve-stretching hours later there was nothing in front of Nester as he swung left-handed round the turn at the bottom of Cheltenham's unkind hill in the last furlongs of the Queen Mother Champion Chase.

The stupendous reverberating roar in the stands didn't penetrate my consciousness as I gazed at the broad channel of green turf that stretched away in front of him, broken only by the two last fences, to the winning post. I didn't consider the possibility of anything having the effrontery to pass him. Nor, it seemed, did Nester. His pace didn't flag for a moment as he landed after the second from home, and even quickened as he pricked his ears for the last.

He saw his stride and launched himself with the grace of a gazelle over the tight-packed birch, powering on towards the finish in a relentless gallop that allowed no challenge.

I could scarcely believe what was happening as the post seemed to rush down to meet him.

Abruptly, it was all over; he'd crossed the line and I was breathing again, suddenly aware of the massive cheers of the supporters of my horse, and the crowd pressing around me in the box.

The first hand to fall on my shoulder was Matt's. 'Well done. It was a brilliant run. I think he'd have done it even if you'd been riding him,' he laughed.

Emma, on my other side, looked at me with her turquoise eyes wet and shining, and squeezed my arm. She stretched up and kissed me. 'Of course he would!'

'And next year,' I said, 'he will.'

Now you can buy any of these other bestselling books by **John Francome** from your bookshop or *direct from his publisher*.

FREE P&P AND UK DELIVERY
(Overseas and Ireland £3.50 per book)

Safe Bet	£6.99
Tip Off	£6.99
Stud Poker	£6.99
Outsider	£6.99
Stone Cold	£6.99
Rough Ride	£6.99
High Flyer	£6.99
False Start	£6.99
Dead Ringer	£6.99
Break Neck	£6.99
Blood Stock (with James MacGregor)	£6.99
Declared Dead (with James MacGregor)	£6.99
Eavesdropper (with James MacGregor)	£6.99
Riding High (with James MacGregor)	£6.99

TO ORDER SIMPLY CALL THIS NUMBER

01235 400 414

or e-mail <u>orders@bookpoint.co.uk</u>

Prices and availability subject to change without notice.